22.7.2025

To Laura

Happy summer reading!

Leilanie Stewart
♡

The Wabi-sabi Doll

The Wabi-sabi Doll

Laurie McGum

To JR and KJ who are always with me on the road less travelled

Chapter one

Kawaii chan

Ugh. Dogshit.

I bent my leg to look at the heel of my trainers. The muck was smeared in between the grooves of the sole. I puffed my cheeks and blew air out, causing my fringe to lift off my forehead.

What a Happy New Year present to welcome me back to my flat in Tottori, Japan, after two weeks at home for Christmas in Southampton. At least it wasn't my professional shoes. I wasn't due back at work teaching English at Voyce language school for another few days after the New Year holidays. Thank goodness; the jetlag was a killer. I needed a few days to ease myself back to my routine.

Having to clean dogshit off my trainers certainly didn't help to ease me in. I would clean the heel later. I kicked them off, leaving them scattered on the doorstep and reached for my snow boots from the hallway. As I slipped them on, it occurred to me that it was an odd place for a dog to have left its mess. My flat was on the second floor of a small apartment block called Villa Libido in Tottori, a small town facing Korea across the Sea of Japan; an expanse of grey buildings surrounded by snow-capped mountains. Besides the funny name of my apartment block, common in modern Japanese apartment blocks as though an in-joke among the developers, there was a rigid set of rules for the tenants; like not having any pets. I had lived in my flat in Villa Libido for the past fourteen months; long enough to know such rules. Did one of my neighbours have a sneaky new pet puppy? Maybe that would explain the dogshit. Still, why would a dog go up a flight of steps and leave its poo on someone's doorstep?

Maybe it was to do with the layout of the apartment block? My flat, and the one below, were the end flats in an L-shaped building. Maybe that gave an animal more privacy to do its *business*.

I shrugged. What did I know, or care, about where dogs did their business, or whether they needed privacy? It was the owner's responsibility to clean up a dog's mess, especially if it was a puppy in the process of toilet training. Our family dog back home in Southampton, Noogie, was eleven years old, long since past his days of toilet training; and when I took him for walks in the park, I always carried a poop-a-scoop bag. Hmph. What an irresponsible pet owner, and among my own neighbours too. I scoffed to myself as I started down the steps, ready for grocery shopping at Jusco shopping centre.

A little girl played under the metal shelter where my bicycle, and others were chained. She must have been three years old, maybe four. I stopped and offered a smile, hoping not to startle the child. She didn't return

The Wabi-sabi Doll

my smile, instead staring up at me with her huge, brown eyes. The girl reached into the basket of my bicycle and lifted a small, cloth bundle out. She set the bundle back into the basket and turned to face the blank wall behind my bicycle. "Atashi no ban da yo! Shitsurei!"

What did that mean, and more to the point, who was she talking to? An imaginary friend? I chided myself; I had been in Japan for a whole year and two months; surely I could translate what a toddler had to say? My cheeks burned under the shame of the sheer brain-power I was having to expend trying to figure out what the child was saying to her make-believe buddy.

It's my turn! Rude!

Yes, I was sure that was what she had said. I took a step closer to her, confident that she wouldn't be surprised by me. "Tomodachi to nakayoku asobimashou ka?" *Are you playing nicely with your friend?*

The girl turned to me, her lip pulled downwards. She lifted the parcel out of the basket of my bicycle and extended a chubby arm towards me, offering the bundle. Whatever it was seemed to be wrapped in a cloth.

"Watashi no puresento desu ka?" *Is it my present?*

The girl nodded, once, and said "Un."

I opened the bundle, unwilling to upset her. Her downturned lip disappeared, replaced by a smile. Inside the cloth was a triangle of sticky rice: onigiri. I wondered what the filling was. Tuna and mayo onigiri from Jusco was one of my lunchtime favourites.

I stared at the onigiri. The girl's mother had probably made it for her, for her lunch.

"Onaka peko peko?" said the child. "Kawaii chan mo onaka peko peko."

What did that mean? Onaka meant stomach. I didn't know what peko peko meant. Sounded like some kind of onomatopoeia. And she was referring to herself as 'cutie' when she referred to herself as *kawaii chan* in third person?

I placed my hand on my own stomach. "Onaka ga suita," I said.

The girl grinned. I understood; she wanted to know if I was hungry.

"Kono onigiri wa kimi no gohan desu." *This onigiri is your food.* I folded the cloth bundle closed and handed it to the girl. She took it from me, staring up at me with those impossibly huge eyes. Oh my gosh, she was adorable; kawaii chan, indeed. I immediately pictured a little girl who looked like a mix of my boyfriend Naoki and I staring up at me. Quick mental shake to dissipate the image; no point getting mushy and confusing the neighbour's child.

"Demo, arigatou," I added as an after-thought. *But, thank you.*

The little girl stood staring at me. For one horrible moment, I thought she was going to blubb, because I had returned her present. Instead, she placed it back in the basket of my bicycle and turned to converse again with her imaginary friend.

Maybe if the girl had a pet she wouldn't have to talk to an imaginary friend. The thought of pets redirected my attention to the dogshit I'd just cleaned from the doorstep. "Kimi wa inu ga imasu ka?" *Have you got a dog?*

She shook her head. "Nai."

Oh well, at least that ruled one neighbour out. Wonder which one of the other occupants in my block had a dog? One that they let out unattended, no less. Not to worry; I was sure I'd find out in due course.

The girl spliced through my musings as she turned back to face me, abandoning her make-believe pal. She dropped both hands to her crotch and crossed her legs.

"Kawaii chan wa ne…" she whined. "Muri sou!"

I knew what she was saying, only from her gesture, not the words. *I need to wee.* A useful phrase, indeed. I watched her with a smile as she hurried inside her house, a small wet patch forming on her dungarees.

Muri sou. Yeah, maybe I needed a wee myself, but I would hold on until I got to the supermarket at Jusco shopping centre. Onaka peko peko. I sure was hungry too. Not enough to eat a child's lunch though. I lifted the onigiri bundle out of my basket and gently set it on the girl's front doorstep.

Chapter two

New Year, new start

Akemashite omedetou gozaimasu.

I peeled the small slip of paper off my forehead and rubbed my eyes, yawning. The New Year's greeting was written in *romaji* letters, the English alphabet, making it easy for non-Japanese people to understand. It had been tucked inside the cellophane wrapper of the airline dessert on the flight back from Heathrow to Kansai airport. I snorted to myself, embarrassed at its unceremonious attachment to my forehead.

As lovely as it had been to spend two weeks at home for Christmas, and introduce my boyfriend of the past three months, Naoki, to mum, dad, and my brother Zac, the jetlag was a killer. Sleeping like I was comatose was probably why I had ended up with the piece of paper stuck to my forehead in the first place.

Where was Naoki anyway? The sliding door between my bedroom and the living room was half open and I could hear the TV beyond. A wave of

The Wabi-sabi Doll

dizziness overcame me as I got up from my futon on the floor; two weeks in my childhood bedroom back in my parents' house and I barely felt acclimatised to sleeping Japanese-style, even though it was much better for my back.

I stripped the duvet and pillows off the futon and folded it in half, then stacked the bedding on top in a neat pile. Japanese living certainly maximised space. Going back to England for a brief visit was nice, but I was happy to be back in my home-from-home, Tottori.

I padded across the traditional Japanese reed mats, *tatami*, that made up my bedroom floor, with the paper slip in my hand and into the living room. Naoki was sitting on the sofa, TV remote in hand.

"I don't know how you can be so chipper. My jetlag's a killer," I said, yawning.

"Chipper? What does that mean?" he replied.

Naoki's English was so good, I often forgot that it wasn't his first language. He had learned English after spending summer with a homestay family in Florida, as part of an exchange programme set up by the international centre in Tottori. Sometimes I even thought that he spoke English with an American twang. Maybe 'chipper' was used more widely in British than American English.

"It means perky, you know, like energetic," I explained.

He smirked. "You learn something new every day."

"Well, it's my turn now." I sat down beside him on the sofa and showed the New Year greeting. "I thought that 'Happy New Year' in Japanese was 'oshōgatsu omedetou gozaimasu'?"

"Oshōgatsu means New Year holiday, but akemashite omedetou is how people say Happy New year," he said.

I twiddled with the slip of paper. After fourteen months of living in Tottori, I had a basic grasp of the language – enough to get by – but I still often made mistakes. "I've been saying oshōgatsu, not akemashite."

"You worry too much, Kimberly. People would understand that just fine." Naoki grabbed my hand and closed my fingers over the greeting. His palm was warm and comforting, melting my insecurities away.

I stroked his hand with my thumb. "It meant a lot to me that you came and spent Christmas with my family. Christmas is a much bigger deal than New Year in the UK."

"I know, it's the opposite here in Japan. New Year is very important – a family time when we make our blessings at temples and eat osechi-ryori, special New Year food."

"I had no idea it was so important. Clubbing with my friends in Picadilly for New Year makes me feel so guilty now." I felt heat sear in my cheeks; Naoki had taken so much time off from work in his family's ramen restaurant in Kawahara, a small village a twenty minute drive from Tottori, and had missed a special New Year ritual with his parents. I couldn't help feeling selfish that he was left with only the weekend free before he had to get back to work.

"It's fine." He dismissed my worries with a wave. "I loved meeting your best friends and the London nightlife was great."

"I'd love to try osechi-ryori with your family. Do you think we could have a belated celebration at your parents' house?"

Naoki dropped his gaze to the remote control on his lap; I couldn't help but notice that he let go of my hand too. "It's not very exciting. I thought we could visit a temple together instead. Have you seen the New Year customs in Japan?"

"Yeah, I went to Sensoji temple on New Year last year, with Jei Pi."

"Oh yeah? How's Jei Pi getting on anyway? Is she teaching back home in Maine?"

The change in topic to my former flatmate, and former fellow English teacher at the Voyce language school, seemed forced somehow. Naoki had got along well with Jei Pi, but he hadn't asked about her in the eight weeks since she had left Japan and gone back to the US.

"Jei Pi's fine. She's has a job in a library, where she worked before she came to Tottori." I took a deep breath. "I'd love to visit a temple in Tottori. We could go to your parents' house after that, maybe?"

A blush crept across his cheeks. "I thought we could spend it here all weekend instead. London was so much socialising, I was hoping to have some quiet time with you after everything."

Normally I would've thought it was a great idea; if I was honest, I felt socially burned out after seeing all of my extended family in Southampton followed by my best friends in London for New Year. But I couldn't help feeling like Naoki was deflecting from a bigger issue. Time to get right to the point, perhaps.

"I was really hoping to meet your parents," I said to the burning red side of his cheek. Naoki continued looking down at the remote control in his lap, and I could feel his thoughts tumbling around, a spin cycle in his head.

"My parents are elderly. I think they would get tired quickly, especially if they had to host New Year festivities. It might be better if we visit them another time," he said, still avoiding my eyes.

"They can't be older than my parents though – my mum is 58 and my dad is 63 and they hosted us for nearly the whole of the Christmas holiday." I could hear the exasperation in my own voice.

"My parents' are both 65, I guess they aren't that much older than yours," he conceded. "My mum is recovering from a hip replacement operation though, and my dad is struggling at the restaurant these days. I suppose it didn't help with me being gone for the two weeks either."

Guilt nipped at me. Naoki wasn't normally one to take so much time off work from his family's ramen noodle restaurant; he had done it for me. He knew that after a year in Japan, I was getting homesick. I had convinced him to come and meet my parents and younger brother, Zac. My family and best friends – Sasha, Aaron and Ronnie – adored him, as I knew they would. Naoki was mild-mannered and personable; who wouldn't love him? Not to mention *gorgeous*, but then that was just for me.

I sighed. "Alright then, we'll leave it to another time, if you think that's best."

"Thanks, Kimberly. I think for the time being, it's for the best. You'll meet them soon enough. My sister, Mitsuko, is keen to meet you though. We could have dinner later this week, if you like?"

"I thought Mitsuko lived in Nagoya?"

Naoki nodded. "She does. Her husband is from there, so she moved to Nagoya after they got married two years ago."

Jealousy reared its ugly head. "Are they both visiting Tottori to spend New Year with your mum and dad?"

An image of two Japanese couples laughing together, one elderly and the other young, popped into my head. My imagination filled in the details of what Naoki's parents, sister and brother-in-law might look like. Their imagined laughter and happiness made me seethe with envy. Why did Mitsuko's husband get to spend oshōgatsu with Naoki's parents, and I didn't?

Was Naoki ashamed of me? Was it because I was a *gaijin*, a foreigner for a girlfriend?

"Only Mitsuko is home for the New Year holiday. Her husband is spending time with his own parents," Naoki said, in a rather flat tone; did he want me to drop the subject about taking me to meet his parents?

Shame burned at me. I felt terrible. Why was my insecure mind always jumping to the worst possible assumptions about people? What reason did Naoki have to be ashamed of me? None. Besides, Mitsuko had been married to her husband for two years, whereas I had only been dating Naoki for three months; Mitsuko's husband was technically part of Naoki's family, in the eyes of the law, and I was just a mere girlfriend. It wouldn't have been unreasonable for Mitsuko to bring her husband if she wanted, and Naoki to not want to bring me.

Not that Mitsuko wanted to bring her husband.

And, not that Naoki *didn't* want to bring me to meet his parents. It simply wasn't the right time – for him, or for them. I took a metaphysical sigh; he would introduce me to his parents when the time was right.

"Is it normal for Japanese couples to split up at New Year and each go to their own parents?" The question rolled off my tongue, without much thought.

Naoki was blasé. "Not really. Families tend to celebrate together. A bit like how you celebrate Christmas." He allowed his face to break into a wide smile at another opportunity to change the subject. "Maybe we can spend next Christmas together? You'll love how we do things in Japan. Christmas is all about couples and romance, sort of like your Valentine's Day."

Once again, I couldn't help but think he was deflecting onto any topic other than family. Or more specifically, his family.

So be it; I would go with his change in topic and win my battle another day. "Well, I'm looking forward to meeting your sister since she's in Tottori. Did Sasha tell you that the guys are wanting to visit us in Tottori this autumn too?"

"The guys? You mean, just Ronnie and Aaron?" said Naoki.

"Sasha too, but I was meaning 'guys' in the casual sense of the word. All three of them want to visit us," I clarified.

Naoki smiled. "That'll be great. I thought they were nice people, and I can see why you four are all so close."

"Yeah, I guess I miss having close friends. Voyce haven't given me any word about a new flatmate yet."

Voyce language school, my employer, did a great job of matching teachers as flatmates based on age, gender and interests, but no new teacher had arrived yet to replace Jei Pi. My other friend at the Tottori branch of Voyce where we worked, Zoe, had recently been spending more time with her new boyfriend Tarou than hanging out with me. I was more than a bit lonely, especially coming home to an empty flat.

Naoki's face brightened with an impish smile. "If you ask me, I think it's great that you don't have a roommate yet. I like being able to walk about in my boxers."

I threw my head back laughing. "Yeah, that wouldn't go down too well if I had a new flatmate, and she came home early only to find us shagging on the sofa."

"I hope Voyce never give you a new roommate, if it means we can have sex in the living room or bathroom, or wherever we want," he laughed.

I let my laughter fade into a placid smile. "Well, you could always move in with me instead?"

Naoki's Adam's apple bobbed up and down as a silent gulp traversed his throat.

Maybe the heavy topics; like meeting his parents, or us moving in together, was a bit too heavy too soon for him. A topic for another day, perhaps. It seemed there were limits to the subject changes that my boyfriend was willing to make. I was keen to take our relationship to the next level, but I had to wait, or I would push him away. I'd broach the issue again when he was ready.

Chapter three

Actions not words

"Hey Naoki, are you there?" I kicked off my shoes in the entranceway of my flat, leaving them scattered. Some of Jei Pei's habits had died hard when she left; like how she had 'house-trained' me to line my shoes up neatly like how Japanese people did.

Maybe not all of them, though. "Tadaima!"

It translated as *I'm home*. Naoki's response was quiet, sounding like he was out on the balcony. "Okaeri."

It was the casual version of 'okaerinasai', which meant 'welcome home'.

Naoki crossed the living room as I entered and met me halfway with a kiss. The balcony door was open and the mosquito screen closed; I saw my futon over the balcony rail and the bamboo beater in his hand.

"Aww, thanks for airing out the futon, that's so sweet of you." I linked my hands in the small of his back and he rested his arms on my shoulders, massaging the back of my neck with his strong, warm fingers.

"That's okay, what are boyfriends for?" he kissed my forehead.

I pulled back from him, wincing with one eye to affect a suspicious look. "Are you being sexist? You aren't saying that men do some tasks and women do others, are you?"

Naoki's large, brown eyes widened and the cutest flush dusted his cheeks and tops of his ears; an adorable reaction that happened when he was embarrassed. "I would never imply that, Kimberly."

I scrunched up my lips and gave him a mushy kiss. "I'm just dicking about with you. You're the most enlightened man I've ever met. I'm not even sure how I got you – never mind deserve you!"

Naoki smiled, his expression relaxing. Was it a bit mean-spirited of me to tease him? Did I take it for granted that because his English was so good, he understood all nuances of the language? How would I feel if the roles were reversed and he teased me in Japanese, and I didn't understand the subtleties?

He tilted his head, studying my face and then rubbed his thumb on my forehead. "Hey, what's with those worry lines? Right back at you – if anything the question is how do I deserve you?"

Guess my face was more expressive than I realised when I was thinking over troublesome thoughts. I was about to tell him what had really been on my mind, when he continued.

"You certainly deserve more than your ex-fiancé. I'm glad you didn't leave Japan early and marry that *asobinin* or else I never would've had a chance to get to know you."

My train of thought turned abruptly to Carl. How had I ever spent seven years of my youth in a relationship with such an emotionally abusive, racist cheater and not realised sooner that he was so bad for me?

Youth, maybe. Naiveté. Maybe–

Wait a minute; what did Naoki call Carl? Asobinin?

"Why do you call him a player? I knew he cheated on me with the sales assistant who worked in Classy Girl, but were there other women I didn't know about?"

A haunted look came over Naoki's face. "Well, it's just something that I heard from another Voyce student, before I quit. He found out I was leaving because we had started going out, and I didn't want you to breach your contract by dating a student, so he told me that he was friends with Shiori and he knew that your ex had cheated on you with her."

Shiori, the woman from Classy Girl. I thought of the last time I had seen her; at least eight months' pregnant with Carl's child, from his affair with her – long after he had ditched her of course – and ran back to London, with his *tail* between his legs.

Naoki was still speaking, so I switched away from my musings. "He also said that there had been another woman, before Shiori. Carl had apparently had an affair with Ayaka from the udon noodle restaurant, next to JCB travel in Jusco."

The udon noodle restaurant. I had eaten there only on a couple of occasions, as I tended to prefer sushi, or something else cold and quick to eat during my lunch breaks. Ayaka.

"She's quite young, isn't she, and she has kind of shoulder-length hair and a fringe? Pretty-looking girl?" I said.

Naoki flushed at my last description of her, offering a hesitant, "Yes."

I waved my hand to dismiss his worries. "I'm not jealous if you think she's pretty – facts are facts. Carl had good taste. Both Shiori and Ayaka were way out of his league. I've no idea why either woman would have wanted to sleep with him though. He was so racist."

"You're out of his league too." Naoki blinked, his long eyelashes sweeping his cheeks. "He was racist about Japanese people?"

I nodded. "He used all kinds of horrible slurs, that some nasty people say about south-east Asian people in the U.K."

"Like what?" Naoki feigned nonchalance, though I noted that he let his arms drop from his embrace around me. He flopped down on the sofa, his legs splayed and one arm across the back in a casual demeanour, but his intense expression showed me that he was serious.

"I don't really want to repeat such slurs," I said.

"Well, like 'slope' or 'Jap'? I already know those words. I heard them before when I was travelling around the States, so it won't offend me," he said.

My cheeks burned. "Similar words, maybe the British version. Carl used to say–"

Naoki understood my pause. "Go on, you can say it. It's educational for me. I love learning English."

"Not this kind of English." My reply was quick, defensive. I took a deep breath. "Alright then – but don't make me say it again. Fanny eyes."

He raised an eyebrow. "You mean, fanny, like butt?"

I shook my head. "That's American English. Fanny is British English slang for vagina."

His mouth widened. "Ah, I get it. Like, slitty eyes? You know, like I've heard a woman's privates being called a slit?"

I nodded, my eyes closed.

"That's okay, Kimberly. I know that you never used those words yourself. I mean – it's not okay that Carl used those slurs, but you dumped the guy, right? So don't be too hard on yourself," he said.

I wrung my hands, standing there in the middle of my living room, feeling like I was a naughty child. "He had an influence over me though, that I can't explain. Even though I never used such horrible, racist slurs, I wasn't so innocent myself. I did have some – uncomfortable thoughts."

"Like what?" he shrugged.

"Well, like, I asked myself would I ever date a Japanese bloke? And–" I lowered my gaze to the floor. "I compared Japanese men to Western men, you know."

"There's nothing wrong with that. People are judgemental." He paused. "Did you judge me?"

Still, with my eyes on the floor, I gave a slow nod. "I put a qualifier on how attractive you were – by saying in my head that you were good-looking for someone who was Japanese. I corrected my own thoughts immediately, of course, by getting rid of the qualifier – that I think you're good-looking, regardless of ethnicity. But it still makes me feel ashamed to remember that first impression."

The Wabi-sabi Doll

I dared to peek at him. Naoki offered an appeasing smile. "That's fine. Your actions spoke differently than your thoughts. We're together, aren't we? To be honest, I had some similar thoughts myself."

I let my gaze rise, with caution, until I saw Naoki's smile.

"I thought you felt softer than the other girls I had dated. I'd dated only two women before you, and one was a surfer, so she was very athletic. I wondered if all western women were 'soft'."

I laughed, throwing my head back. "You mean, fat!"

"Not at all – you aren't fat, Kimberly, not by a mile! Just that you have a–" Naoki's face went beetroot red. "In Japan, there's a saying about a curvy figure, you know."

He gestured an hourglass shape with his hands in the air.

"A bom-te-bom body."

I nodded my understanding. "One of my students told me about that when I first started, after a male student said it about me. He said I had a 'nice hip'."

Naoki was aghast. "That's quite rude. He meant you had a nice ass. It's not quite the same thing as bom-te-bom."

I shook my head, dismissing the sidetrack in the conversation. "The thing is, there is no difference between Japanese people, or English people. People are people," I said.

"Yes, but how many Japanese men had you dated before me?" It was a simple question, but Naoki's tone was enquiring. Curious.

I faltered, wondering if this was a trick. "None."

"And how many did you even know, in London?"

I shook my head. "None."

"So, being attracted to a Japanese guy was a new experience for you, wasn't it?"

He was right. At school, I had dated white boys, black boys, and south Asian boys, as they had been among my classmates. Carl was the only one I had dated from when I had been eighteen until twenty-five – the age I was until my birthday in a few months. There were plenty of people of south-east Asian origin in London, given that it was a multicultural city; but none in my direct social circle.

"You're right. I simply hadn't given much thought to whether I found men of south-east Asian origin my type or not before, as I hadn't known any personally." I flopped down next to Naoki on the sofa, and he wrapped an arm around me.

"There's a world of difference between what you thought and what Carl said. He's racist, you aren't. Uncomfortable thoughts that challenge us are what make us grow as people." He pulled me close for a cuddle and kissed the top of my head.

I let myself sink into the comfort of his warm chest. "You know, Carl brought out the worst in me, but you really bring out the best."

"Likewise. You, and your 'softness' bring out the best in me."

He grinned at me. I grinned back. As with everything about Naoki; his smile, his mood, his whole self – I felt I could finally be me around him. Maybe more than that. I was falling for him, in a big way. Head over heels, hurtling on a journey that I wasn't afraid, for once, to be on.

Chapter four

Water baby

Winter radish. Someone had left a bag of *daikon* on the doorstep.

I lifted the bag of three large, white carrot-shaped root vegetables and looked at the note attached to the handle. Hadn't Momoka in Chat class told me about these? Yes, they were often used in soup like *oden* and were a good low-calorie vegetable. The attached note was written in English letters, with hiragana written above: *Thank you make friends with Nana yesterday. Nana is happy talk to you. Please take delicious winter radish as thank you and make tradition Japanese food.*

How sweet. Much better than the dogshit of two days ago. I put the bag of daikon radishes by the living room door to remind myself to bring them into the kitchen when I got back. No point taking my shoes off to go into the flat when I was ready to go out.

Tottori Kaigan was the plan. You couldn't beat a beach in winter. Best self-therapy there was. Not that I needed any at the moment, to be honest. Life was the best it had been in ages. Naoki and I had been on a lovely trip to London, my family had been enamoured with him, and I sensed our relationship was moving to new heights. My feelings, definitely, had deepened and I suspected his had too. Was the L word on the horizon? That was one of the things I wanted to contemplate, while I pondered the waves.

It took me half an hour to cycle to Tottori Kaigan. I actually hadn't been for a long time. It was somewhere I had been regularly with Carl. On our last trip together, ten months previously, in March of the year before, I had rescued a pufferfish, a poisonous creature.

Maybe that was why I was going back. Now I was the pufferfish, in need of draining its poison. Did Tottori Kaigan subconsciously remind me of my ex-fiancé? I parked my bike and walked along the harbour until the end, looking out across the Sea of Japan. All of the parties that I had been to the previous summer had been at Karo Kaigan, not Tottori Kaigan. Karo was a smaller beach on the other side of the Sendai River but tended to be more of a party spot for the *gaijin* community living in Tottori.

Not that Tottori Kaigan was any less beautiful. I stepped off the concrete harbour path and onto the long, sandy strand. To the east, I could see the giant, undulating sand dunes; another thing aside from Tottori nashi pears that my home-from-hometown was famous for. I hadn't even been on one of the famous camel rides that attracted tourists from all over Japan, and further afield. The camels, of course weren't

The Wabi-sabi Doll

native to Japan, but had been imported specially to provide rides across Tottori's mini-Sahara. Not today, but maybe soon. My thoughts were in charge of the schedule today, not my feet.

I found a spot near the water's edge without too many stones or shells and sat down on the sand. I dragged a lazy finger across the damp grains, writing my name in katakana.

"Keem-bah-ree," I said aloud to the wind.

How to write Naoki in hiragana? I knew all fifty-six of the katakana characters and all fifty-six of the corresponding hiragana characters; enough to read menus and some public signs. My name, as a non-Japanese name would be written in katakana, the script used for foreign words. Naoki's would be written in kanji characters, the script based on traditional Chinese words. Since Japanese was a phonetic spoken language, his name could also be written in hiragana, an alphabet developed as a way of simplifying kanji characters. I didn't know any kanji characters, but I could write in hiragana.

"Nah-oh-key," I said aloud as I wrote the phonetic characters in the sand, above my own. I then enclosed both names in a big heart.

I stared at the heart shape I had just drawn. Did that mean I loved Naoki? Was I in love? What was love?

Maybe it was too soon. Carl had torn my heart to shreds. Not that I had actually, ever loved Carl in the first place. But I had felt affection for him, starting with a schoolgirl crush when we had met while I was eighteen and in my final year of school.

"Manny!"

The loud, brash, London accent ripped me out of my amorous daydreams about Naoki. My ex, Carl's voice. Manny was his unwanted nickname for me; a derogatory moniker coined from the word 'mannequin', as he thought I was slim, blonde and bland like a shop-store dummy. I froze, my shoulders tensing. It was as though a ghost from the past had intruded on present life in the worst, most unwelcome manner. Only, this was no daydream.

"Imagine seeing you here?"

I twisted my body, yoga style, and looked over my left shoulder. Carl strode towards me. He looked the same; tall, scrawny and sinewy, his mousey brown hair standing up against the onslaught of sea air, his jacket billowing behind him. Had he lost weight? Maybe. It gave me some satisfaction to think that our break-up the year before had impacted him any way as badly as it had thrown my life into turmoil. Or maybe not; his oversized jacket bulged at the front. Carl had always been on the wiry side; had he developed a pot belly in ten months since I had last seen him?

What did it matter if he was fat or thin? Why was I sizing him up anyway? He wasn't half as gorgeous as Naoki, and wasn't a quarter of the kind, decent compassionate man that my new boyfriend was either.

"What brings you to 'our' spot on Tottori beach?" said Carl, an annoying smirk on his face.

"I could ask the same of you – what brings you to Japan, in fact?" I spat back.

Carl had visited me in Japan for three months during my first year in Japan; we had spent Christmas and new year together travelling in Tokyo, and he had stayed for the duration of his three-month tourist visa, leaving in March last year. As the spring winds had blown in from China, Carl had blown out on a cloud full of hot air.

Hot air and hubris. Two affairs, with hot local women, behind my back while I had been working hard at Voyce language school to feed us, for twelve weeks.

I fumed at the memory. Carl still watched me with a stupid grin on his face.

"I'll answer first," he said. It took a second for my thoughts to jolt back to realise he was answering my question. He started to unzip his rain jacket and as the panels fell aside, caught by the strong breeze coming in off the Japan Sea, I saw a baby carrier strapped to his front.

My jaw fell, in spite of my need to show no emotion to my abusive ex-fiancé.

"This little princess is called Karen. She came along in November. Can you believe I'm a dad?" Carl turned sideways and my eyes rested on an adorable two month old baby in a pink winter jumpsuit, looking snug against Carl's chest.

If anyone was less deserving of being a dad to a beautiful half-Japanese daughter, it was racist Carl. Was he going to live in the culture he seemed to view as inferior to London culture? Was he in a relationship with Shiori, the woman he cheated on me with?

A petite figure, clad in a long windbreaker coat and thick, woollen trousers, hurried across the beach towards us. As she neared, I recognised Shiori's small form. She was still as beautiful as I remembered her from the year before. The last time I had seen her, she had been eight months pregnant and had come to Voyce school, under the pretence of registering as a new student, so that she could apologise to me. Despite knowing she had stolen my fiancé, I had accepted her apology as we had bonded over our recognition of what a bastard Carl had been to us both: cheating on my and ditching Shiori when she was pregnant.

Clearly he had changed his mind, though. And clearly there was more than one child. My eyes rested on the baby carrier strapped to Shiori's front, below her wide smile that was fixed on me.

"Hello Kimberly san," she said, in a soft, polite tone.

Quite different from the sexy, punk outfits she had worn when out clubbing the year before, and the sour glare she had often given me when we had seen each other around as 'rivals'. Now I understood why her baby-bump had been so big, especially for her small frame. Twins.

"Meet Karen and Naomi," Shiori added, gesturing from the baby Carl carried, to the one she held.

"Did you pick the western names, then?" I looked at Carl, waiting for his response.

"We picked them together." Shiori linked hands with Carl.

"Yeah, turns out those names are used in Japan as well as London, so it's a win-win, innit?" Carl guffawed.

I gritted my teeth, then turned the grimace into a fixed smile; I couldn't give Carl the satisfaction of showing my disapproval.

"Are you living here now?" My thoughts drifted to work. There weren't many jobs that a non-Japanese person could do in Tottori, if they didn't speak fluent Japanese, which Carl certainly didn't. He definitely didn't work at my company, Voyce, one of few options for foreigners who couldn't speak Japanese.

"Nah, I'm over on another three-month tourist visa. You can come over once a year — innit, hun?"

Shiori nodded, giving him an affectionate smile.

Carl's crass colloquial language made me cringe. Shiori was light-years above him; she could have any man she wanted, yet she picked *him*. The urge to suddenly scream, 'do you realise this pathetic excuse of a man says Japanese people have '*fanny-eyes*' crossed my mind, but I suppressed it. What would Shiori think if she knew Carl was a racist bastard? I wanted to accuse the bigoted wanker of so many things; like, did he see his own children as having 'fanny-eyes'?

Instead, I let my thoughts drift.

"He's been over since the girls were a week old. Once his visa's finished next month, we're going over to London. I've never been. It's so exciting," said Shiori.

"Yeah, bruv, can you imagine the look on my old man and lady's faces when they see these two princesses?"

Bruv. How insulting of Carl to call me 'bruv'. He had never called me such a term before. Was it to show Shiori that our seven-year relationship was now relegated to history, and that I had meant nothing — ever?

If that was indeed the case, did it matter? Not really. All that mattered was that Carl would leave Japan; the sooner the better.

"So, what are you doing here? Thinking about me?" he added, scattering my thoughts.

Shiori's mouth dropped open, her eyes full of fire. She smacked him in the arm with the back of her hand. If she looked outraged, I couldn't imagine what the look on my own face was like.

"Joking, joking, just pulling your leg. You're the only woman for me, China doll."

Shiori flushed flamingo-pink. "Don't call me that, it's so embarrassing!"

China doll. China doll and Manny. Both beautiful, both inanimate objects to be used.

"Actually, my other half, Naoki, just proposed to me. I came here to think about planning our big day." I stared defiantly at Carl.

Why did I feel the need to lie to Carl? Was it because, here he was, happy and seemingly well-adjusted, with his ready-made family? What did I have in comparison? In the past ten months since Carl had left, I had been raped by a former colleague, Vince, who had gone home to Arizona soon after, leaving me with both internal and external damage to my vagina. Instead of twin baby girls, I had been left to miscarry my child conceived through sexual assault, finding out the baby had gone at the twelve week scan.

"Go on, show us the big rock then?" Carl nodded towards my left hand, which was bundled in my pocket against the cold.

Since Carl had left, I had removed his engagement ring, replacing it with a gold-plated dress ring that I had treated myself to. It had been a subconscious decision, influenced by the saying that men stayed away from women who wore rings on their wedding fingers. I had wanted the headspace to enjoy being single. Or maybe I didn't like having a bare finger after all those years with a flashy, platinum diamond ring on my hand. Or maybe both.

I lifted my hand, showing the yellow gold band with its single opal flanked by two cubic zirconia stones.

The Wabi-sabi Doll

Carl's face broke into an irritating grin. "Some big spender you're marrying. Good to see what you're worth to him."

My nostrils flared as I sucked an inhale through my nose, my chest swelling with the breath. I had to say nothing, I couldn't rise to the bait. I willed my mouth to stay shut.

"Carl, let's go. It's too cold here." Although she addressed Carl, Shiori's eyes were on me as she spoke. Was that to imply that I was making the conversation frosty?

Whatever. He had outstayed his welcome in any event, invading my personal time – and space – on the beach.

"See ya round, Manny. Hope he pays more for the wedding than he did on the ring. And hope you don't turn out as barren as this beach you love so much."

My gasp was whipped away by the strong, winter wind.

"Fuck you, Carl."

Sadly, the wind whipped my curse away too. But not his response.

"You know I'm joking. You take care," he said with a wink, back over his shoulder.

Always had to have the last word. Thank goodness he didn't see the tear that rolled down my cheek. Carl didn't know, couldn't have known, about the baby that I had lost after what Vince did to me. A baby I didn't know I wanted, despite the circumstances in which she was conceived. I watched Carl and Shiori's retreating figures growing smaller across the sands, before I turned my vision towards the grey, choppy waves where last year I had released my *Mizuyo Kujo,* my Water Baby, back into the care of the world.

Last year, I had lowered my palm and released my kidney-bean baby into the water where she had floated, like a Spanish dancer, surrounded by the red and white strings of my womb, drifting around her like frills in the waves.

Last year I had been truly, irrevocably one with the moment, the essence of Zen as my hand had gifted my Water Child into the Sea of Japan.

This year I was lost. This year, I was purposeless. Empty, and lost, and purposeless, as fast as a single grain of sand on Tottori beach could hit me in the eye. A single grain, whipped up on the wind by a racist bastard's feet retreating across the sand.

Chapter five

Has-beens and hair dye

The black tinted water swirled down the plughole. I watched it disappear into the black hole of the drain. A part of me disappeared with it into the same dark nothingness: my DNA, my essence, my soul.

I wrapped the towel around my head and rubbed vigorously, then pulled it off and shook my hair, like a dog drying itself. My bob had grown out by a couple of inches, now touching my shoulders. My fringe needed a trim. My newly dyed black hair made my pale skin look extra vampirish. It would take some getting used to. I had been blonde all my life, and tended to use lemon juice, or vodka on my hair in summer, giving my natural ash-blonde tones a few sun-kissed highlights. This was my first time going dark.

I blow-dried my hair upside down, peering between the dangling curtain of black strands. Was black too bold a colour choice? Maybe so, but I needed a change.

Looking at the room upside down was a good change too; if only I could have walked across the ceiling. The patterns on the ceiling kind of resembled mitochondria; at least how they looked on the smart board seven years before, when I had been finishing my A-level biology course.

Mitochondria DNA. Changes in the mitochondrial DNA had given rise to a change in modern Homo Sapiens. Humans. Us. Eve had given birth to all of the humans all over the planet. All of us, regardless of skin colour. The whole planet was populated by people who wriggled all over its surface like wriggling mitochondria inside cells, as sausage shaped squiggles crawling across my ceiling, as oblong objects infesting my mind…

Stop. Too much. Desist. Refrain. Halt.

What was wrong with my brain and the odd assortment of random thoughts that intruded in my mind? If I let them grow free, then what would happen? Probably they would grow tall, and wild, and strong as weeds that would become trees with deep roots, deeper underground than the branches visible to the world above ground.

I tossed my dry hair back and smoothed it down behind my head, flattening the fringe across my forehead. My wide-bristle brush did the rest. Once it was sufficiently styled, I walked to the window with the hand-mirror to inspect it in natural light. The colour was very matte, with a faint blue-black tint. Was that because of my natural silver undertones, or because it was a dye designed for Japanese hair, the majority of which was naturally very dark? Who knew?

Below my heavy, black fringe that obscured my eyebrows, my blue eyes sparkled with an intensity like glacial ice. My natural blonde hair didn't offset them so vividly. Did I like the look? Yes, actually, I did. It didn't look natural on me, but it emphasised my features in a way that was different for me. Yes, I decided, I *did* like it. I liked it a lot. Different was good. A new look. A fresh start.

This time last year, my blonde hair had reached down to my lower back, brushing my waist. After the traumatic events of the previous summer, when my ex-colleague and supposed friend, Vince had raped me, I had cut my long hair short, cropped into a bob, with a barely-there fringe. The haircut had been an accidental mishap; that day at Tottori Kaigan was forever etched into my brain. There I was, on the sand, writing the names of the men who had harmed me: Carl and Vince, and the wrongs they had committed against me. I had set fire to the paper in an act of self-healing that had gone wrong. My hair had caught fire. After that, I had been left with no choice other than to lop it all off, short. The change had been refreshing; exactly what I had needed, to cut off the past.

Now this was another new change. Was I tarnished? Was that why I had done it; to look different from the girl who had been in a seven year relationship with brutish Carl? I blinked as I studied my reflection in the mirror, seeking answers that silvery glass couldn't give. Absently, I swept my fringe upwards and looked at my mousey eyebrows. Was there enough black dye in the bottom of the bottle to tint them too? As for my eyelashes, well, black mascara would have to do. I highly doubted that there would be a lash and brow tinting service anywhere in Tottori, when there wasn't a market for it among Japanese people who already had naturally defined eyes. Shiori's pretty face popped to mind, as though to highlight my point to my own subconscious. She had long, black eyelashes that swept outwards in a natural flick and her black eyebrows had a high arch that gave her a coquettish look – at least to me. She was beautiful. No wonder Carl had picked her.

I seethed. What was I doing? Why was I jealous of her? Carl was an abusive, racist creep. If anything, I should have felt pity for her for being stuck with such an unenlightened arse. If I really felt that way, then what did I have to be jealous of?

I stared above the mirror, out into the neutral grey sky. Neutral, bland. It was what I needed to wade through the bland porridge of my thoughts to find clarity. Answers that I could deliver to myself; that I didn't need from any other outside source; only from my own wisdom.

It made me feel inferior. That was the issue; not Carl, or Shiori as individuals, as people. Just the concept that someone else had been chosen in favour of me made me feel inadequate. Incomplete. As though I wasn't a whole, functioning human being who had goodness to offer the world. It made me feel like I was flawed.

It made me *feel*. Not think or know. Feel.

Feelings came from me though, didn't they? I owned them, nobody else.

Was that true? Didn't Carl make me feel bad? Yes.

This was about ownership, wasn't it? I wasn't in control of my feelings; I didn't *own* them. Other people had power over me, the power to do good or ill. They could make me feel happy, or sad. The closer the person was to me, the better, or worse the feeling became; essentially more intense. Was that good?

It depended on the person. I inhaled, letting my ribcage swell. I had a new mission this year: to work on not letting bad people affect me so profoundly. Carl was nothing to me; he was history, our relationship a has-been. I needed to take the power away from him; to restore it to me.

Chapter six

Reflections

I brushed my dark hair flat against my cheeks and smoothed my fringe over my forehead. Confident that my hair looked immaculate, I let my gaze travel downwards over the outfit I had chosen: a white chiffon shirt with black polka-dots over a black cami-vest, matched with a pair of jeans. Time for Naoki's opinion. He looked up as I shimmied into the living room, a conscious choice on my part, for added affect.

"What do you think?" I placed my hands under my hair, my fingers radiating outwards to show the new colour.

Naoki's mouth dropped. He bounded off the sofa like he'd sat on a spike. "What did you do?"

Way to state the obvious. "What does it look like?"

"But – but why, Kimberly? Is it permanent?"

I let my hands drop, rubbing my palms on my jeans instead. "Don't you like it?"

"Well," Naoki faltered, and I knew he was thinking; of probably just the right thing to say. "I wasn't expecting it. I mean, when I walked in and saw the bathroom curtain drawn shut, I knew there must've been a reason for that, since it's only us here. But still, it's a surprise – that's all."

I ran my fingers upwards under my hair, spreading it out Cleopatra-style, then swished it around my face; the smell of the colour sealant conditioner was fresh and welcome in my nostrils. "Surprise is good. And change is welcome."

"But why? You never mentioned wanting a change – normally you would've said something," he said, a mystified look on his face.

I glowered at him. "What, so now I have to tell you if I want to do something? Do I have to ask your permission?"

Naoki's mystified face turned to shock at my accusation. "You know that's not what I meant."

I waved my words away. "I'm sorry Naoki, I don't mean to be such a bitch. I'm just touchy today."

"Are you nervous because we're planning to meet Mitsuko for dinner?" He swooped closer and brushed my fringe to one side with a warm, gentle finger.

I twiddled with the dress ring on my engagement finger. "No, I've been looking forward to it. I've been alone with my thoughts too much this week."

"You didn't dye your hair to fit in more with my family, did you?"

He had a fair point; I couldn't deny that. Was I trying to blend in more without my blonde hair?

"I don't think so. I was kind of upset the other day, after something happened when I went for a winter beach walk near Tottori Kaigan, and I just grabbed the dye at Jusco as an impulse buy before coming home."

Naoki pulled me in for a hug. "I'm sorry I couldn't come over that evening. Dad was really struggling at the restaurant and I had to stay longer than I was planning to lock everything up."

I loosened his arms and walked away to the living room window. The view of Kyushu mountain overlooking Tottori grounded me and I allowed myself to inhale through my nose and exhale through my mouth. "It's not your fault. I shouldn't need you to rescue me every time I meltdown. In a way, it was good you couldn't stay over that night. I never want to become codependent ever again."

"Is this about Carl? Is it too soon for us?"

I let myself turn to face him. Something in his sad, haunted eyes drew me back to him and I returned the hug he had given me moments before, linking my fingers in the small of his back.

"No, Naoki. It *is* about Carl, but not how you think. I'm over him. We're done, finished, history."

He pushed back from me, a little; enough to look me in the eyes. "Yes, but do you still love him?"

"I never loved him in the first place. When we met, I was young and naïve. He was five years older and seemed sophisticated to an eighteen year old girl. He was working, and I was still a high school kid. He lavished me with presents and made me feel grownup."

Naoki lowered his gaze, his long eyelashes sweeping his cheeks. "I'm sorry I'm too broke to buy you presents."

He was getting me all wrong. I inhaled and continued. "I didn't want presents, even though I thought I did at the time. He cheated on me with his ex and bought me flowers to say sorry. He bought me a designer handbag another time, again to say sorry. I found out later it was his sister Chezza's money paying for the gifts anyway – he wasn't rich. He ran his own painting and decorating business that went bust. After that, he got a cleaning job at Luton airport. The presents were a con."

"A con?" Naoki raised an eyebrow.

"As in conman, like a confidence trickster. He basically lured me in when we were first dating, even paying rent on our flat in Croydon, where he's from, while I was in my first year at UCL. But it came at a cost. He became controlling and possessive, using guilt trips and emotional manipulation against me. Maybe that's why I ended up doing my degree course in Clinical Psychology. A psychologist could have a field day studying Carl."

He gave a weak smile. "I understand. I'm glad you're done with him, and that you choose to be with me. But, is there a reason he's on your mind this week? Is it just because it's the first week of a new year and so you're reflecting on the past?"

I focused on his chin, finding myself unable to look at his eyes, though I couldn't say why. "I saw him at Tottori Kaigan."

He blanched; even from my peripheral vision, I saw his mouth agape. "I didn't know he was back in Japan. Did you know he would be there?"

I felt my forehead tighten in horror. "Of course not, or else I wouldn't have gone there. It was the worst coincidence."

A burning sensation started in the corners of my eyes. The next thing I knew, my vision had clouded as tears obscured Naoki, the room – everything. They fell unabated.

"Oh, Kimberly." He clutched me against his hard chest, his strong arms wrapped around my upper back and a warm hand soothing my hair. "That must've been awful for you, opening up so many wounds."

"Even worse, he was there with Shiori. They're back together."

I felt the muscles in Naoki's throat tight against my temple as he swallowed. "Does that bother you?"

My heart hammered in my chest, and I wondered if he could feel it, as I could feel his gulp. "No. I couldn't care less that they're back together, it means nothing to me. But they have babies."

"Oh, I remember hearing that Shiori san had been pregnant," he added.

I puckered my lip. Why did it bother me that he called her *Shiori san*. Use of 'san' was an honorific title in Japan, a sign of respect. Naoki never said Carl san when he mentioned my ex-fiancé's same. Not that he should, of course. Maybe my jealousy of Shiori was simply a hangover from Carl cheating on me with her the previous year.

I wiped my tears away and sniffed. "I think it made me feel inadequate seeing their children. She's so beautiful and fertile, and that bastard even made a joke about me being barren like the Tottori sand dunes, as barren as a desert."

"That's awful. What a wanker."

Amidst my tears, I chortled. He had picked up the British slang from me. Hearing him say *wanker* still amused me, since normally he refrained from swearing generally. Naoki was a proper gentleman, and I had corrupted him, albeit in the most adorable, idiosyncratic Naoki-way.

"Well, it's true. He *is* a wanker. Wanker, wanker, wanker." We laughed together, Naoki clearly understanding why I found it funny. I let my mirth fade naturally; it had been restorative for my soul, so just what I had needed. Now was the time to put words to my thoughts, for Naoki's sake.

"After I lost that pregnancy last year… even though it was through rape and I didn't want to have a baby by that predator…"

"I get it." His voice had a hardness that I knew was about the topic, not directed at me. "You're worried that you won't be able to have another child since you already miscarried one."

Why could I barely look at him, after admitting such a thing? Why was there such a heavy, invisible weight on dating? Looks attracted at first glance, personality bulldozed looks out of the way; but genetics prevailed. If I couldn't have kids, would Naoki be secretly stashing that piece of information away at the back of his mind for the 'long-term relationship' department of his brain to compute whether a serious relationship with me was worth the effort? What if he wanted kids after marriage? Many people did. What about me? I didn't want kids now, not yet ready for motherhood in my twenties, but that didn't mean I might not want them in a few years' time. What if the option wasn't open to me? What if I was unable to have children?

He sliced through all my fears with one gentle finger placed under my chin, tipping my face upwards until our eyes met.

"I'm sure you'll be perfectly able to have children when you're ready. But, even if you're not, it isn't why I love you right now, right here," he said.

I gasped. He had said the L word.

"What's wrong?" he added, his lip rumpling.

"Nothing's wrong. You said you love me."

"I do. I love you."

I studied his face. His gentle smile; the care in his gaze. There was no expectation for me to return the sentiment. I relaxed and let myself sink into his chest, knowing that I could say it back to him, when I was ready. I was sure that would be soon.

Chapter seven

Mindful of the moment

The Italian restaurant was tucked in the midst of a quiet, residential spot behind Tottori train station. I wouldn't have known about it if it wasn't for Mitsuko's suggestion to meet us there.

Naoki must have sensed my hesitation; I could feel his eyes boring a hole in my cheek as we got out of his white Toyota Prius and walked up the short driveway towards the front door.

"It's alright, Kimberly. My sister is pretty chill."

I tucked a stray strand behind my ear and smoothed my hair for the hundredth time. No point lying to him. "I don't know why I'm nervous, I just am."

He gave a half-shrug with one shoulder, one corner of his mouth twitch upwards to match. "Makes sense. I was full of jitters just a few weeks ago at the idea of meeting your family, so I know the feeling."

My thoughts rolled out of my mouth, without giving me a chance to process them. Not that I needed a chance to filter my words of course; Naoki made me so at ease that I could be myself without worry of judgement. "It was really good of her to pick a western place to eat. I mean, not that I would have minded a Japanese restaurant – I love the food here – but it was sweet of her to pick somewhere that she thought I'd feel comfortable in," I said.

He grinned. "Carbonara's also her favourite food, so there's that too."

Carbonara. Mental note to perfect my own recipe if I ever had her over to my flat for a visit. We walked inside the glass fronted building and up a single flight of steps to the restaurant on the first floor. It was a quiet and unobtrusive place where I clapped eyes on Mitsuko right away. Like her brother, she was tall and slender with the same long, sweeping eyelashes and large, soulful eyes that Naoki had, and a set of straight, even teeth. She had shoulder-length hair that was dyed a caramel brown colour, and wore her long fringe offset to the left and pinned with a small clip. Mitsuko was deep in the midst of a conversation with the man at the bar, her demeanour casual as she leaned on the counter. The bell on the door tinkled as we entered, making her turn and smile when she saw us.

Wow, Carl would love her if he saw her. A jolt of jealousy erupted through my core, before common sense overrode my animal brain. What the hell was wrong with me? Why was I still thinking about that abusive creep?

"Hey little bro," said Mitsuko in fluent English, though with a heavier accent than Naoki's.

"Yo sis," he answered, before turning to me. "Kimberly, this is my ane chan, Mitsuko."

Mental note to oneself: ane chan, colloquial usage, big sis. Compartmentalised. Got it. I smiled at her. "Nice to meet you, Mitsuko. I'm Kimberly. Dozo yoroshiku."

"Oh wow, great Japanese." Mitsuko brought her hands together in a single clap, giving a slight bow at the same time. "Yoroshiku onegaishimasu."

"Shall we get a table?" said Naoki.

"Sure." Mitsuko led us to a small table by the window where there was a surprisingly pleasant view over the leafy residential street beyond. Very Zen. Another thing I loved about Japan.

"I love your black hair. Is this a new thing?" Mitsuko added.

Her friendly, yet intimate comment caught me by surprise. My hand flew to the bottom of my dyed black mop. "Oh, actually yes. I did it myself just earlier after my shower."

Such an innocent thing to say, yet my cheeks burned as though a spotlight had been turned on me, melting me bit by bit. How much had Naoki told her about me? I glanced at him, subconsciously maybe, and he straightened his back in his seat; just a tad.

"I sent her some photos from our trip to London," he clarified.

How was it that Naoki seemed to be able to read minds? Or at least, his level of intuition was scarily in tune with mine, at times. Whatever the reason, he knew how to dispel my doubts as quickly as they cropped up.

"Well, it suits you," she said, her long eyelashes sweeping her cheeks as she fixed me with a warm smile. "Naoki's told me so much about you."

Did I sigh with relief too loudly? Not loudly enough? Mitsuko seemed to like me, and it seemed genuine enough. First impressions mattered; she was a good soul. I hoped she thought the same of me.

"He speaks really highly of you too," I answered, unsure of what else to say. It was the truth, though. Kind of. He'd given the impression that they were close, but it didn't seem they saw each other that much, what with her living in Nagoya.

Being around Naoki put me at ease; so why was it the opposite with Mitsuko? They were close, very similar in many ways, so it seemed obvious that I should've felt relaxed in her company. Yet I was tense. She wasn't judgemental, didn't bombard me with personal questions, but being in her presence made me feel on edge.

Maybe it made me think of my relationship with my own brother. Mitsuko was older than Naoki by two years, as I was older than Zac by three years. But the way they got along was so different to Zac and I. Even as adults, me being twenty-six and him being twenty-three, we still fought like cats and dogs. One particularly embarrassing episode played out over the Christmas holiday with Zac accusing me of eating his last two *Babybels* - which I did not – and having to defend myself. Recollecting our argument made me cringe, yet my callous mind enjoyed tormenting me:

Why would I eat your stupid Babybel? I don't even like cheese!

Well, who else would've done it? Are you going to blame it on Noogie?

Leave Noogie out of this, you're stressing him out arguing like this and being such a dick over two tiny pieces of cheese.

The dog had barked then, as though to back me up.

Just admit you did it, Kim. You still eat my food, you haven't changed since we were kids.

The Wabi-sabi Doll

I didn't eat your fucking food!

I had thrown both fists down at that point, like an angry toddler. The cringeworthiness of my memory increased, bringing more and more heat to my face.

You're still harping on about that one piece of pizza that I ate when I was seventeen after a night out? Next time, I WILL eat your Babybel - and spit them at you so that you have proof!

Oh my gosh, so mortifying. I clapped a hand over my forehead as the recent memory assaulted my prefrontal cortex. Naoki and Mitsuko both gave me a quizzical look.

"Are you okay, Kimberly?" Naoki's brow was heavy as he studied me.

I moved my hand off my forehead and flapped it, dismissing the memory. "Yeah, I'm alright. It's nothing. Sorry."

Naoki's concerned face was the opposite of how it had been on that night, back at Mum and Dad's house in Southampton. He had been amused at the fight between Zac and I, and how poor Noogie had been dragged into our childish tiff. Naoki and Mitsuko's sibling relationship seemed much more mature and composed in comparison.

Not one to needle me, Naoki's face relaxed. "As long as you're fine."

His trust in me only made me care for him more. Whereas Carl would have badgered me to admit what was on my mind, Naoki believed what I said and didn't feel the need to know *every* last waking thought on my mind. I was grateful. There was no need for me to rehash the embarrassment of that scene at Christmas. Or of any interaction with Carl.

Carl's words: *Why don't you just say what's on your mind? Are you so stupid that you think I don't realise you're pissed off?*

Me in response: *Because I don't feel like talking, okay?*

Carl again: *Fine, have it your way, grumpy knickers. I'll read it in your poetry journal when you're in bed, then.*

Ugh, why was I still thinking of Carl? Why did I replay the litany of insults he threw at me, on a daily basis?

I wanted to pump my fist against my temple, to knock the memory of my abusive ex out of my head. Why did life have to be so cruel as to keep bad memories locked down, and replay them at the worst times; like meeting Naoki's perfectly lovely sister. A perfectly lovely person, who was unsuspecting about what kind of unbalanced, dysfunctional person her brother was dating.

"It's just quite warm in here." I fanned my face with my hand, willing bad thoughts to leave my head.

If only I could be a blank slate. Empty, calm, ready to respond to the present, rather than get tangled in the messy past. Especially when in front of me sat Yin and Yang. Naoki as Yin, his energy soothing me and Mitsuko as Yang, her curious eyes shining a spotlight on me that made me...

Made me what?

Nervous? Worried? Insecure? I visualised each word in my head, spelling out the letters to keep myself grounded and focused, and then erased it. Drew a mental line through each one, slicing it in half. No; Mitsuko didn't make me feel nervous, or worried, or insecure. I made *myself* feel that way, by having an overstimulated memory and overactive imagination.

Time to make a change; even if only for the here-and-now. I focused on the moment, trying to instil some mindfulness into my actions. Spiritual me.

Mindful me. Ever-present me. How did I feel, in the present? Hungry.

"Onaka peko peko." I rubbed my stomach, my eyes on the menu.

To my surprise, Mitsuko laughed behind her hand. "Kawaii! Sugoku kawaii, ne."

I turned my gaze from her to Naoki. He too smiled.

"What did I say? I thought it meant 'I'm hungry'?"

More embarrassing memories surfaced of slip-ups with the language: saying unko instead of anko to my Japanese colleagues, poo rather than red-bean paste, and asking a cashier if I could have hisho, meaning secretary, instead of hashi, meaning chopsticks, with my sushi.

"It does, but it's a really cute way of saying it – like how a little kid would say it. You know, like a kindergartener," Naoki explained. "Where did you learn that?"

I thought of Kawaii-chan, from the flat downstairs in my apartment building. "I heard the neighbour's kid say it."

They both chuckled.

Why did that make me feel so mortified?

I said nothing. Mental note to use the standard textbook phrase I had learned: onaka ga suita.

Got to be mindful, got to be zen. I inhaled to clear my embarrassment. Decision time; I could ignore it, or I could give them something else to laugh about. Be silly. Get creative.

Yes. Playfulness was the way to handle it. Playfulness for mindfulness. Read the room; if they laughed, I would laugh with them.

I thought of the macho way to say the same phrase for 'I'm hungry'; male usage, definitely not for women to say. I cleared my throat. "Atashi wa hara hetta da zou."

This time, Naoki burst out laughing along with his sister. Perfect. I had made both of them lose their composure, all through my silly combination of girly and macho Japanese words.

I stood up next, and clasped both hands over my crotch, twisting my legs like Kawaii-chan had done. "Boku wa muri sou."

Tomboyish 'I' mixed with childish 'need to pee'.

Tears streamed from Mitsuko's eyes as she was laughing so hard. What had I achieved? Well, I certainly didn't feel nervous anymore. Negative feelings had dissipated into the ether. I felt mindful of the moment, mindful of Mitsuko, and mindful of myself. It was a start.

Chapter eight

Moeru gomi for the mind

What was this, what was blocking the door?

I budged it open, using my shoulder for force. Rubbish, strewn everywhere. A black bin bag of *moeru gomi*, burnable rubbish, had been torn open and scattered outside my front door.

"What is with shit being left on my doorstep? Sheesh!" I deliberately shouted the words loud enough that the perpetrator, if they were still nearby, would be within earshot.

It wasn't all shit though. Black and white, yin and yang, good and bad. First there had been dogshit, which was bad, followed by daikon radishes from the downstairs neighbour, and now rubbish from a random person. This was no accident; someone had brought the bag of moeru gomi up the flight of steps and around the small L-shaped crook to my front door.

They had gone to the trouble of ripping the bag open and shaking it out all over my doormat.

Had I accidently included *moenai gomi*, non-burnable waste, with the moeru gomi? If I had incorrectly sorted my rubbish, then that might explain the aggression in such a hostile move on the part of a disgruntled binman or a judgemental neighbour. But I was always careful to sort my rubbish carefully, mindful that as the *alien* resident, with an alien residential card from Tottori Prefectural office no less, that I'd take particular care not to do anything to make a nuisance of myself.

There was nothing for it, other than to sort out the rubbish and re-bag it in a new bin liner.

Wait a moment, though. As I looked through the *moeru gomi*, I couldn't help but notice that the wrappers showed foods I definitely didn't eat. *Natto*, for one. I never ate the stinky fermented beans, a popular traditional Japanese food. Tomomi and Akemi, the Japanese staff at work, had introduced me to it last year as a practical joke. They had suspected that I would hate it and they were right; I had gagged as the slimy gloop had spread all over my tongue. That had been my one and only experience with natto that I was keen to never repeat.

What else? *Katsobushi*. The fish flakes that went on top of okonomiyaki, Japanese savoury pancakes. As much as I enjoyed okonomiyaki, I tended to eat it at restaurants. It wasn't a food I would have been capable of making myself at home. Nope; definitely not my bag of rubbish.

I seethed. Did that mean that whoever had shaken the rubbish all over my doorstep had assumed that I did it, just because I was a foreigner?

The Wabi-sabi Doll

I gulped. "Racist bastard, this isn't my rubbish!"

I bagged up all of the wrappers, eggshells, soggy tissues and other junk that had been dumped on my doorstep, then went back inside my house to find notepaper. What would be a good message to attach for effect? I wracked my brain. I'd keep it simple – something like, 'This is not my rubbish. I'm sad.' Yes, that would do. In large hiragana letters, I wrote the message using a black felt-tip marker.

watashi no moeru gomi ja arimasen. kanashiku naru.

Underneath, I drew a face with a sad mouth and tears dripping down the cheeks. Then I attached the note to the neatly bagged up rubbish and left it on my doorstep.

Back inside to put away the notepaper and felt-tip and wash my hands after such a disgusting task. Not the kind of start to my day off that I wanted. Not to worry; I wouldn't let it ruin my shopping trip. I would simply need to invest in more retail therapy that I had been planning to make up for the added hurt.

When I opened my front door to leave, the bag had gone.

So, someone had been watching. Someone had watched me tidy the mess and attach the note. I stood on the balcony and looked at all possible flats and houses with a view of my doorstep. The perpetrator could have been any number of neighbours. Guess there was no way I would know who had done it. At least they had removed the bag. Had they read the note? Whoever the bad person was, hopefully they had a massive dose of guilt at wronging me.

If only Naoki could have stayed the night, been there in the living room for a hug. After dinner with Mitsuko the day before, he had seen her off on her train at Tottori Station, then spent the night at home to open the restaurant up first thing in the morning. Just when I needed his long, comforting arms around me.

I really, really needed a hug. Why did I feel so down, and so lonely, and so – overwhelmed. On the face of it, life was straightforward. I was settled into my job as an English teacher. I liked my colleagues, pretty much. I felt confident with the basics of the Japanese language. I had supportive parents and friends back in London. Most of all, against the odds, I had found an amazing boyfriend who was helping my heart to heal. So, what was there to feel lonely and overwhelmed about?

It wasn't Naoki's fault his dad was struggling at the restaurant and needed him to do more and more shifts. It was his family business, something that he might even take over one day, when his parents retired. Family business was important. And I certainly wasn't family.

Family. Was that what was bothering me? Did I want to be part of Naoki's family? I liked his sister, hadn't yet met his parents – but it was too soon. I shook my head, dismissing the thoughts. Not at the moment anyway; the thought of marriage was too soon. No, that wasn't what was bothering me.

I sighed. Years of studying Clinical Psychology and yet I couldn't even unravel my own head. My mind was a bag full of moeru gomi that hadn't been sorted, hadn't been separated properly. The parts that couldn't be burned would leave charred imprints, while the rest would drift into the ether, polluting the atmosphere. Maybe someone needed to rip the bag open, before it got burned, and scatter the rubbish for all the world to see.

Chapter nine

Tipping point

"What on earth did you do to your hair? You didn't tell me it was Halloween?"

My boss, Ben, gawked at me and blinked his eyes in an exaggerated, theatrical way. The young woman who was in a booth with him for a demo lesson giggled at his antics. Just what I needed; to be embarrassed in front of a potential new student.

I sighed. "Yeah well, I like it. I needed the change."

He dropped his theatrics at what I presumed was the look on my face. "I'm just joshing with you, Kimmy."

I shot a pursed smile at him and passed on by the reception desk to drop off my coat and bag in the staffroom. A quick glance at the clock told me I had half an hour before my shift. It wasn't often I had time to kill before work; normally I preferred to relax on Tottori Kaigan, or on the sofa before work. But the

The Wabi-sabi Doll

burnable rubbish strewn all over my doorstep had put a dampener on my mood; work was the distraction I needed.

Time to grab a quick bite of something before my first class. I stepped onto the escalator amidst the shoppers going down to the ground floor of Jusco and turned in the direction of the supermarket.

Carl was standing in the vegetable aisle. One of the babies was strapped to his front. Shiori was browsing nearby with the other baby in a carrier on her front too. I stopped dead in my tracks, almost toppling forward under my own weight. I turned off the escalator and ducked around the side furthest from them, a spot where I could see them, but they couldn't spot me. They were the last two people I wanted to bump into.

They weren't alone. An elderly Japanese man moved to speak to Shiori. The family resemblance was so clear, I didn't need to guess who he was. Next, her mother moved over, taking the *daikon* radish Shiori had lifted and putting it in her trolley. The six family members; parents, daughter, Carl the playing-at-son-in-law, along with the babies, continued down the aisle as a sextet and disappeared around the corner into the next aisle of dried foodstuffs.

The effect was immediate. A numbness settled throughout my body, as though I had been injected with a high dose of sedative. It didn't flow, didn't even trickle; simply stripped my body of all feeling.

Why? Why did Carl get to play happy families with Shiori, their kids, and her parents? Why not me with Naoki, Mitsuko and his parents?

Was I angry? I trained my newfound mindfulness on myself, not thinking, but feeling. Or rather, the absence of feeling. No, I wasn't angry. Numb, not angry. Numbness was the loss of sensation.

I must have done something big – something bad – in the grand scheme of things, to be punished by karma so badly. It didn't make any sense. Carl was a bigoted, abusive person, who had cheated on me; yet he had been rewarded with children and a partner who was there for him. I, on the other hand, had been the victim of domestic abuse and sexual assault, and had been punished by having my baby taken away from me through miscarriage, and now had a partner who was so busy working he couldn't be there for me when I needed him. Not to mention the fact that he seemed reluctant to introduce me to his parents, for whatever reason.

Life was unfair. Just as my mind allowed me to realise the weight of the injustice, my emotions began to return. Anger flooded me then; I balled my fists so tightly that my nails left crescent moon shapes in my palms.

This wasn't the way to handle things. I couldn't take my anger out on myself. I had to address the reasons why I was on the suffering end of a karmic imbalance. In life, there was a reason for everything. What could I possibly have done to lose so much, while Carl – seemingly underserving of life's gifts – had gained so much?

Not fair. Not right and not fair.

My appetite had gone. No longer in the mood for a quick bite before my shift, I turned on my heel and went straight back up the escalator to work. Responsibilities. I had a duty to my students that I would fulfil, even if I wasn't in the mood. Balance. Everything in balance. Even if I wasn't in the mood to teach, it wasn't a one-way process; absorbing myself in a lesson would be a welcome distraction from the overwhelming sense of injustice I felt at the world.

Energy. Everyone had life force, whether they used it for good, or for bad. Carl cared only for himself. He was deceitful, manipulative, one of the lowest common denominators of a romantic partner out of all the boyfriends I'd had. His energy was bad, by any measure. Over the years, both friends and family members had told me that he wasn't good for me. Not just people close to me, either. Whenever we were out on dates in London, I had seen the look on various shop staff or waiting staff's faces, giving me a 'why are you with this bloke?' kind of look.

Thankfully the staffroom was empty when I returned. Ben must've been in a lesson. Good. I liked him, generally, but sometimes his sense of humour could be annoying as shit.

Emptiness. Empty the mind. Deep breath.

I looked at my teaching schedule for the day and pulled out my student files. My gaze skittered over their names and English levels then jumped across to the pile of textbooks, without really seeing any of it. Lessons. Life was always full of lessons. Language lessons. Life lessons.

Love lessons.

Karma. What lesson was it that I needed to work on? My spirit was being tested, and whatever the lesson, the outcome would result in healing; I would become stronger from the test.

A test of what? It was obvious that my path in life was obstructed. I had broken up with Carl, walked away from an abusive, dysfunctional relationship, but he still dominated my mind. I had not yet fully healed.

Being with Naoki was a step in the right direction. Of course, our relationship also had its distance; he wasn't as emotionally available as I'd like him to be, mainly because he had to work so much in his parents' restaurant when I needed him most. Was there a blockage in my energy that was preventing me from attracting *abundance* into my life?

Carl certainly didn't have any blockages; of course he didn't. His energy was at a base, rudimentary level. He didn't overthink anything, didn't have any kind of deep thoughts whatsoever, in fact. Could it be as simple as that? That all a person had to do to 'grow' and move forward in life was to stop worrying about things and go with the flow?

Maybe so, but it still didn't seem fair. Life was unfair.

If there was to be a test, then I would embrace it. I was ready for it. I wanted to move on; past my miscarriage, past my broken ex-relationship, into the new energy that would come of new relationships, and opportunities.

From now on, I would keep my eyes open and react, right away, to whatever life threw in my path. No worries, just to go with the flow.

Chapter ten

Darkness descending

I was being smothered. A heavy weight was bearing down on me from above. My body, lying supine, had no wiggle room; the invisible mass on top of me had pinned my arms tight against my sides and my legs were clamped together.

Help me. Thoughts only; my mouth wouldn't open. Somebody help me. Carl, why don't you help me?

Carl, wandering away from me. Carl, looking back over his shoulder, his face twisted in disgust.

You whore. His thoughts, infiltrating my mind. You sket.

My legs, unclamped, spreading wider. My body, starfished.

Tasukete! Help me. Tasukete!

Naoki, peering at my helpless form, now lying spread-eagle.

An invisible assailant, pressing between my legs. Pressure, a darkness. Shadow. A shadow on my soul.

My body, exposed to the elements, my soul stripped bare. Was there anything more vulnerable and pathetic in the world?

I sat up, panting. I was safe in my bedroom, on my futon – but alone. Gathering darkness outside suggested that it was late afternoon; my short nap had turned to several hours of sleep. I was physically safe. But, as in my dream, I felt psychically raw. I drew my knees up to my chest and linked my hands around my ankles, dropping my cheek to my thighs. Without Naoki there, I had no other choice but to self-comfort.

Why did he have to do so much more work at the restaurant? I hadn't yet met his parents, but I resented them for the extra shifts he had to do, taking him away from me.

The recurring nightmare could've been much worse; I was mindful of that much, at least. It was more symbolic than graphic; I knew it was my subconscious mind reliving the sexual assault I had suffered at the hands of my ex-colleague, Vince. Feeling an invisible weight bearing down was better than having my rapist actually appear in person every time my brain churned out its PTSD-ridden nightmare. Thankfully not every day, but increasingly common, and I was helpless as to why.

For the first time since Naoki and I had begun dating, I reached for my green poetry journal. The words flowed out of my head, down my arm and ejaculated onto the page, in a violent torrent of catharsis:

How long will my soul

suffer this psychic wound
that infests its life force?
Not even coagulating
not yet starting to form

scar tissue, the healing
I so badly yearn for,

separate, a distant entity,
forever,

out of reach.

A wet droplet smeared the full-stop at the end of the poem. My first thought was to look upwards, expecting to see a leak in the ceiling, before I realised the water came from my own tears.

This really was unbearable. A year after Carl had left Japan to go back to London, one year after our relationship had ended, and I still felt like half a person. An incomplete, damaged person.

Was that all I was? Damaged goods?

No. In the aftermath of our doomed relationship, I had been victim to a predator while commiserating seven wasted years through a sea of alcohol. Once I had pulled myself together, I had found a new love – Naoki. A gentle, loving, kind soul who was helping me on the journey to healing.

Naoki. I sniffed, wiped the tears on the back of my hand, and reached for my phone. I needed Naoki, whether he was at work, or not. There was a good chance he would be able to answer his work phone rather than his mobile while in the restaurant; my fingers worked quickly scrolling through my contacts.

"Moshi moshi." Naoki's voice.

"Naoki, it's me. I really need you."

"Kim, I can't talk. I'm so busy." His voice was louder than usual to compensate for the sizzle of batter frying in the background.

"I'm falling apart, Naoki. I need help."

Japanese voices in the background. Naoki's voice, distant, speaking to whoever it was; a customer, maybe. His voice again, closer to the receiver. "I have to go. I'll ring you later when I'm finished."

Click. Line dead. Hung up on. Just like that.

Click. No time for you.

Click. Work first, love later.

Ugh. I scrolled away from Naoki's number to Sasha's, my bestie in London. What was the time difference between Japan and England? My sleep addled brain couldn't think of that; and it didn't matter anyway. I could leave her a voice message.

Which I did.

But still, not enough. I needed Sasha – and Ronnie – and Aaron – right now in my flat. But they were on the other side of the world. My Tottori bestie, Zoe, was nearby. Hopefully she was free.

I stood up from my futon and ran my hands through my hair. I wasn't a damsel in need of saving. I could save myself. If I couldn't rely on me, what good was I to anyone?

A night out. That was what I needed. My phone was still in my hand. I continued scrolling downwards, alphabetically, past N, towards the last contact on my list. Time to see what Zoe was up to.

೫

The Wabi-sabi Doll

"This is nice, Kimmy. Why don't we do this more often?" Zoe stirred her cocktail with her straw.

"I don't know. We should, though," I said.

I meant it. Zoe and I had been too wrapped up lately in our respective relationships; mine with Naoki, and hers with a new flame. I had met him before Christmas, a guy called Tarou. Zoe had seemed reluctant to want to introduce me and I couldn't blame her. I had been the reason for her break-up with Ryuji the previous year. She had blamed him for not saving me from Vince's attack, even though he had been blackout drunk at the party and couldn't possibly have taken care of himself, never mind in a position to rescue me from a rapist.

"How's Naoki, then?"

I shrugged. "I wouldn't know. It's not like I see him much these days."

She gawped. "Did you guys break up?"

"No, but we might as well have, for how little I see him. He's always working at his parents' restaurant." I sighed. "Sometimes I could just do with a man who is there for me, when I need him."

"I know the feeling, though my situation is sort of different. Tarou is lovely, but he's very hands off. He gets all distant if I hug him, even flinches a bit if I reach for his hand," she said.

I sipped my vodka orange and set the glass down. "I don't think I could stand that. I'm so touchy-feely in relationships."

As I talked, Zoe's eyes darted behind me, over my shoulder. As she looked back to me, a smile curled the corners of her mouth. "Don't look now, but there's a couple of guys along the bar who keep eyeing us."

I knew the etiquette; I waited a minute after she had finished, then turned with the pretence of searching my jacket pocket, that was hanging on the backrest of my chair behind me. The two Japanese men looked to be in their mid-twenties. The nearer of the two had closely cropped, bleached blonde hair and very angular features; a pointed chin and high cheekbones. His eyebrows jutted downwards towards the bridge of his nose, giving his face a brooding quality that was quite masculine. Quite attractive, if I was honest. He had an intelligent, if somewhat intense look as he stared at me. His look was at a stark contrast to Naoki's: cropped, bleached hair instead of Naoki's floppy, brushed-forward style; narrow, deep-set eyes rather than Naoki's wide eyes with long, sweeping eyelashes. The only thing they had in common was that both were gorgeous, though in completely different ways; Naoki was attractive in a handsome way, but the bloke at the bar was smouldering hot.

We locked eyes. He didn't even try to look away. Quite the opposite in fact; one side of his mouth twitched upwards into a rather sexy half-smile showing a row of straight, white, even teeth. Bold. Sexy, but bold.

I didn't return the smile, heat creeping into my face. I turned back to face Zoe, who grinned from ear to ear.

"Kimmy, he's still watching you," she said.

"I know, right?" I swept my hair back off my face in a feeble attempt to cool myself down. "What's with that."

"I have to say, both of them are so *hot*." Zoe fanned herself with her hand.

"Yeah, I know. But I have a boyfriend," I added.

The Wabi-sabi Doll

"We both do." She turned herself around to face the counter, though tossed one more look towards both men, before turning back to our conversation. I turned my chair to face the counter too, watching the men through the corner of my eye.

Turned out my peripheral vision wasn't as good as I had hoped it might be. A moment later, the man with the bleached crew cut appeared behind us, his hand on the backrest of my chair.

"Are you American tourists?" he said, in fluent English. His voice had a low, deep quality. I liked it.

I spun in my chair, keeping my face serious. "No. We're not tourists, we're teachers."

"I'm an Aussie and she's a Brit." Zoe tapped my arm with the back of her hand. She might as well have been drooling like a dog, an embarrassing grin plastered on her face.

The man didn't set eyes on her once, his unblinking stare, and sexy half-smile fixed on me. "You ladies work at Voyce school?"

How was it that he made the word 'ladies' seem so dirty? I rubbed both palms on my jeans, uttering a mantra of sanity in my head to keep heat from flooding my face: *I have a boyfriend, I have a boyfriend.*

His companion joined him. Knowing that she had been snubbed by blondie, Zoe turned her attention to his friend, arching her back and pushing out her chest. I wanted to roll my eyes at her shameful display but stayed focused on our intruding guests.

"Listen," I started. "We're just here for a quiet drink. I'm not in the mood to talk about work to a pair of strangers, no offence."

Blondie wasn't so suave any more at that remark. His smile faltered, though he let his eyes linger on me for a few more seconds. I turned away to face the bar again, ignoring Zoe's aghast expression.

"None taken. Nice chat. See you *ladies* around."

His voice was dripping with sarcasm, which he had clearly used to conceal the awkwardness at my rebuff. A moment later, fading footsteps gave way to the sound of the squeaky door hinge and a blast of cool, night air. I ventured a glance and saw that the men had left.

"Oh my God, Kimberly Thatcher, you are such a bitch!"

Zoe smacked my arm with the back of her hand in a playful way.

I jerked one of my shoulders up in a half-shrug. "Yeah? Well, I didn't ask them to come and talk to us."

"You handled it better than me though, hey?" She fanned herself again.

"You know what you need? You need to go home to Tarou and have a good shag," I guffawed.

She chuckled. "You're kidding, right? He's so frigid, if I try it on, he might actually turn to stone."

We both let loose our laughter. The mirth felt good, even if momentary. How long had it been since I'd had a good belly laugh? Too long.

"At least Tarou is physically there. I'm back to sleeping with my plushies again. It's easier for Naoki to stay at his parents' house as he's doing so many shifts."

Laughter simpering, and gone.

Laughter and lightness in the bar with Zoe. What then? I looked out through the glass pane in the door. Beyond was nothing but the black night. Zoe was there for me, when I needed her. In the bar. But nobody would be with me afterwards.

Just darkness.

Darkness descending, bearing down, squeezing all the light, and life, from my soul.

Chapter eleven

Playing nicely with pain in the heart

The world ebbed, to and fro, on a tide of vodka and orange. The world was orange. The world was cold. The world was wet.

Orange sunlight cast an orange glow over the sand. So that explained the tangerine glow; not the copious vodka oranges I had been drinking. Too many screwdrivers; alcohol on the brain.

I spluttered. Water washed all around me. I pushed myself onto my hands and knees; I had been lying prone. There was sand all over my left cheek. I rubbed it off then massaged a crick in my neck from where I had been sleeping, belly down, my head turned to the left.

Where was I? A beach, somewhere, with the tide coming in. Not Tottori Kaigan, as the famous sand dunes were nowhere in sight. Karo Kaigan? How on earth had I got there? I staggered to my feet as more waves rushed up the beach and swirled around my ankles.

Where the fuck were my shoes? I spotted one, floating in the swash nearby. The other? Who knew? My handbag? I turned in all directions and spotted it, abandoned on the sand. My cash, flat key and makeup were all scattered nearby.

What the hell had happened? I recalled nothing much after the two men had left the bar. Zoe and I had necked more drinks. We'd gotten into some drunken sing-songs with the bar tender. How on earth had I ended up on the beach, alone?

Not good, Kimberly, not good at all. I smacked my palm against my temple. After the mess I had got myself into the previous year, when I had ended up so intoxicated that I had become ragdoll to a violent rape, I should have known better. Why didn't I know any better? Another smack, to my other temple. If my mother was here, she might have done the same.

That is, if she knew what had happened to me.

It wasn't something you could tell your mother; not if you didn't want to break her heart. My mother's heart would probably have broken into a thousand pieces and fallen on the floor if she knew what had happened to her only daughter.

I swallowed a lump in my throat. I had to take better care of myself – if not for me, then for my mother. Getting so inebriated that I had memory blackouts, and falling asleep, exposed and vulnerable, on a beach wasn't a good way to reward either of my parents. What would happen if it wasn't rape next time, but murder? What if my parents were forced to come to Japan to identify my dead body on some mortuary slab.

Hot tears pricked the corners of my eyes at such a thought. For now, I was alive, and I was thankful for my life, and I would do better to take care of what I had.

I picked my sorry arse up off the beach, dusted the sand off my jeans, put the contents of my handbag back inside it and walked towards the roadside. It was only a short walk to the bus shelter, and from there, my bleary eyes scanned the times. Not long to wait for a bus.

And not long for the bus to bring me back home. The short, and uneventful journey, weaved alongside the Sendai River and over the bridge into Akisato. I got off on the main road near Lawson's convenience store and walked around the corner to my flat.

Kawaii-chan was playing in the parking space out the front of the apartment block. Looked to be some kind of fishing game, judging by how she waved a stick around, pretended to catch something on the end of it, play-cook the invisible something-or-other, and eat it. The little girl caught sight of me, turned around, and flapped her fingers in a gesture that looked like she wanted me to go away.

"Oh, sorry I interrupted you, sweetie." Of course, the child couldn't understand me. What was that phrase that meant 'sorry for getting in the way' or thereabouts? "Ojamashimasu."

The little girl kept doing the same gesture, like she was flicking her fingers to sweep me away. Wait a minute; hadn't I seen something about that? Wasn't the gesture for 'come here' in Japanese the opposite of the western one; instead of waving the fingers towards oneself, as I did, brushing the fingers outwards, palm down meant the same thing.

I walked towards Kawaii-chan and sat down on the bottom step of the stairs leading to my flat, where the girl indicated. She stood in front of me and clapped her hands together, palms flat, then began singing. As she sang, she pushed her hands upwards and spread out her fingers like the branches of a tree, then tapped her nose with one finger, followed by mine. I listened to the lyrics, which sounded like a Japanese nursery song. Google translate to the rescue; I quickly typed the first line, *ōkina kuri no kinou shita day* into my phone for an English translation.

Under the spreading chestnut tree
You and me
Playing nicely
Under the spreading chestnut tree

Warmth spread through me; much like the chestnut tree in her song. It was exactly the pick-me-up I needed. Human connection. Someone who cared for me, even if I was only an ignorant gaijin, and she, a preschool child.

"Nakayoku asobimashou." I repeated the words meaning 'playing nicely together' and Kawaii-chan grinned.

Our sweet moment, which could have – should have – lasted an eternity in my opinion – was cut short by a grey van in my line of sight behind Kawaii-chan. Horrible memories flooded back; the previous summer, men in vans pursuing me when I was a lone female travelling home after a night out. Ben's advice, about groups of men kidnapping and raping women, dumping them in the mountains. My brush with the Yakuza at Karo beach.

I channelled my rational mind; no, this was simply an innocent van. I was suffering a mild form of PTSD after the previous summer. Nothing more, simply that. Except...

Except then, just as I rested my eyes on the dark-clothed driver, his face obscured by the van's sun visor, the engine revved up and the van sped away, its tires squealing.

What was that? Was I being watched? Who by? For what reason? I was an English teacher, not a hostess girl working in a sleazy snack bar. It had to be a coincidence. Didn't it?

I said my goodbyes to Kawaii-chan, needing the safety of the four walls in my flat. In any event, I had a thumping hangover. *Futsukayoi*; I needed an *Ukon* drink, the Japanese miracle medicine for hangovers, and a warm bath. Forget my troubles. Forget vans. Forget men. If only the alcohol could have permanently erased the pain in my brain, and in my heart.

Chapter twelve

Mystery doll

Knock, knock, knock.

Oh fuck. Oh shit, oh fuck, oh shit.

Go away. Like, literally, what did he want? It had to be the driver wearing dark clothing in the grey van.

My thoughts launched immediately back to the previous summer. When the van had followed me home, after a night out, someone had knocked on my door, cat-calling, "Woo-eee. Hah-low baby. Let me in."

At that time, I hadn't answered the door, had stayed perfectly still in my flat with all the lights off, pretending I wasn't home. Who knows what might have happened if I had answered the door?

I certainly wasn't going to answer the door now either.

Knock, knock, knock.

It wasn't a light rap, though wasn't a heavy thump either. It was the firm knock of someone who knew I was home. I closed my eyes, willing the man to go away.

Five minutes. Ten minutes. Fifteen. Time enough to check? I peered out the peephole first and saw that the landing outside was clear. Pity there wasn't a chain on my door. I armed myself with a large kitchen pot, ready to hit him on the head, if necessary.

My heart raced as I opened the door. What if the man was hiding, just to the left or right of the peephole? Or, what if he was crouching down below it?

I swung the door open, ready to catch him unaware.

Nobody. But not nothing. My eyes dropped to my doormat where someone had left a Japanese doll. It was dressed in a pink satin kimono. It had a white porcelain face and long black hair with a heavy fringe. There was a small button nose, a wide-eyed expression and red painted lips.

What on earth? My thoughts tripped on the possibilities. A bomb? Ridiculous. A gift to pique my curiosity, to lure me out of my flat where I could be grabbed by a potential kidnapper? Maybe too paranoid.

Should I take the doll? I hesitated before picking it up. The thing was about the size of a Barbie. I turned it over to see if there was a compartment in the back; somewhere to hide a dangerous item: a knife, or drugs. Nope, nothing.

Why did I feel creeped out? There was no note, nothing to explain why it had been put there.

I shut the door, harder than intended, and strode through into the living room. What to do with the doll? I flung it, frisbee style, onto the sofa.

Knock, knock, knock.

The Wabi-sabi Doll

The sudden intrusion jolted me back to the present. I spun in the direction of the front door.

"Fuck off, or I'll call the police. Er... keisatsu ni denwa suru yo!"

"Kimberly, are you okay? It's me."

Naoki. I hurried to get the door before throwing myself into his arms, making him stagger backwards a couple of feet under my weight. He smelt delicious, like *chashumen*, my favourite pork ramen with egg slices. Yum.

He grinned at me. "Woah, did you miss me that much?"

I buried my face in his chest. "I've had quite the week, that's all I'll say. I missed you."

"I missed you too."

Was it just me, or did his response sound as emotive as if he'd just said, 'I had toast for breakfast'?

I led him through into the living room. "So, I guess it's been busy over at the restaurant?"

"What's new?" He pulled a mocking face. "Who were you threatening to call the police for?"

I sat at the kitchenette table, near the sofa, my arms folded. "Nobody. It's nothing."

"It didn't sound like nothing," he said, his voice gentle.

"Well, you weren't there, so it's not your problem."

I knew I was being an asshole; I could see the hurt in his lowered eyes. Why was I being an asshole? Maybe to pay him back for being too busy for me when I needed him; putting his family business ahead of everything. Yes, it was selfish of me; but I couldn't help myself. I wasn't perfect.

Far from it.

He sat down on the chair opposite me at the kitchen table. "What's with the doll?"

Naoki gestured to the creepy, porcelain thing lying on the sofa where I had chucked it, hair and dress askew.

"Someone left it on my doorstep. It's probably cursed," I spat.

Naoki guffawed. "You really crack me up. Why would you think that?"

I shrugged, still feeling petulant. "What am I supposed to think? It was left there with no note. All sorts of stuff has been dumped on my doorstep lately – first dogshit, then rubbish tipped everywhere. Someone is out to get me, I'm sure of it."

He raised an eyebrow. "Didn't you get some nice things too – daikon from your neighbour?"

I flapped a hand. "Fine, then Mr. pedant. With the *exception* of the daikon."

Naoki surprised me then; he strode to the sofa, picked up the doll, smoothed its hair and dress and set it on top of the TV.

"Oh-kay," I said, in as sarcastic a tone as I could muster. "And you're trying to tell me the doll *isn't* cursed? Why the hell else would you get up and lovingly place it on top of *my* TV?"

He turned around, one side of his mouth raised in a smirk. "Not *lovingly*," he argued. "This was clearly a thoughtful gift. People think highly of you around here, Miss *Gaijin*."

I rolled my eyes; albeit in a playful sense. He was complimenting me, and I knew it. "But, in all seriousness now, don't you find that doll just the tiniest bit creepy?"

The Wabi-sabi Doll

He shook his head. "It was handmade, by someone with skill. I really think it was a present."

"Nobody gives a present with no note. Nor do they leave one randomly on your doorstep. I'm convinced that whoever put it there did it for sinister reasons." I pointed, dismissively, at the doll.

"And I really think you're too cynical, sometimes for your own good, Kimberly Thatcher."

Kimberly Thatcher. The only time anyone used my full name was when they were scolding me. My teachers had done it at school, as my parents had at home when telling me off. Zoe did it too, on occasion, to tease me. Naoki's use, in this context, felt like a dressing down. He was demeaning me; and not being light about it either.

"Well, you know what? This isn't up for discussion anyway. That thing is going in the bin. It's probably haunted. It's probably possessed with the soul of some poor unfortunate child who only wants someone to love it."

I was joking, so why did I feel cold? Why did my own glib words leave me feeling chilled. I stared at the doll, and it stared back, benignly. Innocuously. Or did it? Was there a trace of cognition in that cold, hard porcelain? Did it judge me; did it watch me from its ivory tower on top of the TV, waiting to strip my soul right down to its bare essentials, one spiritual fragment at a time, and destroy them all.

"Hey, are you okay?"

Histrionics.

"Hel-low? Earth to Kimberly, come in Kimberly."

Naoki's hand waved in front of my face, severing the invisible laser beam from the doll's creepy, dark eyes to my face. I turned and looked at him, but my retinas were still imprinted with creepy white face, red grinning mouth and wide, dark eyes boring a hole through me.

He laughed. "You're taking this doll stuff too seriously."

I snapped back to reality. "What? No way. I was done thinking about that. I was wondering what to have for dinner, as a matter of fact. I forgot to grab something from Jusco."

"Yeah right." His dimpled grin would've been downright cute if it weren't for the mocking tone. Never mind the doll; my boyfriend saw right through me. "We could go and get something from Lawson? What about oden?"

I wrinkled my nose. "Nah. I need something with more stodge. Let's get tonkatsu."

His phone rang then, piercing the silence in my flat. He walked across my living room, slid the mosquito screen and sliding door aside, and stepped out onto my balcony to take the call.

I couldn't help but feel dismissed. Was he trying to be private? It was an impossibility in a flat with paper thin walls. I could hear everything he was saying anyway; even if I couldn't understand the Japanese.

A moment later, Naoki came back in. He looked apologetic. "I'm so sorry. My mum isn't feeling well. She needs me to cover the afternoon shift at the restaurant until nine."

"On your day off? But it's the first free time you've had in, like, forever?"

His hands hung at his sides, his mobile in one hand. He opened his palms in a wide, apologetic gesture and shook his head.

"Fine. I suppose you should go then. I don't know if there's any point in you stopping by anyway, when you always seem to have to leave straightaway."

I sank back into my chair, folding my arms. I knew I was huffing and puffing like a toddler who wasn't getting her way, but I couldn't help myself.

"I'll make it up to you. We'll have that tonkatsu next time," he said.

"Will we? I don't see how."

Naoki stood, an awkward silence between us, the tatami mat rustling under his socks as he shifted, unsure of what else to do. Then, without a word, he left. The door clicked as he shut it gently.

"Don't bother coming back. This isn't working." I said it in a quiet undertone; more to myself than intended for Naoki to hear. But honestly, in that moment, I really felt that way. I meant it.

Chapter thirteen

Drunken Doll

I put the bottle of imported *Glens* vodka to my lips and glugged, feeling the sting of liquid as it ran out of the corners of my mouth. I wiped the trickle that had escaped down over my chin, rubbing it with the back of my hand.

Strewn around me was evidence of my feast for one: empty *Pocky* cartons, a jumbo-sized crisps wrapper, the long ago finished bowl of instant ramen and the foil wrapper from a *Krunky* bar that I had demolished in two greedy bites.

Another swig of Glens. Had I nearly demolished the whole bottle of vodka by myself? Didn't feel that way. I was barely buzzed. Or, maybe tipsy. Well, alright then; on my way to drunk. I certainly had a warm flush. If anything, my lack of true inebriation after having drunk such volume of liquor *probably* wasn't a good thing. Was I an alcoholic? A functional one at any rate; I gave myself a pass.

Alcohol helped smooth the edges of my life. It lubricated the parts of me that got stuck: mainly my brain. It stopped the parts that got hurt; like my heart.

Did my heart hurt? Yes. Why? Because nobody loved me.

That wasn't true. Mum and Dad loved me. Zac did too, even if he didn't show it often. My friends loved me: Sasha, Ronnie and Aaron.

Why did I still feel empty, then?

Because Naoki didn't love me. He *said* he did, but then acted differently.

I understood his need to help his aging parents with their family business, that they'd been running for decades. Why did Naoki have to be so secretive about it, though? Why did he dash out of the room to take phone calls with his family? Why was he so reluctant to introduce me to his Mum and Dad?

Was he ashamed of me? I took another swig, feeling the liquid spill down my neck, and the tears dripping onto my chest.

Maybe no man could ever love me. Carl didn't love me, and now Naoki had abandoned me. Maybe I was unlovable.

Nobody for company, nobody to give a care. No flatmate after Jei Pi had left, and now, no boyfriend either.

Nothing for company except a creepy doll.

The doll. It was still on top of the TV where Naoki had set it. I stared at it, and it stared back.

"Someone gave you to me, but you don't even love me."

No response. Of course not; the doll couldn't talk.

"Did the man in the grey van give you to me, as a present? Is he infatuated with me?"

Still no response.

Another swig of vodka, though I didn't take my eyes off the doll.

"If you were really a present, as some kind of nice gesture, there would've been a note."

The doll stared back at me, with its wide, unblinking eyes.

"I'll bet you're haunted. You are, aren't you?"

I was joking, of course. The words had barely left my mouth when the doll toppled forward off the TV and nosedived onto the tatami rug. It landed on its back, so that the smiling porcelain face could still stare upwards at me.

A cold sense of unease rippled through my body, starting from the head down. I stared at the doll, half-expecting it to suddenly stand up. That was ridiculous, wasn't it? Or not; not when a supposedly inanimate object had all of a sudden toppled off the TV. There hadn't been a breeze in the house, and it hadn't been standing at a precarious angle. It had been standing, erect on its feet, for hours where Naoki had left it.

"Oh my God, you *are* haunted. You must be."

I pulled both legs up onto the sofa, tucking my feet under my bum; a reflex action. Was I being ridiculous, sitting alone, giving myself the creeps?

The creeps. A cold, creeping unease coagulated in my gut. Spirits. *Mizuko Kuyō*. *Water Child*. I thought back to the rows of stone babies, wearing red knitted hats and bibs, displayed in shrines across Japan for the lives of miscarried, aborted, or stillborn babies. A sore, dry lump formed in my throat.

The Wabi-sabi Doll

What if the doll was inhabited by the spirit of my miscarried baby?

Yes. What if.

What if she had come back to me?

Mummy, she might say, why did you kill me with your hurt? You didn't believe in me. You saw me as half-monster, caused by the rapist who hurt you.

I clapped my hands over my ears; another reflex action. So silly; such an action couldn't stop the words. They came from inside my head. My tortured, tormented head. Slithering like slippery, slimy snakes, sojourning from my subconscious. So silly, so stupid. Only sobriety could stop them, but I was sozzled, senseless.

Stop.

Halt, desist.

If I was sober, I would have written down my stream of consciousness in a poem. Silly sibilance. Instead, I needed an outside perspective. I needed reassurance. I needed…

I needed help.

My fingers were on my keypad before any conscious thought could kick in.

"Kim?" Naoki's voice, with a twinge of irritation.

"Naoki, I'm freaking out."

A pause. "Are you drunk?"

"I've had a bit, but I'm not even tipsy."

"You're slurring." Another pause. "Can we talk later? I'm at work."

I ignored him. "There's something really creepy about that doll. Can you come and take it away?"

I heard him sigh; long, deep and slow. "Not right now. If it's really bothering you, put it outside on the doormat and I'll get it in the morning. It'll be gone before you wake up."

I pulled a cushion close against my stomach and hugged it. "Alright then. As long as you'll get rid of it. I think it's haunted."

Laughter. Was I really hearing that right? Was my supposedly caring boyfriend really laughing at me?

"Listen, forget about it. I'll ask Zoe to come and get rid of it. Don't bother coming back round. You're never here for me when I need you anyway."

"Wait, Kim—"

"It's over. Goodbye, Naoki."

Enough. Yes, I was being petulant. Yes, I was absolutely puerile. Okay, pusillanimous too, since I was on the Ps. Too cowardly to deal with the doll, petrified of a one foot tall porcelain object. Pissed as well.

Petulant.

Puerile.

Pusillanimous.

Pissed.

Petrified of porcelain.

And a poet. Still a poet, with a sensitive, poetic heart. Maybe I wasn't being supportive of Naoki, but he had failed me too. Keeping me apart from his family. Keeping me distant, at arm's length.

I had to be brave, for me, since all I had to rely on was myself.

I stood up. Knocked the cushion aside. Let the vodka bottle roll away. In one swift move, adrenaline giving me momentary sobriety, I grabbed a fistful of the doll's clothing and scooped it up, then threw it outside my door onto the rainy doorstep. It gave me satisfaction to see dirt smeared on its porcelain face, its dress askew and the hair in disarray.

Now I could rest easy. Now, hopefully I would have a dreamless sleep. I had rescued myself; my own knight in shining armour to the damsel in distress that was my inner child.

I didn't want to be alone. But at least I could rely on myself. That, at least, was something.

Chapter fourteen

Haunted Doll

Sunday morning. Thank fuck. No work today.

My banging hangover from Saturday night spent alone with a haunted doll for company, had got the better of me. All I wanted to do was roll up in my duvet and hide from the world, for another day at least.

Except.

Except my curiosity was too strong. Had Naoki done what he said he would do; had he stopped by my flat while I was asleep and removed the creepy porcelain thing from my doorstep, where I had tossed it?

Oh wait. Hadn't I broken up with Naoki while I had been drunk?

Had I?

I crawled out of my futon and used the wall to pull myself upright. I had to know. I had asked Naoki to get rid of the doll, told him how important that was to me, and if he was any kind of good boyfriend, the doll would not be on my doorstep.

Dressing gown on, fluffy slippers on, door unlocked.

The doll was still there. I had left it smeared with mud and in disarray, yet it stood upright. Its dress had been smoothed into place, the hair neatly combed and the face pristine.

"Aah!" I screamed, leaping back, so that my back banged against the entranceway wall. "Help!"

What was the point in shouting for help? I lived alone and my neighbours, even if they heard me, didn't understand English.

"Tasukete!" I repeated in Japanese. "Ningyo wa obake ga haite imasu!"

Help! The doll has a ghost inside it!

At least, I thought that was what I had said. It was hard to quickly translate my thoughts in English into Japanese; speaking another language involved translation, not free thought. I wasn't fluent enough in Japanese to know how to speak the language at will; especially when in a panic.

Saying it out loud highlighted how silly I sounded. My rational mind told me that it wasn't haunted – of course not. But, my fear-ridden self told me that there were weirder forces at play. Forces that were bigger than me, overseeing me, and my life.

I had half a mind to phone Naoki, tell him breaking up had been a drunken mistake, but what was the point. Even if we got back together, he was never there when I needed him. Always at the restaurant. Fuck the restaurant! What about getting rid of the creepy fucking doll on my doorstep?

Who could I call who wouldn't let me down?

Zoe. She had Sundays and Mondays off, so at least one weekend day was an overlap for us both. I left the doll standing outside on my doorstep and hurried to find my mobile phone.

"Hey Kim." Her voice was croaky with sleep. "What's up? It's so early."

"It's half eleven," I clarified. "I really need company. I'm home alone and I've seriously got the creeps."

I gave her the rundown of events since our night out on Friday evening: sleeping on Karo beach, singing with Kawaii-chan and being watched by the strange man in grey van, and then the doll. The mystery doll. The haunted doll. The creepy doll. How I had thrown it outside in the dirt, only to find it upright and immaculate.

"Hmm, well, that does sound odd. Not the haunted part – ghosts aren't real, Kim, come on! But it's weird how someone obviously cares about it enough to have cleaned it up after you threw it away, but then they left it on your doorstep without an explanation – again."

"What should I do with it?"

Zoe sighed down the phone. "It sounds like a Hina doll, from what you've described. You know, the Hina Matsuri is coming up. It's a festival to celebrate little girls, at the start of March. That's probably why someone left it for you."

I couldn't help but feel affronted. "That makes it worse. I'm not a little girl. What an insult!"

"Oh Kim, be a bit open-minded! Why don't we go out for dinner and a few drinks? You need to let your hair down. You're getting too wound up about everything."

"Maybe. I broke up with Naoki, so I *am* a bit overly sensitive."

A gasp. "What? When did this happen? Spill the beans!"

Why did Zoe sound so happy about that? Irritation coursed through me. I needed to suppress my annoyance; she was right, of course. Setting my cares aside – even for one night – was a good thing.

"Where are we going to meet? It's easier to fill you in on everything when I see you."

ଓ

Dinner. Drinks. More drinks. Too many drinks, after which, Zoe and I had ended up at yet another bar. A snack bar, called Bar Nightfall. Was I an alcoholic? What a stupid question; of course I was. The question was, was I a functional alcoholic, or a chronic alcoholic?

Chronic. Air, food, water, sleep and – alcohol. Lubrication for the soul.

"Do you know something?" I slurred. "I heard a story once about a twenty-one year old girl who could drink a whole litre of vodka, straight, without even getting more than buzzed. It was because her mother started plying her with alcohol once she hit her teens, and you know why? To boost her tolerance and help prepare her for men, so that no man could ever get her wasted and take advantage of her. Isn't that a good idea?"

I fell sideways off my stool, to an eruption of laughter from Zoe.

"Kim, oh my God, a breakup fucks with your head even worse than it does to mine."

She heaved me back onto my bar stool with one hand under my armpit. With my screwdriver-addled brain, it took me a moment to catch on to what she was saying.

"Have you and Tarou broken up too?"

Her smile faded; she gave a one-shouldered shrug to counter it. "I'm surprised we lasted as long as we did. He's so stand-offish and I'm so full of fire. Hot and cold just makes lukewarm."

A cold draught of late-January air made me shiver as the door of the snack bar opened. Two men walked in. My stomach jolted as I recognised the man with a bleached crew cut and sharp features who had tried to flirt with us several weeks before at the same bar. He looked my way, one corner of his mouth twitching upwards for a brief second, then turned his attention to the bartender.

Zoe and I glanced at each other. Her cheeks were flushed, a devious sparkle in her eyes.

"Well, if it's fire you're looking for then I think we're in luck," I said, in an undertone.

As if on cue, the bleach-haired man swooped over to us in a cloud of expensive smelling cologne.

"Hello ladies, mind if this Samurai buys you a drink?"

It was such a random, offhand comment that I couldn't help myself from bursting into laughter. Either that, or I was more blocked than I thought.

"Is that a yes?" he added.

I let my chortles subside. "Go on then, why not."

"What'll it be?"

"Shochu for me," said Zoe.

He raised his eyebrows. "Hardcore. I like it."

The Wabi-sabi Doll

Potato-derived alcohol sounded good, but a familiar variety was more my thing. Maybe my New Year's resolution to drink less alcohol would have to wait. "Screwdriver."

I was about to elaborate on what that meant but didn't have to; he ordered a vodka and orange in Japanese, as I recognised the katakana words in the sentence. The few exchanges we'd had so far had been in perfect English in any event, his accent with a slight American twang.

"Why are you ladies always sitting here at this bar alone? Two *bijin* like yourselves should have company," he went on, as he handed the drinks that the barman passed across. I noted his gaze passed over me before he averted his eyes – and smile.

"Well, we don't have to be alone." Zoe batted her eyelids as she took her shochu from him.

Bijin; beautiful women. A fleeting sense of smug satisfaction surged through me before I centred myself to be more *zen*. The men led us to a crescent-shaped booth at the side of the room with a red, u-shaped, faux-leather seat. Zoe slipped in first and I noticed that the blonde man hung back, leaning against the frame that separated it from the next booth, allowing his friend to slip in beside Zoe. He held his arm out, indicating for me to go into the booth beside Zoe, and then sat down on the curved seat next to me. Zoe's fleeting disappointment was obvious; she clearly had her sights set on the same bloke as I did and didn't like that he had chosen to sit next to me. Petty, but I couldn't help smiling to myself that he'd picked me.

Interesting booth. A series of seemingly random memorabilia lined the wall behind the curved seat: there was a small gold gramophone; a matching pair of white theatre masks; a statue of a fertile woman carved out of a dark wood like mahogany, or maybe ebony, with gold leaf around her eyes and highlighting her lips; a bongo-style drum that had been made out of half a coconut and a framed, A4 sized poster advertising Guinness that looked Victorian in style. Maybe they were knickknacks collected by the owner on their travels, who knew?

"Why don't we start with names then?"

The question jolted me out of my musings. I turned and looked at the blonde-haired man, who watched me with a smile that suggested amusement and intrigue.

"I'm Kimberly," I said.

"As in, Kim?"

"Yeah," I smiled.

"I'm Shinichi and he's Keitaro." He thumbed towards his friend in an offhanded manner. "Which do you prefer? Kim or Kimberly."

Why did the question make me feel hot? A simple query, nothing to put me on the spot. Yet I felt so exposed, felt his intense eyes boring into me, like he was seeing my soul.

What a silly thought. I dismissed it in one, fell metaphysical sweep of my mind.

"Kimberly, I guess. Nobody really calls me Kim, apart from some of my students, who find Kim easier to say."

"So you're an English teacher. At Voyce school?"

"How did you know?" My suspicious mind was about to jump to conclusions, but there was no need; Voyce was the biggest language school by a mile. Of course he would assume I was a Voyce teacher before thinking of any of the other smaller schools.

"I saw you going into work one day."

The Wabi-sabi Doll

Or not; paranoid fears jumped into my head. Men in vans, strange knocks on my door, creepy dolls being left on my doorstep.

"I was in the optician next door," he continued. "I have to get my eyes tested regularly as part of my job."

His follow-up comment assuaged my mistrustful mind. I chided myself; I needed to relax. No assumptions. A new year, a new person, a new start. Carl was a thing of the past, Vince as well, and sadly now Naoki too.

Another metaphysical shake to my brain; blank slate. Why was I already comparing Shinichi to men from my past – however recent? It was simply a drink between acquaintances; I couldn't assume any further connection would come of it.

Too soon for a new man.

Too soon for romance.

But what about a fling; some much-needed fun?

I couldn't deny I enjoyed the attention.

I cleared my throat, hoping to dispel the heat from my cheeks. "What sort of work do you do that needs you to get your eyes tested so much?"

"I'm a fireman," he said.

Made sense; he was in good shape with a gymnastic physique. The shallow part of me was impressed. An old adolescent fantasy resurged of wanting to marry a man in uniform. I pictured Shinichi in a sexy fireman uniform with a domed hat, carrying an axe, looking more stripper than rescuer.

Got to put a stop to such thoughts before the lava showed on my face – and my volcano erupted. Granted, Shinichi could hose me down any day. I forced my chortle down with another swig of screwdriver, that sufficed to cool me down.

Whew, what an evening so far, even if half of it had been in my head.

I looked to my right, focusing on Zoe and Shinichi's friend to get my mind off my own amorous thoughts. It helped with my composure, kind of giving me a metaphorical *cold shower*. They were cosied up on the u-shaped curve of the seat, heads almost touching, and his arm stretched across the back of the booth behind her. I smiled; it was good to see her so happy after her break-up with Tarou. Maybe this evening would work out for us both.

I turned back to Shinichi. Instead of settling on his face, my gaze fell to a point just behind his left ear.

How had I not noticed it before? Half visible behind him was a Japanese doll, about a foot tall. It wore a blue kimono and smiled with red painted, slightly parted lips. The heavy black fringe and cleopatra-style hair framed its moon-white face. The painted, dark eyes seemed to suck the soul out of the room, two black holes swirling in the ether, pulling the air from my lungs, and the energy from my body—

"Are you okay?"

Shinichi leaned a little to his left, almost instinctively, and enough to block the doll from sight. I found myself unfrozen immediately; my heart able to beat, the breath able to flow in my lungs. What had happened?

"You kind of just, zoned out there for a moment," he went on, pausing before the word 'zoned'.

I swallowed to wet my adrenaline-stripped throat. There was no mistaking it was exactly like the doll that someone had put on my doorstep, except wearing a blue kimono, not pink. It hadn't been among the memorabilia before, or I would have noticed it, surely.

Had it? I'd looked carefully at all the objects: gramophone; masks; ebony statue; coconut drum and Guinness picture – but no doll.

"That doll." I gulped and raised a shaky finger, enough to point at it, before dropping it. "I didn't see it before."

Zoe scoffed. "Oh, come on Kimmy, not this again!"

I ignored Zoe, as irritating as her scepticism was. "Was it there before?"

Shinichi turned his head half an inch, before stopping, his eyes not leaving me. "Could be? I didn't pay attention, to be honest. Is it bothering you?"

I gave myself a mental shake-up, before they all thought I was mad. "It looks familiar, that's all. It reminded me of something. Forget it."

He gestured with his thumb over his shoulder, towards the door. "Do you want to step outside for some air?"

I had never heard more appealing words. Unable to speak, I simply nodded.

Shinichi grabbed both our drinks and led the way outside. I slipped out of the booth without even a sideways glance at the doll.

How could I explain it? It would seem insane. If I thought rationally, it did seem insane, even to me. How could a porcelain doll, an inanimate object, change her clothing for a night out and follow us from my flat to the snack bar?

I felt sick. The cold January wind whipped my hair back off my face, keeping me grounded in that moment.

"What happened in there? Is the drink not agreeing with you?"

His words grounded me in the present even more. "I'm alright. I got spooked for a moment by something — not you."

Why did I feel the need to elaborate? Why was I so defensive?

He cocked his head sideways. "The doll bothered you?"

My mind. My unstable mind. "Yeah, maybe. Something like that."

"Well, you know what I do, when something's on my mind?" He had a cheeky glint in his eye, the corner of his mouth curled upwards. "Try to have some fun."

With that he leaned in, and I found myself turning my head upwards to meet his. And we kissed.

Chapter fifteen

Jellyfish by moonlight

And then we fucked. Shinichi was right. Having fun was the best thing for me.

Outdoor sex wasn't anything I had ever done before, never mind on the beach. There was something liberating about it; being outside on the sand, with only the stars above to watch over us. Maybe there was something else too that excited me; the risk factor, probably. Of course, the early hours were a safe bet that no dog walkers would be up yet, though there was a good chance that other people might head for the beach after closing time at the bars, like we did.

If they did, we would give them quite the show. Shinichi was quite the gentleman, laying his jacket on the sand for me, and our innocent star watching had rapidly turned amorous as he had leaned over me for a kiss – at first. No late January chill for me, what with my inebriation and his warm weight on top of me.

Drunk as I was, I had at least made sure he had pulled protection out of his wallet. Not up to a man necessarily to bear responsibility for such things, but I was never preferred, never carried intimate items in my bag. Maybe that needed to change. Change was always good.

It was different than with Naoki. Apart from the fact that we always did it in my apartment, the sofa being the most adventurous we'd been; Shinichi smelled different. He tasted different. His body felt different. Naoki was in good shape, but a fireman had a different physique. More taut. And he kept his eyes open; not for the kiss, but to watch my pleasure, with a satisfied smile that I found quite... Quite what? Not charming. Sexy? Perhaps. Maybe I needed to see a man's carnal lust for me. Maybe I needed to feel – needed.

Nothing wrong with that.

An icy wet chill over my bare feet and legs forced a cry from my chest and caused Shinichi to gasp. Waves. Had the tide come in to serenade us? Maybe the moon wanted in on our action.

"Oh, fuck that's freezing!" I shrieked.

Shinichi's teeth chattered. "A cold dip is good for the body."

Laughter erupted, replenishing the air in my lungs. "Yes, your dip must be cold."

He laughed too. I really could be crass sometimes.

Maybe it was his sheer stamina, or being used to more extreme weather through his job, but he was able to finish, even in the frigid winter Sea of Japan. His excitement brought me to a climax too; just in time as the swash swept further up around us, lapping along the outside of my thighs to sting my hips. Any higher and my clothes above the waist would be soaked; Shinichi's too. No post-coital hypothermia, no thanks.

"What are the twinkling lights in the water?" I said, my teeth chattering. They weren't bioluminescent, instead reflecting the night sky above, creating stars on the crests.

Shinichi scooped me up in his arms, bundled in his jacket. "It can't be jellyfish. It's not the season. But let's not wait to find out."

He huffed as he carried me up the beach and we both tumbled onto the soft dry sand, then rolled side by side, laughing.

"A sting in the nether regions would've been even worse than hypothermia," I chuckled.

He guffawed too, his chest rising and falling. "I think that's the craziest thing I've ever done."

"Me too." I rolled over on top of him and kissed him. "Pretty wild ride."

He helped me look for my jeans, pants and boots, which had been scattered around on the sand. Thank goodness I had thought to throw them over my head, landing further up the beach, and not near the shoreline as they would've been drenched. It was only once I was dressed that I saw him shaking, as his trousers were drenched to above the knees.

"Oh my God, you poor thing, you're soaked!"

He shook his head, but even in the starlight, I could see that his lips looked almost blue.

We hurried up to the main road. While he phoned a taxi for us, speaking in Japanese that was far too quick for me to understand anything of, I stared out over the moonlit sea.

Would I have done that – had wanton sex with a strange man on a beach like a teenager – if I was back where my parents lived in Southampton? No. Of course not. Something about living abroad, maybe, had triggered the 'holiday reflex' in me. Was that it? Was I treating Japan like a holiday?

Japan wasn't a holiday; it was my home from home. It was the home of my soul. I had freed myself from Carl's malign influence, and from Vince's. Naoki had good energy; he was a good man. But he was too busy for what I needed. I needed love, and attention, in a partner.

Shinichi ended his call and tucked the phone in his trouser pocket. "Taxi's on its way."

"Good. I'm freezing."

Despite shivering himself, he rubbed my shoulders. Quite the gentleman.

He flashed a boyish grin. "Were you thinking of jellyfish?"

I chortled. "You're so cheeky!"

Our taxi pulled up and the automatic door swung open. We both slid into the back, me on the beach side. As Shinichi chatted in Japanese with the driver, I let my thoughts drift back to the waves. Jellyfish. Out of season jellyfish. Jellyfish on my mind; but not in the way Shinichi's inuendo might have suggested.

Jellyfish floating on the gentle crests, glittering, diaphanous at twilight on the day I had released my Water Child to the sea. The Sea of Japan had opened her aqueous arms and received my baby after she had left my body, a perfect red kidney bean delivered into my hand, a part of me for the last time.

Were the jellyfish tonight a sign? None had stung Shinichi and I, just as I hadn't been stung before when I released my baby into the sea. Were they looking out for me, maybe giving me a sign from her that she was okay?

Are you safe, my sweet Water Baby?

I directed my thoughts at the black expanse before the taxi turned inland and the view was gone.

Chapter sixteen

Fever dreams

There I was. There he was. What a whirlwind romance we'd had.

Shinichi turned and smiled as I walked along the aisle towards him. The *obi* fastening my white silk *shiromuku* was so tight, my breath came in laboured gasps. Who knew traditional kimonos could be as tight as a corset?

He looked perfect in his *hakama*, the contrast with his dyed platinum hair offset nicely against the black silk. My *geta* clicked against the floor as I took dainty steps towards the altar, clutching my small posy of white roses.

The Shinto priest waited for me to arrive, ready to perform the ritual purification for our union and to offer prayers to the Gods. After today, we would be husband and wife.

The Wabi-sabi Doll

Three faces among the guests distracted me. Three men. Three exes. Carl sat nearest the aisle, glowering upon my approach. My ex-fiancé's green eyes seemed to burn with an envious fire. Next to him sat Vince, smirking as he always did. Calling him an 'ex' was a stretch. My rapist ex-colleague at Voyce school was more apt. Beside him sat Naoki, who looked sad. His large, dark eyes glistened, as though if he blinked, a shower of tears would fall over his cheeks.

I tore my eyes away from the three men and focused instead on my soon-to-be spouse.

A sudden tempest blew along the aisle, whipping my hair around my cheeks and tugging the hem of my shiromuku. I gasped as cold water swirled over my feet and around my ankles. Waves.

Shinichi took my hand, and without a word, we hurried outside. The beach had been consumed by a tsunami, black water eddying over the sands. I could see twinkling lights in the water. Under the bright reflection caused by the moonlight, they seemed to dance on the surface.

Jellyfish. Hundreds of them were swarming out of season.

For some reason I was drawn to one in particular. The dark water lapped to my shins as I stepped onto the flooded beach. It crept higher, swirling around my knees. The cold, dark waves stung my thighs, yet I couldn't peel my eyes away from the bobbing jellyfish. It was bigger than the others, seeming to increase in size, the closer I got.

The tsunami water receded, sucking all the other jellyfish with it, leaving the biggest one behind. It was a deep blood red colour and resembled a Lion's mane jellyfish. The long tentacles that massed around it, like a halo on the sands, were translucent. The sight of the large, gelatinous blob triggered a memory, the details of which wouldn't come to the forefront of my mind.

What did it remind me of?

A red blob, with flowing, sinuous tendrils.

I was transfixed as I watched it, unaware if Shinichi was even by my side anymore. His hand was no longer linked with mine; that much I knew, though I dared not turn away to see if I was alone. I didn't want to take my eyes off the jellyfish. It pulsated on the wet, muddy sand, and with each rhythmic motion, it seemed to grow in height, like a giant, beating heart increasing its life force with each pump.

What *was* that thing? It couldn't be a jellyfish. Stranded jellyfish died on the sands; they didn't thrive.

The umbrella of the reddish blob began to form into a dome. The membrane on its surface thinned out, as a black mass pushed from underneath. The black protrusion pushed, and the membrane split as a human head emerged. The dark colour was black hair, dangling long as it hung in wet strands over the person's head. The slim, white neck that followed gave the impression that it was a child, a girl.

The girl crawled out of the jellyfish, on all fours. She wore a pink kimono. As she raised her head, the dark hair parted and I saw a heavy fringe on her brow, followed by a pretty heart-shaped face and red painted lips.

The child stood up, her wooden geta sinking into the soft sand. Her formal dress reminded me that I was there, near that beach, for my wedding to Shinichi.

Shinichi.

Finally able to turn away from the child, I looked over my left shoulder and saw him, standing further up the beach, watching the girl and I with a helpless expression. A wide, deep stream of water had formed behind me; a strong, black current of water keeping him away.

I turned back to the girl and jumped to see that she had closed the gap between us, now standing right in front of me. Her wide, dark eyes peered upwards, and her red lips parted in a crescent moon smile, showing a row of even, white teeth that were porcelain-perfect.

"Mama," she said, in a squeak, one hand rising to caress my cheek. The splayed white fingers were doll-cold as they touched my skin.

૮૩

"Aah, get away from me! Don't you touch me!"

I sat bolt upright on my futon. My hair was saturated with sweat and my nightdress clung to my back.

My body heaved as I sucked life-giving air into my chest, as though I had been holding my breath in my sleep. I visualised myself healing with each long intake of breath, and my heart, which had been hammering in my chest, began to slow.

A guttural cry ripped through the room. It took half a second to register that the pained sound came from me. My bedroom faded into a wet blur as tears poured down my face.

"I'm going mad. Somebody help. I think I'm insane."

My bedroom door clicked open. I let out a short shriek and pulled my duvet to my chest as Shinichi burst into the room.

"Kim, you're awake. I heard you scream. Was it a nightmare?"

Who had I been expecting to come into the room? The porcelain doll. The creepy doll. The possessed doll.

I really was, truly insane. Driven insane by a haunted, inanimate object.

"You're here. I'm not alone!"

A series of strange, clipped giggles broke from my chest and escaped into the room; maybe all the air had gone to my head, making my brain float in an osmotic haze.

"I'm not alone," I said, as the giggles faded, and my skin erupted in goosebumps.

"Of course you're not alone. I stayed over. You caught a chill on the beach last night. I feel so bad. I shouldn't have taken you there after the bar."

The previous night came back to me in a tumble of fragmented images: snack bar with Zoe, screwdriver upon screwdriver, random memorabilia in the bar and among the items, the porcelain doll that tormented me. Shinichi had come to my rescue, ferrying me outside, offering healing kisses. Not just kisses. A long, drunken walk to the beach while we talked about topics that escaped me in my inebriation. Had I poured out my soul to him? I had certainly given him other parts of me, on the cold, winter moonlit beach.

Sex on the beach, by the Sea of Japan, in January. Was I mad? What sort of *Peter Pan complex* was I dealing with? I was twenty-six, a woman far from her teens by any measure, yet acting like an adolescent.

No time for psychoanalysis of my damaged, fragile self. I was clearly in the throes of a fever. The goosebumps disappeared, replaced by scorching heat, searing through my body.

"I was making you some soup. It's ready."

Shinchi disappeared into the living room, leaving my head full of thoughts of my mum's restorative chicken soup, made with bone broth. I imagined the smell and my mouth watered.

He returned carrying a steaming bowl and dropped to his knees on the tatami mat beside my futon. I saw tofu cubes floating in the dark brown liquid, among spring-onion rings. Miso soup. Shinichi scooped a spoonful, blew on it, and brought it to my mouth.

"Eat," he said.

I obeyed, opening my mouth to accept the spoon. The soup was hot, and delicious. No; it was the best thing I had ever tasted in my whole life.

"More," he ordered.

I opened my mouth again, allowing myself to take the life-saving elixir. Mouthful by mouthful, the healthful broth filling my ravaged body.

Shinichi stood up. "I've made you rice with *ume*. Pickled plum. Don't lie down."

Despite feeling so ill, a tremor of excitement rippled through me. Did I enjoy being ordered about? His direct imperatives combined with tender care was rather… Rather what? *Sexy*.

Time to ponder over that when I was better. The simple fact of the matter was that he was present. He was *there* for me. I needed that, more than ever. More than anything.

Shinichi returned with a bowl of plain rice that had been stained yellow by a pickled plum, placed in the centre. He mixed it using chopsticks, scooped up a bite of the sticky rice mix, and offered it to me. It had a sweet and sour taste, with a savoury vinegar aftertaste that I found delectable.

"Incredible. Rice and plum sounded so plain, but this is amazing."

He smiled. "My mum used to make it for me when I was sick and had no appetite."

"It's so simple, but it's truly delicious." I took the bowl and chopsticks from him and ate with good appetite.

"I love to see you getting your strength back." He took the empty bowl from me. "But you should sit up after eating."

He set the bowl aside and wrapped my duvet around my shoulders, then helped me to my feet. We made it to the living room, moving slowly, and tucked the duvet around me so that not even the tiniest breeze could reach my clammy skin.

What could I say? Too early, too soon, but had I finally found the perfect man for me? Is that what my dream – the first part of it – had been telling me?

Maybe my subconscious knew a 'keeper' when it came across one. I allowed my mind to focus on such a happy thought, and nothing else, as Shinichi busied about doing the dishes.

Chapter seventeen

Over the edge

The doll was coming for me, closing in on me, suffocating me.

It was too late. It had been in my flat long enough that even its presence had begun to seep into the fabric of my space, like a disease, infesting every surface. Black lines had begun to form on the ceiling. I thought they were cracks at first, hairline fractures in the plaster, maybe, but they seemed to spread like tiny roots.

I was a prisoner on my futon, forced to lie and stare at the ceiling, forced by my own oppressive weight bearing down on my soul. A metaphysical suffocation of sorts. Oh, I was dying, definitely. Being killed, stripped of my own essence, invaded by a foreign, alien, tormentor.

My futon was soaked. A waterfall of sweat had saturated every fibre. I had no choice to lie on the waterbed of my own effluence, as my body might as well have been a sack of potatoes.

How did my mind work, when my body didn't? If anything, it was doubly as active as before, my thoughts tearing through my brain twice as fast as the speed of sound. A sonic boom of delirious day dreams.

The longer I stared at the black lines, the more my own meandering mind tormented me. The lines looked less and less like roots and more and more like hairs.

Black hairs. Black hairs like those on the head of a black-haired doll.

Yes, it was the doll again. I had to get rid of the doll.

I had tried and failed before. I had tossed her outside my front door, into the rain and dirt, only to find her cleaned and presented on my doorstep. I had then found her following me, watching me from the snack bar while I had been on a double date with Zoe. Shinichi had rescued me from her noxious aura. Who would rescue me now?

I would rescue myself. Bad luck came in threes, or so the saying went. I would make a renewed effort to purge her poisonous presence from my flat, for once and for all.

I tried to sit up, but my efforts transpired into a weak stomach crunch, before I flopped back on my pillow, lead-headed.

The doll. One way or another I would *will* my body to find its strength, to get myself into my living room.

I rolled myself off my futon and landed belly down on my tatami mat, then pushed myself onto my hands and knees. A short crawl out of my bedroom, across the living room and I pushed myself up onto my knees to snatch the sinister object off the top of the TV. My arm muscles shook as I hauled open the sliding glass door onto the balcony open, and then slid the mosquito net back too.

With my last reserve of strength, I dropped the doll off the balcony and heard a rustle as it landed in the field below. Then, I collapsed face down on my living room floor, what little energy I had now spent.

ତ୍ୟ

Hands. Firm hands and strong arms. I was being flipped over and scooped up.

My head lolled and my arms dangled as Shinichi picked me up and gently set me on the sofa.

"Here, drink this. You must've been lying on that floor passed out for hours."

I took the bottle of *Pocari Sweat* that he handed me. I wasn't a fan of sports drinks normally, but right then it tasted divine.

"The doll. She was tormenting me."

My voice sounded weak in my own ears, my words a mere mumble.

"It was fever dream," he soothed.

"No, she's been tormenting me. She comes to me in real life as well as my dreams. Outside my flat, clean and tidy after I've tossed her out, and at Bar Nightfall wearing a different coloured kimono – blue not pink. I know who she is. She's real."

"Drink," he ordered. I sipped more Pocari Sweat. He was right; I felt a little better, the more I drank.

"You don't believe me. She haunts me. If you're around me enough, she'll haunt you too."

"What did you do with the doll?" He spoke so matter-of-factly, his tone serious and sober, that I couldn't help but wonder if he believed me after all.

"I threw her outside, over the balcony. She's in the field below." I pointed at the window, just in case there was any avenue for doubt.

Shinichi followed the invisible line my finger made and slid the glass door open. He stepped outside, looked over the balcony, then returned inside shaking his head.

"I don't see anything in the field below."

"What?" If my body had lain slumped before, it was bolt upright on the sofa now. "Don't tell me she's on her way back up here?"

Shinichi's expression fell somewhere between concerned and alarmed. "It's a Hina Doll, Kim. It can't walk anywhere."

"You sound like Zoe. I'm right though. It's possessed. I know that sounds crazy, but I'm right. It's following me, tormenting me."

"You have flu – and a high temperature. A high fever can make all sorts of things seem real."

I sighed. "Just hear me out – and then you can tell me if all this seems irrational, or whether there's a more supernatural explanation for everything that's been happening."

"No – you hear me out. You need to rest. You're sick. If you still feel this way when your fever breaks, then I'll listen. Until then, I don't want you worrying yourself about haunted dolls, alright?"

I didn't like it, but it looked like I had no choice. I nodded.

Shinichi smiled. I returned his smile. But the moment we looked apart from one another, I turned to the balcony, just to be sure my tormentor wasn't waiting for me with an even bigger, satisfied smile of her own.

Chapter eighteen

Valentine's Day

Was it really mid-February already? Where had the weeks gone?

I leaned close to the mirror to reapply my red lipstick, after my meal. Shinichi had taken me for *Yakiniku* in Yayoicho at a restaurant called Café Throwback not too far from Tottori train station. Our Valentine's Day date was far from over. Drinks, and maybe clubbing later on.

I pulled back from the bathroom mirror to observe myself. Not too bad. I was thinner than normal, after two weeks of flu. My black jeans hung off my thighs, whereas they had been a tight fit only weeks before.

Maybe reapplying the black hair dye hadn't been the best decision following my illness. It made me look even paler than usual, almost anaemic. My straight, black fringe brushed my eyebrows, and my hair now reached down past my shoulders. Worse still; an involuntary shudder seized me as I looked at my appearance. It hadn't occurred to me that having long black hair with a heavy fringe against my pale complexion would make me look so – look so…

Like the creepy porcelain doll.

I hadn't thought of the doll since ten days before, when I had thrown it off my balcony. I was glad that it hadn't reappeared at my front door, as I had been expecting. Since it was gone, I had been devoid of any nightmares about it.

There was a hair elastic in the back pocket of my jeans. I scraped my hair into a high ponytail, leaving only a strand on either side of my fringe to frame my face. Good; now there was no resemblance between me and the creepy doll.

Shinichi was on his phone when I went back into the restaurant, but he wrapped up the call when he saw me approach, and greeted me with his usual sexy smile, his hands on the table with fingertips touching lightly. In his black, three-piece suit with satin side strips on each leg, he was suave and refined for our dinner-date. How I couldn't wait to strip it off him later; we hadn't had sex since the night on the beach and I was eager to consummate our relationship properly, minus the inebriation.

"You look stunning. Your hair up gives you a different look," he said.

I sat down opposite him with a grin. "It makes me look – less like a doll, shall we say."

His eyes had a mischief in them. "Is this about the Hina doll?"

I braced myself. I hadn't spoken of it to him since my feverish delirium, but it had been on my mind every day. I slowly nodded.

"Alright then. I told you a couple of weeks ago that I would listen once you were better, and you're well now. I'm all ears," he went on.

I took a deep inhale. "This is going to sound crazy."

"Try me," he said, still smiling.

I bit my bottom lip. "I think the doll is haunted by somebody that was close to me."

A weight had been lifted off my chest, as though by voicing my fears, I had removed some of the oppressive energy that had dominated me since coming into possession of the doll.

"A grandparent?" he guessed.

I shook my head. "A baby. My baby."

If Shinichi felt any surprise by what I said, he didn't show it. His face remained calm and serious as he listened: about my miscarriage; how my Water Child had been taken into the sea, surrounded by jellyfish; the mystery doll outside my flat and how it had returned, clean and pristine after I had thrown it out; the doll appearing in the snack bar where we had shared drinks; the out-of-season jellyfish on the beach serenading us while we had sex and my nightmares.

"It certainly does sound strange," he said, his face stoic.

"You believe me then, that it's haunted?"

He didn't answer. A distant look set on his face, his eyes narrowing with a sleepiness and his mouth pursed in thought.

"I mean, if it was a present, the person would have left a note, or let me know in some way, wouldn't they?" I continued.

He still didn't speak. Why did I feel a sudden, desperate urge to babble at him – to convince him that

I was right. What if he thought I was mad? It probably sounded insane.

"I believe you. Spirits are everywhere. The ones we love are around us, unseen all the time. Here in Japan, we celebrate the festival of Obon in August, to honour our dead." He sat back, linking his fingers together. "I'll make sure to get you an *omamori*, to keep you safe."

How very thoughtful. I wasn't Buddhist, but appreciated the kind gesture. The small, fabric amulets with gold lettering on the front, were believed to bring luck and protection, as well as warding off misfortune. I definitely felt in need of good blessings.

"If you really believe it's the spirit of your baby, then why are you afraid of it? Do you worry that it was corrupted somehow, if it couldn't pass on?"

His question caught me by surprise. Just like Naoki and Zoe before me, humouring me, disbelieving me, I had assumed he wanted to end the conversation; instead he was not only perpetuating the topic, but adding insight that hadn't occurred to me. Is that what I thought; that the lost spirit was back to haunt me, or cause me harm in some way? What if the spirit was angry at me because she had lost her life so soon? What if she was angry that she had been conceived through rape?

I was unable to answer. Shame besieged me at the idea of admitting to my lover that I had been raped. I knew it was ridiculous; Vince was to blame for that, not me. But, what if Shinichi *judged* me for the sexual assault? Rape was taboo. It carried a stigma. Would he see me in a different light if I told him what I had been through?

The Wabi-sabi Doll

I had to be brave. "She wasn't conceived in very happy circumstances. I'm worried that she's angry at me for that and that she can't forgive me."

Shinichi continued to sit with his back straight, his fingers interlaced, hands on the table. I couldn't help but think of how Naoki might have shown affection in that moment; how he might have leaned towards me and caressed my hand. Shinichi's face held the seriousness of an interviewer quizzing an interviewee. Whether he was affectionate or not, he was there. He was present with me; Naoki hadn't been there for me, which was why we were no longer together.

"Do you forgive yourself?"

There was no tone to his question, nothing implied. It was a simple, straightforward question that cut through me like a dagger in my heart.

"I... um..."

Did I?

"Well, I..."

Why should I?

His face relaxed. His hands relaxed. He placed both palms down on the table.

"I'll take you to a temple tomorrow. We can place an offering to a *Jizō* statue and hope that her soul will be at rest."

I recalled all the rows of stone baby statues that I had seen the previous summer. All were dressed in red bibs and caps, each one a memorial for a miscarried, aborted or stillborn baby. *Mizuko kuyō*: Water Child. Yes, Shinichi was right. I needed to have a proper ceremony for her, so that she could rest.

So that my own heart could rest too.

Shinichi peered up at me from his seated position, a half-smile on his face. "Is there anything I can do to cheer you up? It's still Valentine's Day, isn't it?"

He reached into his right trouser pocket and brought out a small, black box. My heart nearly stopped. It wasn't an *engagement* ring, was it?

With one, smooth flick of his thumb, the lid popped up. Instead of a ring, I saw a yellow-gold tennis bracelet with alternating diamonds and rubies.

"Oh my gosh, Shinichi!" My hand flew to my mouth.

"May I? he said, his sexy half-smile reaching his eyes.

I extended my left hand, allowing him to link the clasps around my wrist.

"It's an eternity bracelet, twenty-four carat gold."

A nervous guffaw slipped out. "Are you proposing to me?"

"Think of it as more of a get-well present. You were dangerously sick there, for a while. I was worried about you, over here, with no family to take care of you."

"You did a pretty good job nursing me back to health," I said, marvelling at the bracelet. It must have cost a fortune. How much, exactly, did firemen earn in Japan?

A cheeky glint formed in his eyes. "You know, technically I didn't have to get you anything for Valentine's Day. Over here in Japan, it's traditionally a day for women to offer chocolates to their intended – did you know that?"

"Yeah, one of my students at Voyce might have mentioned that. Normally because it's more conservative here, men can only ask out ladies. So

Valentine's Day is the one time when ladies can make a move on the men they fancy."

"Right," he smirked. "And if they accept her proposal, they give her white chocolate on White Day on the fourteenth of March."

"And if they reject her?" I asked.

"She gets cookies," he grinned.

"Sounds like a win-win to me," I laughed.

"So where's my chocolates then?" he joked.

I reached into my bag and pulled out a small box of dark chocolate liqueurs. "You read my mind. Happy Valentine's Day. I'll expect white chocolate in a month's time then."

Shinichi looked at the box. "Are you trying to get me drunk?"

"Trying to," I giggled.

A waiter sped to our table, as if prompted by telepathy, to settle our bill. The man bowed low, almost horizontal to the floor, and held the pose for half a second; enough for me to take note. I noticed that he didn't make eye contact with either of us as he processed the payment that Shinichi handled, though he was impeccably polite, using formal language.

"Wow, that was incredible service. I mean, Japan has amazing customer service in general, but I swear that guy treated us like royalty, or something," I chortled.

Shinichi gave a blasé shrug. "We're probably both so good-looking that we make the place seem classy."

I watched the same waiter settle the bill at another table, with a group of businessmen having an *enkai* party. He definitely didn't bow as low for them, even though they were all well-dressed in suits and ties.

"Guess so," I added. "He treated us differently to those older men."

"A bunch of fat salarymen haven't a patch on us. Now, let's get out of here and, as you English like to say, let's do a pub crawl," he said, with a wink.

Chapter nineteen

Jizo

The stone *Jizo* was about twelve inches in size. With its rounded, bald head and plump cheeks, it looked like a sleeping baby. The dome shaped body had no arms or legs, but a series of diagonal lines running across its front, and a flat base on which it could stand among the rows of other stone babies.

I placed the red, woollen hat I had bought on its head, and draped the red, felt bib around its shoulders. Next, I tucked a windmill in the neckline of its bib. That would help my *Mizuko kuyō,* my Water Child, walk to the afterlife. From the water of my womb to the water of heaven, it would help my child to be reborn.

Shinichi lit a stick of incense, bowed, and offered a blessing to my *Kaimyo,* the temporary name of my child between worlds, while she made her way to heaven. After he was finished, I placed a small posy of peonies in a vase next to it.

"Farewell, my Akari. May you return again someday in a happier life." My voice wavered, and I swallowed to control the tears. Despite the sadness I felt, Shinichi was right. A weight had been lifted off my shoulders. I felt comfort in the statue, as though it would protect the spirit of my unborn child from harmful spirits and help her find her way to heaven.

"Akari. I like that. It means 'bright' in Japanese. Is that why you picked it?" said Shinichi.

I nodded and wiped a tear away with my finger. It was hard to turn away from the statue, but I let Shinichi lead me away from the temple. A Buddhist monk passed us by in the grounds; the monk bowed to Shinichi then hurried on his way.

"What was that about? Do monks bow? I would've thought people paid their respects to monks, not the other way around." I turned to watch the monk rush into the temple; he gave a backward glance and saw me looking, then quickly averted his gaze forward to the temple.

Shinichi tightened his protective grip around my shoulders and steered me towards the roadside. "He knows why we came. I bought the Jizo from him."

I couldn't say why, but my gut feeling told me he wasn't telling the whole truth about the monk's odd behaviour. Maybe it was simply another element of protectiveness; he seemed to feel responsible for my emotional state. If I was honest, I quite liked that fact.

Shinichi certainly showed a level of care that I looked for in a partner. He seemed to go above and beyond when looking after me: being physically there for cuddles when I needed them; cooking me food when I had flu; supporting me to grieve for my lost child; the list went on. I felt bad about breaking up with

The Wabi-sabi Doll

Naoki, but at the same time, I knew I had definitely made a better choice in being with Shinichi. Part of me wanted to be cared for; needed a 'knight in shining armour' and there wasn't anything wrong with that. Choosing to be with a man who met my emotional, as well as physical needs, made me feel more confident in my decision-making abilities. Contrary to making me feel that I was being co-dependent in choosing such a partner, it gave me a freedom, and confidence, that was liberating.

"Do you think the Jizo will help Akari to be at peace now?"

He nodded. "It'll help her to find the right way to heaven. I think what happened before is that she got lost, and her spirit saw you in the darkness. Was her father Japanese?"

I lowered my gaze. "He was American."

"What did he look like – if you don't mind my asking?"

"He had black hair and dark eyes and kind of, like, fake suntanned skin. Why? Does it matter?"

Shinichi's eyes travelled upwards to my hair. "Your hair is dyed black, is it not?"

I touched the crown of my head reflexively. "Yeah. Is there a problem?"

He shook his head, but his face was contemplative. "And you say Akari's spirit presented itself to you in the form of the Japanese Hina doll?"

Where was he going with this? I paused, trying to gauge the direction of the conversation, but couldn't.

"Yeah. I'm pretty sure the doll was moving by itself, and also in my dreams, she appeared as a human version of the doll."

"As in, shoulder-length black hair with heavy black bangs?"

"Yeah, thick black fringe."

Why did I feel the need to correct him? American 'bangs', British 'fringe' – what difference did it make? None, other than I was being defensive.

Shinichi didn't follow up with a comment. Instead, he pointed at my hair. A simple gesture that made it obvious to me what he was saying.

"She was lost between our world and heaven. She's dark haired, like her father, and you dyed your hair black, which made her go to you instead. She saw you in the darkness, and went towards you."

Alarm bells went off in my head. "What if she gets confused and leaves the Jizo to follow me again?"

His eyes flitted to my hair once again. Without saying a word, I knew what he meant.

I ran my hand across my hair, smoothing it flat. "Alright then. I didn't like the black dye much anyway. It made me look too much like that creepy doll."

A fresh start. Hopefully for real, this time.

Chapter twenty

Want for nothing

"Woah, you look incredible."

My hair felt plastered to my head with hairspray and conditioner, more of a helmet than a hairdo, but I appreciated the compliment nonetheless. Shinichi's face lit up the minute he saw me entering the café. He made a beeline across the room and embraced me in a public display of affection that surely went against what Japanese people generally considered *saving face*. Not that I thought he gave a crap about that anyway. Shinichi seemed to play life by his own rules; and people seemed to give him a wide berth for that fact. Everywhere we went, he drew the focus, as though he was the centre-point of gravity in the room. It was nice to have such a charismatic man turn his attention all on me.

Stripping the black dye out of my hair had taken a professional job; not anything I could've done myself with a home DIY kit. The black dye had clearly been so strong that the hairdresser couldn't entirely remove it from my hair. The resulting ash brown colour was a new experience for me; I had expected that my natural baby-blonde colouring would simply reappear. The brunette halo framing my face would take some getting used-to.

"Do you think so?" I ran my splayed fingers through my locks, loosely combing the strands.

"Of *course*. You look *hot*. I somehow imagined you might be a blonde, but I like this colour. Sexy brunette, huh?"

Should I tell him? The thought crossed my mind, but I decided against. I needed to leave the past behind, however temporarily, and the new brunette me was a way to do that while I figured out my current path. Besides, on a shallow note, if my hair had returned to its natural colour, we might have clashed. His bleached crew cut alongside my natural colour might have made us both look a bit *Village of the Damned*.

I smiled. "There's no way Akari would get confused by this look," I said, smoothing my hair with both palms on either side of my head.

Shinichi nodded his agreement. "Of course not. She'll be carrying on her journey, no problem."

Such a thought was liberating. I finally felt like I could let go of some things I had clung to for the past half a year. Shaking off the emotional baggage was such a weight off my mind.

"Thanks for waiting for me here. I hope you weren't too bored?"

"Not at all. I couldn't wait to see what you looked like."

The Wabi-sabi Doll

I tilted my chin downwards, deliberately coy, my hands linked behind my back. "Glad you aren't disappointed."

"Never." He swooped upon me and kissed me; again, unafraid of showing his affection in a conservative society. "How about we go back to your place and I'll show you how not-disappointed I am?"

༄

And he did. The sex was wild.

And again, later that evening.

And later that night.

"Hey Kim. There's this thing I'd love you to do."

"Oh yeah? What thing?"

He licked his lip and flashed me a devious grin. "Something in Japanese I'd love you to say."

"Say? Like, when we're in the middle of it?"

He shook his head. "Before we get started."

"What do you want me to say?"

"*Shitai.*"

"Shitai?"

"It means, I want it. Let's try it."

I made my lips into a pout. "Shitai."

"Sexy, Kim. More sexy."

"Ssh-tai!"

He made his eyes into cold, narrow lines. "Beg for it."

"Shinichi, shitai!"

He practically leapt on me, kissing me all over. "Can we do something else?"

I grinned. Where was this game going? "What is it?"

"I'd love to do it on your balcony. You know, like I bend you over the railing?"

A nervous giggle escaped my lips. "What if the neighbours see?"

He let out a puff of air from the corner of his mouth. "Like anyone's around at this hour?"

"Well... maybe that would be okay."

He grinned. "Even if they are, we'll give them a show, right?"

Another nervous giggle.

"What about if I give you a gentle tap with the futon beater too. Gently, on your ass."

My nervous giggles began to crescendo; I stifled them with my hand.

"Um, sure. Just gently, though?"

"And would you let me tug on your hair? It's just, I love your natural colour. You look so hot, babe."

Natural. Not so. Tight-lipped. "Un-hun."

"Alright then."

Out on the balcony we went, the sliding doors askance. I strapped myself over the balcony rail then looked back over my shoulder and adopted a coquettish expression, one finger on my lip. "Shinichi, ssh-tai!"

Shinichi grabbed my hair from behind and tugged with one hand, while he used the futon beater to tenderise my backside; only gently, as promised.

The sex was rough, and hard, and wild.

Shitai. I want.

I wanted for nothing.

I couldn't have been in a better bliss if I had tried.

Chapter twenty-one

Tied up

"So, Kim. There's this thing I want you to do."

Hmm. What could it be this time? Shinichi was an adventurous lover, I would give him that.

He produced a red rope. Was it a skipping rope? Did he want me to skip for him? I hadn't used a skipping rope since I was ten.

"You wouldn't mind if I tied you up, just a little?"

Ooh, kinky. I didn't say my thoughts aloud, but I couldn't help a little wiggle of my hips as I sat on my haunches on the bed. Shinichi seemed to cotton onto my physical cue and grinned.

"Have you ever been tied up before?"

I shook my head. "I've been love-cuffed once, but that's all."

The words poured out of my mouth before I even had time to filter them, and heat seared across my cheeks in a horizontal flood. It felt weird to be talking of past sexual trysts to a current lover. Would he mind?

His grin widened and one eyebrow shot up in a devious arch. "I didn't think you were into – you know – deviant things."

"Well, I wouldn't call it *deviant* but just, a light bit of S&M. Is rope tying deviant?"

He tipped his head to the left, then right, pulling his lips into a straight line. "In Japan I suppose it is. It's called *shibari*, a form of bondage tying."

"In England I suppose it would be considered *deviant* too. Like, you would buy kinky stuff in certain shops. It's not something you'd admit to generally. People would only do it more openly for hen and stag dos, that kind of thing."

His forehead wrinkled as he raised both eyebrows hopefully. "Are you up for giving it a go then?"

I nodded.

"I'm guessing that when you were hand-cuffed, it was to a bed?"

"Not even that. Just my wrists in front of me while I was blindfolded."

He smirked. "Alright then, we'll start with that."

I held my wrists out willingly for him to tether them together. His smirk became lopsided as one sneaky corner of his mouth rose higher than the other.

"I have a different idea. How about a bit of roleplay?"

A giggle escaped my mouth. "Oh-kay? What sort of roleplay?"

"Would you – resist?"

Now it was my turn for my eyebrows to shoot up. "Resist? Like, pretend I don't want to be tied up?"

"Would you be comfortable with that?" He peered upwards, like a puppy dog.

It was just harmless fun. "Okay then, I'll try it."

I imagined myself as a criminal, who had been caught by Shinichi, as a police officer. The visualisation helped me to get into the *role*, even though I said nothing, and nor did he. He whipped the ropes around my wrists so quickly he actually *did* seem as accomplished as a police officer. Then again, he was a fireman by trade. He must have been used to tying tight bindings.

I switched the image in my head as we fucked, my wrists bound and strapped across my stomach. I imagined him in his sexy fireman uniform, tethering me because I was a hysterical bystander in a burning building, tethering me for my own good. And then? My fantasy ended. What suitable narrative could explain a heroic fireman having sex with someone they had rescued from a burning building?

Oh well. I let the sex take over, focusing on the sensuality between my body and his instead. If Shinichi's sexual tastes were anything to go by, I would most likely have plenty of time to develop more elaborate narratives within my fantasies, besides.

We rolled over, splayed on the tatami mats in my bedroom, a sweaty mess of pure ecstasy. I watched Shinichi's muscular chest rise and fall, letting my head loll on his arm, my tethered wrists strapped across my stomach and my legs spreadeagled.

"That was the best fucking sex I've ever had," I gasped.

He winked at me. "We're only getting started, baby."

If my energy wasn't completely spent, I would have been up for another round. My wrists hurt with the tightness of the ropes; but I found that I kind of enjoyed the pain. Not kind of. *Quite* enjoyed the pain.

As I stared at the ceiling, sailing on a tide of bliss, an object in my peripheral vision drew my eye. I rolled my head to the right.

There it was. It hadn't been there before, not as far as I was aware. The doll was immaculate, its black hair perfectly sleek, the shiny red lips pulled in a shy smile, the wide, dark eyes staring at me. Its pink kimono stood out among the more muted beige and pale green colours of my bedroom; why I hadn't noticed it before was beyond my comprehension.

A shrill scream filled the air. The noise in my ears startled me, before my brain registered that it was me who had screamed. I leapt up onto all fours in a burst of adrenaline and scuttled to the other side of Shinichi, cowering behind him.

"She…" I pointed a shaky finger at the doll. "She came back. You said she wouldn't."

Shinichi looked as baffled as I did. He pushed himself up and sat cross-legged on the futon. "Calm down. Let's think through this. Akari is protected by a Jizo, she can't come back."

There was no way I could calm down; my mind was on a turntable, a mile a minute. "What if something happened to the Jizo? What if she saw what we were doing and got offended, so she decided to come back? What if she got jealous – like, thinking that we might be replacing her?"

Dead air filled the space between us, as Shinichi stared at me, and I stared right back at him.

I let my eyes drop from his face, down over my breasts, to my flat stomach.

Was it flat? Was there a curve that hadn't been there before?

"Oh – my – God. You've got to be shitting me. It can't be... can it?"

Shinichi looked pale as he blinked at me and said nothing. His eyes followed mine down to my stomach. "You're not late, are you?"

Was I? I legitimately hadn't thought about it. When was my last period anyway? Shinichi and I used contraception; apart from that first time on the beach while we'd both been fairly intoxicated. When was that? Several weeks ago? Like, two weeks ago? Two weeks ago I had been several weeks through my cycle already. I tried to count on my fingers and gave up. I was useless at keeping track.

Shit. Could it be? I put my palm flat against my stomach and spread my fingers wide across my bare, warm skin.

"If I was – late – would it be a problem?" I dared to raise my eyes away from my stomach and peered up at Shinichi.

Shinichi's blank expression dissolved as a wide smile spread across his face; sunrise chasing away the shadows of night.

"Never. Don't worry. I'm here."

I leapt onto his lap, straddling him, with my arms wrapped tightly around his neck in a big, comforting, bearhug.

Whether or not I was tied-up – metaphorically, as well as literally, judging by our recent sexual adventures, I knew I wouldn't be alone.

Chapter twenty-two

Late

Two weeks late.

Six weeks since my last period.

My stomach was flat as a pancake. How long before it started to curve and swell?

I walked through the vegetable aisle in Jusco. I needed to be mindful of eating more healthily than I had been lately. No more instant ramen or fatty cuts of meat. I had to eat lean chicken and fresh fish, as well as lots more vegetables.

I picked up a large daikon radish and inspected it, pretending I was a pro. Not that there was any such need; all of the fruit and vegetables on display were picture perfect, some even wrapped in what looked to my unknowledgeable eye as foam *doilies*.

I was so distracted putting all manner of unusual, brightly coloured veg into my basket that I didn't notice the quiet voice behind me.

The Wabi-sabi Doll

"Hi Kimberly."

I jumped and spun. "Naoki. Hey – how are you?"

It was a reflex action; if I hadn't been caught by surprise, I might have been inclined to make my voice more stiff and hostile to him. But seeing his kind smile, and his long, sweeping eyelashes enhancing the look of affection towards me, made my hardened heart melt somewhat.

"I'm hanging in there. I was hoping to see you. Maybe get some coffee and catch up?"

I bristled, giving myself an emotional shake-up. I had broken up with him because he was always working at his family restaurant and not there for me; not only that but for the past month, I had been in a committed relationship with my sexy fireman, Shinichi. Not to mention the fact that our kinky tryst on the beach had left me with a bun in the oven.

My hands instinctively flew to my stomach. "It's not a great time for coffee, I'm busy."

Naoki's gaze dropped to my stomach for half a second then back to my face, his eyes ever so slightly wider. He swallowed. "How about going for ramen then? I really do owe you one, after I cancelled last time."

"I'm not in the mood. I'm trying to be healthier." I turned away from Naoki back to the sweetcorn in husks, choosing a large, ripe one for my basket; but not before I saw the hurt in his eyes.

"Wait, Kimberly, I'm sorry."

I paused, turning back to him. "You don't have to be."

With that, I walked away. It was easier to do than I thought it might be.

Naoki and I had only been together for three months, from October the previous year until January of this year. Three fleeting months. In that time, he had met my entire family. I had really believed him to be the *one*.

Things had certainly changed. My family and friends knew about Shinichi; I had told them in Facetime calls, and talked expansively about him, but I sensed they were humouring me, like, 'Here goes Kimberly with a new man, living it up now that she's free of Carl after seven years'.

What would they say when they found out I was pregnant? I cringed at the thought. Better leave that until after the twelve-week scan.

Naoki swooped into view in front of me, blocking my path. "Kimberly, please wait. I only have one more question. Hear me out."

I let him catch his breath, tempted to think that his desperation was a bit cute, but after I overrode my feelings, my logic found it irritating.

"What is it, I don't have much time," I huffed.

He didn't beat about the bush, his eyes fixed on my stomach. "Is there something I should know?"

A glimmer of hopefulness twinkled in his gaze, endearing him to me once more; momentarily, fleetingly. I shook the feeling away. "Nothing that you need to worry about."

I walked on, leaving him looking lost. His arms hung at his sides, and his head hung a little closer to his chest. Guilt stabbed me at the image of him there, a lost puppy. Maybe I had been too much of a bitch; maybe my response had been uncalled for. I knew in his gaze that he knew I was pregnant and that it wasn't his. I had known him for a year, been romantically attached to him for a quarter of that time, and I had never seen him look so devastated.

I was a bitch. A bitch who would rot in hell. A corner of my poisoned heart turned black and peeled off, dropping into my rotten guts for what I had done to him.

Why couldn't it have been Carl? Why couldn't I have hurt Carl by telling *him* that I was pregnant with a new love's child? Why couldn't *Carl* have shown the pain of emptiness and loneliness and desperation instead of Naoki?

Why did I still care about hurting Carl?

Had I *still* not gotten over Carl, even now, after relationships with two other men? Or was it because he had hurt me, on Tottori sand dune beach, by showing off his twin babies and his new romance with Shiori, my one-time nemesis?

I *still* had much work to do on my soul. I *still* had so much to unpack in my psyche, clearly.

Shinichi. I visualised my sexy fireman and his smouldering hot, lopsided smile. Sizzling, sexy, Shinichi. Naoki and Carl were instantly forgotten.

For now, I had to focus on nurturing my body to give our baby the nutrients it needed. I grabbed a couple of fresh corns on the cob and put them into my shopping basket. Corn was loaded with folic acid. Carl had his family time with Shiori, and I would enjoy mine later in the year with Shinichi.

Life felt good, being late.

Chapter twenty-three

Hina Matsuri

Haru-ichiban. The Spring Winds from China. More new words to add to my ever-expanding Japanese vocabulary. The Spring Winds ushered in a change of weather for a new month – March.

I had been to Kyoto before, but not with Shinichi. As he took me around the sights, I tried to push memories of going there the previous year with Carl out of my head. This time, instead of my ex's negative, energy-draining bad mood and snide comments about how the Victoria and Albert memorial statue in London was more impressive than the stunning gold-leaf covered Kinkakuji temple, my new boyfriend was a knowledgeable and articulate tour guide. Not only positive in his attitude to life, but gorgeous too.

"Why are there so many dolls on display? Is this a 'Kyoto' thing?"

The Wabi-sabi Doll

Shinichi shook his head. "They're for the Hina Matsuri, or in English, the doll's festival. It's a celebration for girls every year on the third of March."

"Girl's Day. I like that. There's no celebration for girls in the U.K. We have Christmas and Easter for the kids, but it's mostly stuff like Mother's Day and Father's Day and Valentine's Day. I quite like that children get that sort of respect here. Is there anything for boys?"

"Boy's Day is on the fifth of May and that's called *tango no sekku*," he added.

"That's so lovely. There's so many respectful things in Japan, I just love it." My hands jumped to my stomach. "Not that I think I'm having a boy. My gut feeling tells me I'm going to have a sweet little girl. She's going to look just like you."

Shinichi held his chin aloft, a proud smile plastered across his face. It was lovely to see; he was proud as a soon-to-be father, as I was to become a mother. Why shouldn't we be?

"We'll need a new name for your doll," he said.

For a split second, I didn't know what he meant; then I recalled the porcelain doll.

"I've already got one." I gave him a knowing smile. "Her name is Kami."

"The doll, or our daughter?" he said.

"Both, why not?"

I slipped my hand into his as we walked along through the dangling decorations and past rows of *Hina* dolls on display for the Girls' Day festival.

"You know, the funny thing is, I no longer fear that doll. After I started to suspect that I'm pregnant, it was like, all the fear just ebbed away. I even brought her with us – Kami, I mean."

"I figured you would." There wasn't an ounce of surprise in his voice.

"I put her on my pillow just before we left the hotel." I cast a sideways glance at him, wondering if I might catch a fleeting look of derision, or the wide-eyed expression of worry over my mental health state; but no. Nothing like that. Respectful and supportive, as always.

I needed to let go of the Carls — and any Carl-like behavioural assumptions about current boyfriends — in the past.

"You're so *kawaii*, Kim, you know that?" He wrapped his arm around the small of my back and squeezed my waist. "Hey, you know what? I've got a great idea to celebrate the Hina Matsuri. There's this thing I want you to do."

I couldn't help but grin at him; probably a wide, goofy grin, but I didn't care. Those words were my signal that he had yet another kinky plan in mind.

He grinned back. "You want to get dressed up as a geisha? It'll be great. You'll look like a Hina Doll."

"Really? Where can I do that?"

"There's a place where we can go for you to do the whole Geisha and Maiko dress up experience."

"You mean, like all the white make-up on my face with red lippy, plus the kimono?"

He nodded.

"And then what? You want to have some kinky sex with me dressed like a geisha?"

He pulled an exaggerated expression of shock. "Is that what you take me for? That everything is about sex?"

I laughed. "Okay, Mr. Purity. What would I do instead then, once I'm dressed as a geisha?"

"Get a few pictures of you looking stunning to send home to your family, or post everywhere on social media."

I narrowed my eyes at him, on purpose. "And *then* what? You're up to something, aren't you?"

He chortled. "Okay, you got me. We can get ourselves a sex shop geisha costume for you to give me my own private show, back at our hotel."

I roared with laughter. "I knew you had an ulterior motive. Alright then, let's do the respectable dress up part first, then go and get the rest for the sordid follow-up. Sounds like fun."

Chapter twenty-four

Geisha cosplay

I fixed the black wig on my head and skewered it onto my own hair-bun using a pin with plastic cherry blossoms attached. My face was painted white with powder and my red lipstick gleamed. Together with the pink yukata and *geta* on my feet, I looked every inch a demure maiko.

Well, not quite. It was the second time that day for some dressing up, only this time, it was for Shinichi's own private show. The red and gold silk kimono that I had worn earlier at the Maiko and Geisha experience had seemed much more regal, helping to give my look an old-world feel. Now? I felt much sexier and more fun.

Shinichi lounged across the sofa in our hotel room. "You look gorgeous, my little maiko."

"Don't maiko have to sing and dance and entertain? I can't do any of those things," I laughed.

The Wabi-sabi Doll

"In that case, I'll have to train you to be a good apprentice geisha, then," he teased.

I twirled, to show off the pink floral yukata he had bought me earlier that day for *ichi man en:* ten thousand yen was about fifty pounds. Although I thought traditional heavy silk kimonos were much more beautiful than yukata, the summer kimono versions, their light cotton fabric made them easier to put on without help. The set he bought me came with a bow that clipped onto the obi sash at the back. Kimono sashes required the help of a knowledgeable attendant to wrap them as tight as a corset, and Shinichi was the first to admit that he hadn't a clue how to do such a task. My yukata sash had two strings on either end, so that all I had to do was wrap it around my waist and secure it with the strings, then tuck them inside the fabric and disguise the knot with the pre-made bow. My yukata not only made me look the part but was perfect for our cosplay purposes; I knew he would want me to wear an outfit that would give quicker access than a kimono for our kinky dress-up fun. Together with the black geisha wig that we had bought from a hyaku en store, a one-pound shop, and my makeup from the maiko and geisha experience he had paid for earlier that day.

"If I have to be a geisha, then what's your role?" I pulled aside one hem of my yukata aside to reveal my bare leg underneath.

Shinichi licked his lips. "You'll find out later. How about dinner first?"

A knock at our door announced a waiter, on cue, who came into our room. He pushed a trolley of mystery food, hidden under silver domes, and a bucket of ice with a bottle of wine cooling in it. The man didn't bat an eyelid at the fact I was dressed up like a maiko, yet embarrassment burned at my face; thank goodness for the white powder to conceal my self-consciousness. Before he left our room, he bowed low to Shinichi, as though he was the emperor. I couldn't stifle my chortle, and it ended up as a splutter that I tried to conceal under one of the yukata's long, cotton sleeves.

"What was that all about? Everywhere we go, people seem to treat you in such a formal manner. I mean, I swear if I brought you to London, the Royal family would bow low before you!"

Shinichi grinned, his eyes narrowing to lines. "Japan is a formal country, haven't you noticed?"

"But that waiter. I pointed to the door. "He practically bent himself into a bloody right angle!"

He scoffed. "Oh that? That was part of the act. You're my geisha, remember? I'm supposed to be a distinguished gentleman, so I arranged with him to play along."

That made sense. It certainly explained the waiter not even batting an eyelid at me, either. "Okay then, distinguished gentleman of mine. What would you like this demure geisha to do for you today, since she can't sing or dance?"

"Hmm, what indeed?" He stroked his chin in a theatrical manner, a sly grin on his face. "Why don't we start by you showing me a hint of leg?"

I gave a pantomime gasp and touched the tips of my fingers against my open lower lip. "Why, that wouldn't be proper! I'm a delicate lady, I couldn't possibly!"

"You'll have to do it. I'm paying a lot of money for you, I expect to be rewarded for my efforts. His taunting voice had an edge of faux danger to it."

I bent my leg at the knee and inched the cotton hem of my pink yukata up, slowly across my bare skin. "Will that be all, Mr. Distinguished gentleman?"

He waved his finger from side to side, like a metronome. "Uh uh, uh. I'm not finished with you yet. Next, I want to see your shoulder. Go on, slide it off your left shoulder."

I affected a coy smile and did as I was told.

Shinichi whipped his phone out of his trouser pocket. "Beautiful. Stunning. I'd better take a photo of my most gorgeous model."

I narrowed my eyes in mock suspicion. "Wait a minute. Distinguished gentlemen didn't have cameras when geisha were a thing, did they?"

He cocked his head, giving me a playful look. "There are still geisha today. Who said we're pretending this was in the past?"

Fair point. I raised my bare shoulder close to my ear and jutted my naked calve at a more prominent angle, exaggerating the coy pose even more.

"Why don't you go just that little bit further? Lift your yukata just the *tiniest* bit more. I wanna see some thigh, baby."

I giggled behind my fingertips in mock embarrassment, then slid the yukata up over my knee and along my thigh and tipped my chin downwards, batting my eyelashes at him.

Before he took another snap, Shinichi stretched his leg out and used his toe to flick my yukata aside, exposing the edge of my lacy, red, thong.

"How dare you, good Sir! May I remind you that I am a lady of class?" I peered down my nose at him in mock outrage, then grabbed a fistful of fabric and pulled it back over my bare leg and smoothed the yukata in place.

Shinichi got up and stood in front of me. He peered down his nose at me, acting every bit the outraged gentleman, then circled me, looking me up and down. "You are certainly a lady of status and fine form. But I am still a paying customer and I have bought your time. I expect to be entertained," he said, affecting a posh, if exaggerated English accent.

I tried not to grin; keeping up the charade of disgruntled gentleman customer and dishonoured geisha was a fun roleplay. Shinichi stood in front of me, waiting for my response.

"Well, if it's entertainment you're after, then let me try *this*." I swept the fabric off my left shoulder, then right shoulder, and crossed my arms across my midriff, pushing my bust upwards to reveal my cleavage above the yukata.

Shinichi furrowed his brow and puckered his lips, the perfect thespian. Then he grabbed both folds of my yukata and pulled them apart, revealing my bare breasts, which bounced at the intrusion. Before I had a chance to fix my clothing in place, he raised his phone camera.

Heat rushed to my face as I broke my role. "Hey, that was sneaky! You didn't take a picture of my bare boobs, did you?"

He leaned forward and cupped my face in both hands, kissing my squashed lips. "I did, but it was all part of the fun."

"Can you delete it, please? I don't want any nude pictures on anyone's phone. My red thong is showing too."

"Aww, but you look so gorgeous. Hey, you're my *bijin*," he protested.

I folded my arms. "Delete it, Shinichi."

He pouted, shooting me a puppy dog look. "Don't you trust me?"

"Now," I said, in my best school-teacher voice.

Shinichi sighed. He unlocked his phone, scrolled to the photo, and hit delete. "Are you happy now, ma*dam*? Am I back in your good books?"

I glanced sideways at him, still keeping my arms folded, and narrowed my eyes to cast a roving eye over him. As he grinned, I couldn't help returning his sexy smile with a cheeky one of my own.

"I'll forgive you – but just this once. You're on thin ice, mister."

"I know how to make it up to you," he said.

He didn't *half* make it up to me. He held me up, braced against the wall, with my legs wrapped around his lower back. Impressive as his stamina was, my mind wandered. I hadn't checked whether or not he had permanently erased the photo. Sure, he had deleted it; but had he wiped it completely from his recycle bin? Bit late to ask now; it would seem like I didn't believe him. There was no reason to doubt him, was there? Nothing he had done so far gave me any reason to mistrust him. So why did I have my reservations?

Chapter twenty-five

A message from Kami

My stomach looked like a harvest pumpkin. I turned to look at myself side view in the mirror, and it was as though a basketball had been shoved under my skin. The past eight months had really crept up. Our little girl would be arriving soon, making a mother of me and a father of Shinichi.

The mirror began to shake, distorting my appearance. An index finger appeared around one edge, creeping from behind, followed by a second finger, then a third, and finally the pinky finger. I realised with horror that the wall-mounted mirror was, in fact, a door. The door widened and a crop of mouse-brown hair announced a man peering in, his green eyes full of wicked glee.

Carl! My strangled scream caught in my throat as my abusive ex gestured to me with one finger to follow

The Wabi-sabi Doll

him inside the hidden room, a gloating smile wide on his face.

A hidden room. The grey walls had been covered, ceiling to floor, with hundreds of eyes. Blue, green, brown, hazel; all were watching me. Scouring my pregnant bulk, boring beneath my skin into my mind, scrutinising my soul.

☙

I sat up, gasping. Another nightmare. Were the bad dreams a symptom of pregnancy? My hands both jumped to my stomach, feeling the small curve below my belly button. I was only eight weeks, not eight months and the only eyes that watched me were those of the porcelain doll.

She no longer gave me the creeps, as she had done when possessed by the spirit of Akari. Now, she was possessed by the spirit of Kami, and when born, the soul that resided in the doll would enter my newborn baby.

Shinichi wasn't there with me. He had been on night duty as a firefighter; hopefully not attending to something dangerous like a burning building, or chemical explosion. My mind tortured me at times with such imagery. I liked that he had a heroic profession saving lives, and imagined him looking sexy in his uniform, although I had never actually seen him dressed in it; but didn't like that his shifts meant he couldn't spend the night with me that often. How ironic that I had broken up with Naoki for doing so many shifts at his parents' restaurant, and now I was with another man whose job often took him elsewhere for days on end.

Where did he live, I had asked him? Shinichi had been vague, mentioning an apartment in Iwami and didn't seem to want to talk about it much. I had asked if I could see it. Another time, maybe, he had said, as it was messy. I didn't care about mess, and knew what to expect of a bachelor's pad, and I had asked again, to no avail. He told me he would get round to cleaning it and bring me there sometime for dinner. But then we had dined again at mine. Then again, another time. And so on, and so forth. I stopped asking after that, and he didn't voluntarily bring it up.

What was *with* men? The ones I dated all seemed to be headstrong, set on their ideas and with no way of changing their minds.

I rubbed the tiny curve of my stomach. Our daughter, Kami, would soften Shinichi; of that, I was sure. Didn't girls always have their daddies wrapped around their little fingers? I sure did, as the only daughter in my family. Zac was a mummy's boy, and I was a daddy's girl.

What about that massive pumpkin-stomach in my dream? I counted on my fingers. I would be due around Halloween, just in time for my two year anniversary in Japan. Maybe for my Halloween costume I would paint my baby bump to look like a Jack-o-lantern. The thought gave me a chuckle.

What about the other parts of my weird nightmare, though? The painted eyes watching me? Time for some psychoanalysis. Hundreds of wide-open eyes watching me. That had to represent excitement caused by a new undertaking. Motherhood was certainly the biggest undertaking that I could think of; more life-changing than even moving to Japan for a new life.

Where would we live, the three of us? Iwami, in Shinichi's bachelor pad? Or back to London, where my family could be nearby to support us?

I turned to my Kami doll for inspiration, and gasped.

She was facing the opposite way, towards the window. What had caused Kami to move; and why?

I peered out my bedroom window and saw Shinichi outside my apartment block. He was talking to Kawaii-chan's mum, standing close enough so that their voices didn't travel.

Why wasn't he sleeping after his night shift? In his black trousers and black bomber jacket, he looked well rested and cut a sharp figure as he talked to my neighbour. Curious, I went into the living room and opened the sliding door onto the balcony. I craned my neck so that I could see them without them noticing me. From there, I could hear Shinichi's deep voice and the animated, flirtatious sound of Kawaii-chan's mum.

Who could blame her; my boyfriend was a hottie, after all. What could they be talking about, so deep in conversation, though? Maybe he was making pleasantries with her while on his way to see me.

I closed the sliding door to the balcony and went through to my kitchenette to make breakfast, while waiting for a knock at my door. Fifteen minutes passed, and none came. I snuck another peek out through the sliding door and saw that Kawaii-chan's mum tended to her vegetable garden, but there was no sign of Shinichi.

Odd. Wonder why he didn't stop by, considering he was so close to my flat? I flopped down on my sofa, clamping my slice of buttered toast between my teeth, so that I could fire off a quick text to him:

Hey sexy. Hope you aren't too tired after your shift. Free for dinner later? I fancy some yakitori.

Send. A moment later, my phone pinged as he texted back:

Yo, gorgeous girl. Was a busy one, slept like a log after, just woke up. Wish I was in bed with you instead of cold and lonely. Tell me what you're wearing and that might warm me up…

Doubly odd. Why was he telling me he was just awake when I had seen him a few moments before outside my flat? My thumbs hovered over the keypad; what to write back?

My pink cami vest and shorts. What about you?

Black bomber jacket and black jeans, maybe? I waited for his answer.

Just my boxers. Bet you look hot. Send me a pick, babe.

Hmm. Doubly triply odd. I set my toast on the sofa, wiped away the crumbs, folded myself into a sexy pose and snapped a selfie with my tousled hair and skimpy, pink pyjamas.

How do I look? Your turn now. Let's see those tidy whities…

I resumed munching on my toast while I waited for his answer, which came a few minutes later. A photo appeared that he had taken in his bathroom mirror. His phone was held high in his right hand, and he winked at the camera with his left eye shut. The dim illumination from the strip light of the bathroom mirror highlighted the ripples of his abdominal muscles and his tight-fitting Calvin Klein boxers left little to the imagination.

I chuckled to myself as I texted my response. *I'll have you for breakfast, please.*

How on earth had he managed to get home and get stripped off so quickly? It wasn't possible.

The Wabi-sabi Doll

There was only one explanation; I must have been mistaken about the person who had been talking to Kawaii-chan's mum outside. It must have been a man who resembled Shinichi and my brain, which had only just woken, had assumed it was my boyfriend. Besides, I had never seen Shinichi wearing a black bomber jacket.

A moment later, another photo text pinged on my phone. As if reading my thoughts, the picture showed Shinichi bare-chested and wearing a black bomber jacket, like the one the man outside wore. He had his hands tucked into the pockets of his black jeans with only the thumbs outside, pulling the open jacket to either side of his hips and giving a smouldering look to the camera. The photo was overwritten with Japanese text. Why on earth did Shinichi send a message in Japanese to me? More to the point, what did it mean?

I held my thumb over the text to highlight it and copied it, then pasted it into a search. Relying on auto translate was still preferable to my rudimentary Japanese ability, even after sixteen months in the country.

How's this one? I know you like the J-pop look. I tried my best. See how I pander to your fetish, Eri?

I stared at the translation. Huh? Who was Eri?

A moment later, the photo disappeared. I stared at the grey circle with a strike through it, indicating that the image had been removed.

I hovered my thumbs over the keypad, my mind whirling, then started to type.

Um, bit confused here. Who's Eri?

A few minutes later, his reply popped up below my text.

Sorry babe. I sent that to you by mistake.

I sat back and folded my arms. My mind was in a muddle. Was he cheating on me? If so, at least it seemed he was coming clean.

Another text followed. *I meant to send it to a friend.*

What the *actual*? I held my phone at arm's length. Yeah *right*. A *likely* story. I forced my thoughts to condense.

Do you usually talk about fetishes, and send half-naked pictures of yourself to your 'friends'?

There was a longer gap before he replied.

I know it seems strange. She thought I looked like a J-pop star and asked me for a pic to compare. It was just stupid fun. Didn't mean anything. Honest, babe. It was done as a joke to make fun of her.

Hmm.

My thoughts drifted to the doll. Kami knew something was up. Kami had inclined herself towards the window. Was Shinichi lying? Was she telling me that he was, indeed, the man I had seen outside, talking to Kawaii-chan's mum, and wearing the same black bomber jacket as in the deleted photo? Was he cheating on me? Was he making a fool of me, just like Carl did, when he cheated on me with Shiori?

Why was the little voice of doubt calling loudly in my ear, for the second time in less than a week? I massaged my belly as I pondered my reservations.

Chapter twenty-six

A visit from Kami

I was going mad.

I had to be, to meet Shinichi despite my reservations. Whatever the deal with him was, I had to have faith in myself. I wasn't repeating the mistakes of the past with Carl. I wasn't with another man who was using me, cheating on me, making a fool of me. Shinichi had *never* belittled me like Carl had, who had verbally abused me, chastised me for being stupid and the like. Shinichi was the opposite, in fact. He didn't take me for granted. He was there for me, physically and emotionally. Our sex life was incredible; the best I'd ever experienced.

But I still had doubts. Was he too suave, using his obvious masculine charms against me to manipulate me sexually? Meeting him was the best way to either assuage my doubts, or to reinforce them. Essentially, his invitation to meet was a make or break.

I walked through Yayoi-cho, the restaurant and pub district of Tottori and saw him waiting outside Café Throwback, where he had offered to meet me. He was dressed in a dark grey satin, three-piece suit – unusually formal – and carried a bunch of red roses.

Why did his effort strike me as trying too hard?

I nudged the doubt to the back of my mind. Not the time or place; besides the fact that he looked incredible. Had Carl ever dressed so formally and taken me to a fancy new restaurant, making me feel a million pounds? Nope. Naoki hadn't, for that matter either. Not even to his own family restaurant.

"Hey babe. You look beautiful," Shinichi said, swooping in for a kiss.

I turned my face at the last second, deflecting his lips onto my cheek, then gestured down at my burgundy pencil dress. "Not especially. I wore this to work. But I'll take the compliment anyway."

Treat him mean, keep him keen. Well, not exactly. More like, keeping him at a healthy distance until he explained the meaning of the shirtless text to his so-called friend, Eri; with a better excuse than trying to make a fool of her.

Shinichi jolted forward, almost crashing into me, as someone behind bumped into him. I peered around his shoulder and–

What a coincidence.

Shiori and Carl had stopped abruptly in the middle of the footpath. Shiori was looking rather 'deer-in-headlights', her cheeks flushed and eyes wide, as she peered up at Shinichi. The schoolgirl act poked at my defence mechanisms with a sharp, thorny stick and I stepped closer to Shinichi's side. He wrapped a protective arm around my waist and pulled me close. Another weird coincidence how it had been a year – almost exactly – since I had found out that Shiori had stolen Carl from me. Now it seemed she was flirting with Shinichi too.

"Sorry. I didn't mean to bump into you," she said, in English.

Weird. Why didn't she say it to him in Japanese? Was her use of English for the benefit of Carl and me?

Speaking of Carl; he stood gawping at me while Shiori made her apologies to my boyfriend. Was that a lustful smirk on his face too? So bold. So brazen. The cheek of—

"Alright there, browner," said Carl, his eyes on my hair.

Maybe mocking, rather than lustful, then.

Shiori turned to me with a tepid smile. "Kimberly. How nice to see you."

Shinichi looked from Shiori to me and back at her. "You two know each other?"

Hmph. If that wasn't the *half* of it. I ushered the thought away as Shinichi's eyes landed on Carl, then jumped to me, then back to Carl.

Carl, noticing that he was under scrutiny, stood upright and straightened his shoulders. I had seen that posture before; he was squaring up.

If the atmosphere between the four of us hadn't been so tense, I would have laughed; there stood Shinichi and I, clearly the more attractive and smartly dressed couple, while Shiori and Carl looked every bit like new parents; bleary-eyed and wearing baggy casuals.

"I see," said Shinichi, with a nod of understanding. "Well, my beautiful girlfriend and I are late for dinner. Excuse us."

"Bye Shiori," I said, then turned to Carl and fixed him with an unblinking stare. "See ya."

As Shinichi and I turned into the foyer of the restaurant, I heard an argument break out between my ex and his latest fling outside.

"What was that look for? Like you found her so sexy?"

"What?! I wasn't even looking. She's a pig. That's why I dumped her ass. You're the only one who's beautiful, China doll."

A *pig*. I smirked to myself recalling a similar argument the previous year, a few weeks before I found out Carl was cheating on me with Shiori. We had been walking through Jusco, the department store where both Shiori and I worked, and she had come out of the clothes shop, Classy Girl, where she was a sales assistant. She had held up a dress from one of the racks and asked, "How do I look? Sexy?" Carl had answered "yes", causing an argument between us, where he had been forced to defend himself by saying that she had put him on the spot; that he thought all women were pigs except for me. Of course, little did I know at that time that he had already been seeing her behind my back.

I scoffed. All of it, both the memory and the scenario that had happened moments before, was funny. Pathetic, but funny.

I glanced at my handsome, sophisticated boyfriend. An inadvertent benefit of the happenstance outside the restaurant was that I appreciated Shinichi much more. While Shiori and Carl were consumed by petty jealousy and arguments, Shinichi and I were about to enjoy a romantic evening together. Not only that, but he only had eyes for me.

That was the confidence boost I needed for myself. I had to believe in my own decisions; I had chosen to be with Shinichi, and he had picked me too. If he said his photo text to his friend Eri was just for fun, then I had to trust him. I couldn't let petty jealousy from a failed past relationship colour my view of my current relationship. Shinichi lavished his attention on me, taking me on trips to swish hotels and fancy restaurants. Money aside, he gave me something even more important: his time. I had no reason to have any doubts in my boyfriend.

The restaurant staff in Café Throwback greeted us with low bows as if we were royalty, then led us to a window table. As my eyes lighted on a familiar object, I momentarily stopped in my tracks. On top of a *shoji lantern*, a traditional Japanese box lamp, next to our table was my Kami doll. She was wearing a sky-blue kimono and had a matching blue flower behind her right ear. I looked around the restaurant. All of the other tables had a shoji lantern next to them too, but none had a doll.

"How on earth?" I trailed off pointing at Kami.

Shinichi lowered my finger, and rubbed my hand with his thumb as he held it in his own. "Don't ask how. She's your guardian. Who are we to question the mysteries of the universe?"

He placed his other hand on my stomach and gave it a quick rub. I placed my hand on top of his and squeezed to show my understanding.

Kami. Yes, it was true that sometimes things happened that were hard to explain; like thinking about a person and suddenly getting a phone call from them or having a sixth sense about not going a certain way home, only to find out later that someone got murdered later that night. But this was different. Over the past two months, Kami had appeared, pristine at my door after I had tossed her outside in the dirt. She had appeared at Bar Nightfall wearing her sky-blue kimono rather than the pink one she wore in my flat. She had appeared in my bedroom after I had thrown her off my balcony. She had turned to face a different direction, alerting me to my neighbour outside talking to man who bore an uncanny resemblance to Shinichi. Now, she had moved out of my bedroom and arrived at the restaurant where my boyfriend had arranged to take me for a surprise date, wearing her 'going-out' blue kimono again.

Yes, the universe worked in mysterious ways; but it was getting increasingly hard not to question how. Or why.

Chapter twenty-seven

A guardian for a scan

Short breaths in through my nose for one – two – three.

Slow breaths out through my mouth for one – two – three.

This wasn't happening.

It was exactly the same room, and exactly the same doctor as a year before, when I had attended my twelve-week pregnancy scan. When I had been made pregnant by a colleague after he had raped me.

This *was* happening. I was having a full-blown panic attack.

What an unfortunate, and unexpectedly traumatising coincidence.

I cupped both hands over my face, as I lay on the gurney, and breathed in the recycled air that I had already exhaled.

The only way to get myself out of this was to focus on the present. It was a different situation; I was with my caring boyfriend, not a predatory ex-colleague. I was glad that he had come back from a toilet trip just in the nick of time, as my post-traumatic stress had started to crescendo.

Slow breaths in and out.

In. Out.

Shinichi seemed to read my mind; he squeezed my arm. His touch gave me the confidence to remove my hands from my face.

The sonographer spoke to Shinichi in Japanese and let him translate what I already knew was coming. First the standard question: did I have a full bladder? Apparently it worked better with a full tank of urine in there. Then the instructions: that he was going to apply gel to my tummy. That it would be cold. That I would feel pressure on my stomach and to let him know if it hurt. That it shouldn't hurt, but might feel uncomfortable because of my full bladder.

I continued taking deep breaths as the sonographer pressed the wand all over my stomach. Shinichi kept a close watch over me, standing next to the gurney. I appreciated his protectiveness, but on the other hand, I couldn't see the screen.

I raised my head up off the gurney and tried to peer around him. "Shinichi, I can't see the screen."

"Ssh, it's okay. Just focus on taking deep breaths," he soothed.

"But I want to see the baby," I protested.

He stroked my hair and placed gentle, but firm hands on my shoulders, guiding me to lie down on the gurney.

"The baby is fine, don't worry."

The Wabi-sabi Doll

More Japanese as the sonographer spoke to Shinichi. I listened to his tone of voice. Not grave, as he had been last year when he had spoken to Zoe about my dead baby. This time his voice was animated; almost irritated, as they talked.

"What's he saying? Can I see the baby?"

"He says the baby is well. It's growing just fine."

"Not *it*, she's a *she*," I corrected. "Kami is growing just fine, you mean."

The sonographer shook his head and spoke quickly, his intonation giving weight to the words that I didn't understand; all I knew was that he was getting frustrated at Shinichi.

"Why did he shake his head? What's going on?" I propped myself up on both elbows, managing to see the screen around Shinichi. Without the wand on my stomach, the screen was completely black. It didn't help that Shinichi, taller than the sonographer, seemed more doorman than supportive boyfriend, acting as a blockade between me and the medic. Eventually, the sonographer put up his hands to Shinichi and swiftly left the room.

"Why did he leave? What did he say?" I could feel my heartrate speeding up again.

"He said there's nothing to be concerned about, that's why he shook his head." He gave me a reassuring smile. "And he left because he's so busy – there's another couple waiting for their scan after us."

I paused, forcing my brain to work. "If everything was fine with no concerns, why didn't you want me to see the screen?"

He turned to me with calm composure. "It's more important to me that you stay calm. Part of becoming a mother is to put your own needs first for the benefit of the child."

I lay my head back down on the gurney and looked at the ceiling; he spoke words of wisdom. If my body was full of adrenaline, from having a panic attack, it would be bad for Kami as well as me.

The sonographer came back into the room, red and flustered. He handed me tissues to wipe the gel off my stomach.

"Do I get a scan of the baby?" I asked the sonographer.

He avoided eye contact as he replied to me in Japanese before leaving the room. I turned to Shinichi to translate.

Shinichi gestured towards the corridor. "He said he's printing it in the next room. I'll go and see if I can get it, while you're straightening up your clothes."

I'd just jumped off the gurney, when Shinichi appeared as quick and silent as a ninja. He held out a black and white print. In the middle, the tiny foetus was curled into a C-shape.

I stared at the scan photo. Should I have felt something? Why did I feel nothing? Was that normal?

"You're really sure he said everything is alright with Kami?"

He kissed the top of my head. "Yeah, sure. Don't worry about everything so much, just relax."

I stared again at the scan photo and blinked and stared some more. It was a generic photo, the size of a polaroid photo. At the top there was information in Japanese along with the size in centimetres of the baby. She had a five centimetre crown to rump length and a gestation age of twelve weeks and two days.

"What happens now? Am I going to have maternity appointments?"

"Not much will happen until your next scan at twenty weeks. There'll be more appointments closer to the time."

I glanced sideways at him. "You seem so sure."

His long, narrow eyes crinkled in a grin that seemed, for a moment, more devious than placating. "The sonographer gave a lot of information."

He held my elbow as we left the room, a gesture that gave me a chortle of amusement. "I'm not about to pop. You can give me a shoulder of support in a few months when I'll doubtlessly be needing you to help get me out of chairs!"

As we passed the open doorway of the next sonography room, I did a double take. There, in the furthest corner of the room, was Kami. Her face was inclined towards the corridor, with her red-lipped smile welcoming smile. She was wearing the pink kimono that she originally had worn when I found her on my apartment doorstep.

"Kami's here. She came with us." I walked into the room and lifted her off the shelf where she stood, then cradled her like a baby.

"Of course she's here. She's your guardian, watching over us until her spirit can enter the baby."

I studied his face, which seemed to be full of Zenlike wisdom. "At what point do spirits enter babies?"

"They go in and out, but don't fully attach to the child's body until the moment of birth," he answered.

"What a beautiful thought. Isn't it lovely to think that a good angel is watching over us all the time." I stroked my stomach, even though it was still mostly flat. Only a tiny bulge, like the kind I had after a slap-up lunch, gave any indication of the little life within me.

I hooked one arm around Shinichi's back and held my Kami doll close to my stomach with the other, visualising the spirit of our soon-to-be daughter flowing out of the doll and into my body, then back again.

I had never felt so full of happiness in my life.

Chapter twenty-eight

April showers, May flowers

I had never felt so full of emptiness in my life.

Mid-April. April showers. Before May flowers?

Not for now, at any rate. Just emptiness, usurping happiness. I had never felt so tempted to reach for the vodka bottle than at that moment. I never would have, of course. No alcohol for nine months.

Thirteen weeks of pregnancy, unlucky for some. I should have been happy. But my emotions were constantly a rollercoaster. What had triggered it this time?

Shinichi. With a woman.

It had been my day off. Normally I avoided Jusco on weekends since it reminded me of work. But I fancied a shopping trip to get a lovely floaty chiffon top that would work well as both a maternity top, and still be wearable after I had given birth. I deserved a treat, why not?

Then I had spotted him with her, and my shopping trip had turned to spying torment. The woman with Shinichi was a well-dressed Japanese lady in her early twenties. She had dyed auburn hair and large, brown eyes that peered out below a straight fringe. Her rosebud lips made a cute heart-shaped pout and I seethed with jealousy as I tailed them through the department store. Whereas I was beginning to look big and bloated, she was petite and lithe. Intrusive thoughts of the attractive brunette enjoying Shinichi's incredible sex slipped into my brain, poisoning my mind.

Eri. She must have been Eri. The one that he had been trying to send a half-naked picture of himself to, but had mistakenly sent it to me. The one that he claimed was simply a friend.

I was being too paranoid, wasn't I? What if they were just friends and I was jumping to conclusions? He was being friendly and chatty with her, but nothing untoward had happened. Nothing other than my pregnancy hormones running high.

Nothing untoward until that hug. That hug out in the carpark, when they had parted ways. Yes, she had initiated it, but it was where Shinichi had placed his hands that concerned me; low on her back, almost resting just on the groove above her backside. Was that how friends hugged? It hinted of something more than a platonic friendship. I had never wanted to slash someone's tires more at that moment more than I did to that bitch's white Nissan Note.

Should I have confronted him? Maybe. I could easily have slipped out from my hiding place in the bike shelter and confronted them both. But fate had again intervened.

Naoki. My ex-boyfriend had spilled out of Jusco's large automatic doors at the right moment. Or maybe the wrong one. He had seen me looking frumpy in my oversized, bump-accommodating top, and in floods of mascara-streaked tears.

"Kimberly." His voice had a note of concern, bordering on panic. "What's wrong?"

What's wrong? What was *right?*

I sniffed and wiped my face on the back of my hand. "Nothing. I'm fine."

"If you don't mind me saying, you don't seem fine. I was hoping to call you, but I didn't think you wanted me to. I thought about calling so many times."

I raised my eyes. "You did?"

He ventured a soft smile. "I see you stripped the black dye out of your hair."

I smoothed my hair with one hand. "Not entirely. I think it'll be this mousey brown shade until it grows out."

His eyes travelled downwards to my stomach, as if he had a sixth sense about my condition. "Are you – keeping well?"

My hands flew to the small curve below my belly button, and I cradled it, linking both fingers together. "Yeah, well enough. I'd better go. I don't fancy cycling if the wind gets stronger. It feels like a typhoon."

"We call these '*haru ichiban*'. The spring winds from China. They cover everything with yellow dust from the desert." His gaze settled on my hands, cradling my stomach. "Is it safe for you to cycle?"

I stared at him, trying to glean any hint of information. He knew I was pregnant. He must have to make such a cryptic comment. Better play Devil's advocate. "Of course it's safe. Why wouldn't it be? I've cycled home in strong wind loads of times."

There. I dared him to follow up with another insinuation. Whether I was pregnant or not was none of his business.

His hopeful face was full of naïve wonder. "I could give you a lift?"

I paused, looking from my wind-lashed bike huddled in the shelter, to Naoki's familiar Toyota Prius, parked near the exit. "I suppose that would be alright. Thanks."

An awkward air fell between us as we walked to his car and got in. What were we now? Exes? Friends? Neither of those things? I was committed to Shinichi, but as I cast a sideways glance at Naoki, I couldn't help but feel butterflies in my stomach when our gazes connected and I saw the warmth in his expression towards me.

Enough already, Kimberly Thatcher. I gave myself a mental slap in the head to come to my senses. Why was I acting like a hormonal teenager instead of a mother-to-be in a committed relationship?

"If you don't mind me saying so, you look well. You have a glow about you – and you've changed." Naoki's eyes dropped to my stomach for less than a second. He *did* know, and was goading me to tell.

He went on. "Are you going to stay in Japan? What about Voyce? Will you be able to continue working in the school?"

It was a good question. I had been so wrapped up in the bubble of my relationship with Shinichi that I hadn't thought about it. I opened my mouth to answer, but no words came out. Naoki turned off the bridge and into my neighbourhood of Akisato. I was thankful

The Wabi-sabi Doll

that my apartment was so close to Jusco as it saved me from an awkward conversation.

"Forgive me for saying so, as I know it's not really my business, but I heard rumours about who you're seeing. He's not a good person. Take care of yourself."

Not a good person? Unexpected anger welled. I wanted to say so many things to Naoki, but they wouldn't come out. Like, how I wouldn't have been seeing another man at all if Naoki actually cared more about our relationship than his family restaurant. Like, how it was rich of him to judge Shinichi, a respectable fireman and committed boyfriend, when he knew nothing of our romance. Like, why did he bother to care at all now that we were exes. More like a case of, closing the stable door after the horse had left.

"I'll be staying in Japan, and I can take care of myself, so please don't worry about me. Thanks for the lift home. Bye, Naoki."

I got out of his car, leaving him with a gobsmacked expression. Neither of us waved to the other; I turned towards the stairs leading up to my apartment without a backward glance. The sound of him pulling away from my apartment block preceded the swish of a car pulling in. As I fumbled with my keys, I turned with more than a hint of annoyance. I wasn't in the mood for more probing questions, or nosey judgement, from Naoki. But it wasn't Naoki coming back. My boss, Ben, pulled into my allocated parking space instead.

"Kimberly, I'm so glad I caught you. I just finished my early shift and I saw you coming out of Jusco with Naoki there, so I followed."

Ben wasn't going to reprimand me for getting romantically involved with an ex-Voyce student, was he? It was in the Voyce teaching contract that any relationships, whether platonic or romantic, between students and teachers was forbidden. Technically Naoki was an ex-student, a point I would argue if it came up, besides the fact we were no longer romantically involved, in any event.

"You know, I always thought you and Naoki would make a great couple," he said, with a wink.

My cheeks burned with hot, embarrassed fury. "Well, we're not, I'm seeing someone else."

Was my reply too hasty, reeking of too much of a cover-up?

Ben gave me a sly grin. "I'm glad you've moved on from your ex. What was his name again, Chris?"

"Carl," I answered, my voice falling flat.

All of the interest in my love life was getting boring. I found myself jutting my backside outwards in an attempt to make my rounded stomach appear smaller and more concave.

Ben seemed to have taken the hint, for he cleared his throat. "Anyway, I didn't come here to talk about who's dating who. I actually wanted to let you know that you'll be getting a new roommate soon."

My former flatmate, Jei Pi, had gone back to Maine just before Halloween the previous year. I had been expecting Voyce school to find a replacement, but with five months of no roommate, my initial loneliness had given way to enjoyment at having my own space. Living by myself meant I could walk around in my undies, or naked. Naoki, followed by Shinichi, could stay over as much as they liked. I could leave unwashed dishes in the kitchen sink overnight without having to keep clean and tidy for someone else's benefit. If I was honest, I didn't relish having to get used to living with another new roommate anytime soon.

"Oh yeah?" I managed.

Ben raised an eyebrow. "You must have been lonely living by yourself?"

I twitched one shoulder up and down. "Kind of."

"Well, she's Canadian, and the same age as you. You're twenty-six, right?"

I nodded. "For a few more months. What's her name?"

"Victoria. She's from Vancouver."

"Victoria from Vancouver. At least the Vs will make it easy to remember." My voice sounded much more sarcastic than I intended. Hopefully Ben didn't pick up on my tone.

"She's getting in on Thursday, so you'll have a couple more days to yourself."

I sighed. "That's great. I'm looking forward to meeting her."

Ben grinned and turned to leave. As I watched him go, my head was flooded with thoughts. Like, what would happen once my bump expanded; it wouldn't be right for me to stay with a new flatmate. On the other hand, what was the future for me and Shinichi, after that hug with a mystery woman in Jusco's carpark? I couldn't picture us moving in together after that; not when I was feeling so suspicious of him. And sooner, rather than later, I would have to tell Ben, and work, about my pending maternity.

April showers, May flowers. Maybe a new roommate would be the catalyst I needed to making change happen. Life seemed up in the air for April, but May would bring better days.

I hoped.

Chapter twenty-nine

Room for change

"Oh, hey yah, roomie. How's it hanging?"

Blonde. Blonde and bubbly, like a flouncy cheerleader. V for Victoria from Vancouver stood grinning in the entranceway of my flat, waving at me with both hands as if I was standing on top of bloody Kyushu Mountain instead of four feet away from her in the living room doorframe.

I cracked a grin in return. "Um, hi, how's things? Did you have a good flight?"

"It was ay-okay." She dipped her head left then right with the 'ay' and 'okay', in the most nauseatingly sweet manner, then spun around, her mouth agape. "Wowee-zowee, isn't this the cutest apartment? Don't you just love Japan?"

Wowee-zowee? I refrained from an eyeroll; what would she know about Japan, as wet-behind-the-ears as she was? "Have you been over here in Nippon before?"

She kicked off her shoes and I couldn't help but notice her ankle socks had pink frills around the rim; like, what age was this person? Didn't Ben say she was twenty-six, like me? Frilly ankle socks were for preschoolers, sheesh.

"I back-packed for three months with my boyfriend at the time, but not here in Tottori," she said, in a sugary-sweet, high-pitched voice. "We went to, like, Tokyo and Osaka, and Kyoto and Nara. Oh, and Kobe."

I watched her count on her fingers as she listed each city, her eyes turned upwards to the ceiling, in an attempt to help her recollection, no doubt.

Having a new flatmate brought back memories of Jei Pi. How, at first, I had thought she was annoying, with her garish, larger than life clothing and colours, and her irritating catchphrases, like 'hey roomie' and 'oy vey' even when she wasn't Jewish. How I had judged her – wrongly – and had written her off in my mind from the outset, until we gradually had become friends after I had broken up with Carl. It was a good reminder not to judge a new flatmate so harshly. Why was I being closed off to Victoria? It said more about me than it did about her.

"Well, it's lovely to meet you. Welcome to Japan. As they say here, yokoshiku onegaishimasu. That basically means nice to meet you."

"Oh yah, sure. Kochira koso." Victoria gave a quick bow and followed it with a giggle.

So, my assumptions were wrong. Why had I assumed Victoria didn't speak Japanese? Was it because I didn't know any Japanese when I arrived, sixteen months ago, so I expected everyone to be the same as me?

I stepped aside as Victoria entered the flat, her eyes wide with childlike wonder. Her honey-blonde curls bounced above her shoulders as she walked, her blue knee-length pleated skirt swishing with every step. Despite trying my best not to make judgements, her appearance conjured up images of a fairy prancing around my flat. *Our* flat. I needed to stop thinking of it as my own space anymore; it was a shared flat, owned by the school we both worked for: Voyce.

"How've you found living here, Kimberly?"

"You mean, in this flat, or in Tottori?"

"In Japan," she elaborated, with another twirl, and a smile.

"Well, obviously I love it, since I'm here." Was there a touch of sarcasm to my voice? I cleared my throat.

"And how long has that been?"

"Um, nearly a year and a half."

Victoria peered out the living room window, then gasped and clapped her hands together, just the once. "Wowee-zowee, is that a balcony?"

She slid the door open and stepped outside, her eyes landing on Kyushu Mountain overlooking Tottori. "I can't wait to explore. I mean, I'm looking forward to teaching, but I'm *waaay* more excited about travelling and meeting people, if yah get me."

I could relate to that. Teaching for me was a means to an end; it wasn't my chosen career path, but it kept me living in Japan.

She turned to me then, with an impish grin. "What about the men? Are you single?"

Way to get overfamiliar too soon. I couldn't help but fold my arms across my chest. "I have a boyfriend."

"Ooh," she purred. "A Japanese guy, I take it. Is he hot?"

What on earth? Who was this entirely inappropriate blonde in heat?

"Yes, Japanese, and yes, he's a nice guy," I answered, taking the diplomatic approach.

"Does he have any friends? You'll have to introduce me. I broke up with my ex five months ago and I'm *aching* to meet a new hottie."

Chapter thirty

Fresh Fridays

This was a mistake.

A big mistake. What was I thinking? Halfway through my second trimester and out on a double date with V for Victoria, along with Shinichi and a friend. The same friend, Keitaro, who had tried to charm Zoe when we had been out for drinks one night. He certainly seemed to have forgotten Zoe, as besotted with Victoria as he was.

Come to think of it, V for Victoria was rather good at monopolising all the male attention in Bar Nightfall. She threw her head back every time she laughed, tossing around her bouncing, blonde curls. Once was fine, but she laughed at every other joke. Her low cut, black satin top that showed off an impressive cleavage helped too. I rolled my eyes and took a sip of my orange juice. Not much fun when Shinichi, Victoria and Keitaro were all getting hammered while I was

The Wabi-sabi Doll

sober as a judge and hiding my pregnant, bloated body beneath a sensible tunic top and leggings.

What on *earth* was I thinking?

I didn't even like Victoria. Not much, anyway. In the two weeks since she had moved in, her irritating girly laugh grated on my nerves more and more each day; not to mention the attention that Shinichi seemed to lavish on her, both at our flat over the past fortnight, and right in front of my face at Bar Nightfall.

A nudge on my arm switched my brain back to reality.

"Are all blondes as screwy as this one?" Shinichi jerked his thumb towards Victoria and she reacted by throwing her head back once more and laughing in a crass, uvula-wobbling display.

"I don't know, why don't you ask her, since you two seem to be getting on like a house on fire," I said, jerking my shoulders.

Victoria's smile faltered. "Oh, hey now, don't be like that, K?"

K? As in, 'okay' or as in K for Kimberly, a new, unwanted nickname that she had given to me?

"It was just a joke, no offence intended." Shinichi shot me a smarmy smile and kissed the top of my head.

I tossed my mousey brown hair off my shoulder. The black dye still hadn't faded. Shinichi clearly thought I was a natural brunette if he had made a comment like that about Victoria's blonde hair; and it also seemed blondes were his type.

Was that why I had never mentioned to him that, unlike V for Victoria, I was a natural blonde? Because I was testing him, somehow? Hmm. A question I needed to ponder, clearly.

A nudge on my shoulder also piqued my attention. Keitaro tilted his head at me in an enquiring way. "Why are you drinking that boring stuff?" He nodded towards my orange juice. "I'll get you something stronger."

"Shouldn't you be getting a drink for your date and not trying to offer alcohol to your best mate's pregnant girlfriend?" The words oozed out of my mouth with more bitterness than intended.

All three of them: Shinichi, Keitaro and Victoria, watched me with surprise, all conversation dying. Why was I feeling so hostile?

I shrugged. "Don't mind me. Pregnancy hormones, I suppose."

Another excuse. Why was I angry?

Because my boyfriend was flirting with my new flatmate. Simple.

Maybe I deserved better than a man who flirted with other women, right in front of his pregnant girlfriend. Yes, maybe; though worrying about something so petty wasn't the best, either. Flirting wasn't exactly *cheating*. Was I tarring Shinichi with the same stick as Carl? Was I blaming my new boyfriend on crimes he hadn't committed; projecting my angry insecurities onto him? I couldn't sit back and flood little Kami, nestled in my stomach, with negative hormones. I needed to fill my body with serotonin, and oxytocin. Kami had to come first now, not Shinichi; not even me.

I stood up. "Who's up for clubbing? I haven't been in ages. What about Club Passion?"

Shinichi's smile faltered. "Is that really a good idea?"

"Why not?" I shrugged. "Exercise would be great for both me and the baby and it would make being sober more fun, while you all drink."

"I don't know," he went on. "What if someone drunk knocks into your stomach?"

I rubbed my rounded belly. "She's well protected in here, don't worry so much."

"I'd prefer to stay here." He forced a wide smile. "We're having fun, aren't we?"

Hmm. Why was he so dead set against going to Club Passion? His staunch attitude was making me suspicious.

"I'm not having fun watching you three get tipsy while I'm on soft drinks." I folded my arms across my girth.

Victoria looked from Shinichi to me, then back to Shinichi. "I'm with K. Clubbing sounds fun. Let's go to Club Passion."

"See, she's with me?" I turned from Shinichi to Victoria. "And it's Kimberly, not K."

Victoria's face fell.

"I don't like the vibe at Club Passion much." Shinichi squirmed; or did I simply imagine that he did? "What about we go to Club Three-Six-Five instead?"

"No way, Club Passion is far better than Three-Six-Five," Keitaro said, with a dismissive wave.

Shinichi fixed him with a glare; I definitely hadn't imagined it. My boyfriend was hiding something from me about Club Passion.

An image popped into my head: my Kami doll, dressed in her pink kimono, standing behind Shinichi's left shoulder. Her dark eyes focused on me and her red lips peeled back as she opened her mouth to speak.

What you want to know is over at Club Passion. Go there and you'll find the answers you need, she seemed to say.

I stood up. "I'm walking over to Club Passion. You're welcome to join me, but I'll go on my own if I have to. I fancy a dance."

I didn't bother to look back to see if anyone was following me. Did it matter anyway? Somehow, I felt numb. Maybe a combination of seeing Shinichi hug the mystery woman in the Jusco carpark, or flirt outrageously with my new bimbo flatmate, was too much sensory overload. Was Shinichi simply Carl-lite? Another possessive, controlling womaniser, but on a microscale? I couldn't be bothered to find out. Right now, in the world, it was simply me and Kami. Kami and me.

Kami and Kimberly and good karma.

My feet skipped a light step all the way to Club Passion. It was only as I neared the front doors of the nightclub that I heard a flurry of feet approaching from behind. A moment later, Shinichi swooped in front, blocking my entrance.

"Hey Kimberly. You took off so fast there, I almost couldn't catch up. I feel like I've been a jerk. Have I been a jerk?" He swept his hand back through his hair, in a manner that I might have found endearing a few weeks back. But not now.

"You haven't. I just want to dance. It's okay if you don't like Club Passion. I'm not making you come with me." I stepped around him.

He stuck his arm out and placed his palm, flat, in the middle of my stomach. It wasn't a protective gesture, not even a kind one. It was a cold one. A controlling one.

"Club Three-six-five are letting women in for free tonight, as part of a new promotion. If you go there, I'll definitely come with you."

I pushed his hand off my stomach, with a rough swipe. "Have fun. I'm sure Victoria will be happy to go with you."

I marched on inside the entranceway of Club Passion and there was nothing Shinichi could do. The man at the ticket desk's eyes widened as he saw me. What was with the strange reaction? It wasn't because I was beautiful. Quite the contrary; I looked dowdy in my plain tunic top and leggings, with minimal makeup. He gave me my ticket and stamped my hand. It was only as I pushed on through the double doors into the nightclub that I understood his reaction.

A large LCD screen near the bar showed a scantily clad geisha. Her O-shaped mouth matched her O-shaped blue eyes as her pink, floral yukata spread wide, exposing two pert, bare breasts. Stars had been superimposed over both nipples, but they did nothing to hide the geisha's modesty. Below, her bare leg jutted out of the yukata, showing everything right up to the red string of her thong at her hip. Above the exploited girl was a large, blocky slogan in English and katakana reading:

Gaijin Geisha presents
Fresh Fridays
At Club Passion

I swallowed the rising sickness in my stomach as I stared at myself on the screen, recognisable even with the black geisha wig on. My hands jumped to my stomach, as though to shield Kami from the sight of her mother looking like such a tart. My eyes jumped sideways to an A3-sized poster on the doors leading to the toilets. There I was again, *Gaijin Geisha*.

"Kimberly, listen. I can explain."

Shinichi had both hands up in a pleading gesture.

"Go on then. I'd *love* to hear the explanation for this." I jabbed my finger at the LCD screen, its light dominating the dark nightclub dance floor.

"I thought I had deleted it from my phone. But you'll never guess what happened," he went on.

I folded my arms across my chest. "No, I'm afraid I can't guess. Enlighten me."

"Instead of delete, I accidentally hit send. You see, I'd been chatting to my friend, Koji, just before we got back to our hotel room, so when we took those photos, I didn't realise the messages were still up on my phone."

I pressed my lips together. "Yeah right. A likely story. Please don't insult my intelligence."

He put his hands together in a praying pose. "I'm not, I swear to you. I wouldn't lie to you about something like that. It was a slip of the button and the photo got sent to Koji. He's one of the management staff here. He loved it. I told him to delete it, but he said it was too late. He'd sent it to the events company for use in the promotional flyers and materials."

My eyes bulged. "Promotional flyers too? So, my tits are all over thousands of flyers to promote these 'Fresh Fridays' nights?"

Shinichi averted his eyes, letting his gaze jump around the revellers; but I noticed he didn't look remorseful.

I glowered at him. "How much did you get paid to use my face as your freebie model?"

"Nothing, I promise you. It was a genuine mistake. I'm not lying."

"You betrayed my trust. You betrayed Kami's trust. You used me." I paused, struggling to find the words. "I mean, I've heard of revenge porn. But this is even worse, as we hadn't even broken up. I trusted you. I believed you when you told me the photo was deleted."

He let his jaw drop, his eyes wide and pleading. "Oh, come on Kim. What was one mistake? It's not like you look awful in the pictures – you look hot."

"Oh, and that makes it alright?" I turned my back on him. "You better leave now, Shinichi, or I might break your nose."

"Don't be angry, babe. It was an honest mistake. Forgive me?"

I felt his hands on my shoulders, trying to turn me back around. Was this asshole for real?

I put both hands in the flat of his chest and pushed him back, then followed with a warning kick to one shin. Nothing more than that, or I risked flooding my body with cortisol, and then Kami would have been bouncing off the walls of my womb.

"Forgive you? We're through. Don't contact me again. I'll be blocking your number."

He smirked, though it seemed defensive. "What about the baby?"

"Kami and I don't need you. Goodbye, Shinichi."

Chapter thirty-one

May madness

I wandered across the grass in front of Tottori hospital, heel to toe.

Heel-toe.

Heel-toe.

Heel-toe.

Touching heel to toe kept me grounded. Reminded me of physical reality, keeping my mind present. I needed to stave off any early warning signs of an impending panic attack. It wouldn't be good for me, or the baby.

Sixteen weeks. After my twelve-week scan, I hadn't heard anything from the hospital staff. Wasn't that strange? Surely medics would want to keep up to date with an expectant mother? I hadn't had any communication at all about any upcoming appointments. No check-ups, no baby preparation classes; nothing.

The Wabi-sabi Doll

What should I do? Not only was I single, but I hadn't even told my family yet. It wasn't that I didn't want to; it was more the fear of disappointment, or shame. What would they think about me getting knocked up by a boyfriend that they hadn't even met, who I had now broken up with? Twenty-six years old and my life was falling apart.

Now that I was a soon-to-be single mother, I needed to take charge. I would go into the hospital and request a check-up; find out how Kami was doing, and then I could make a plan. It was already May. Only five more months and Kami would be due, at the end of October. My teaching contract was due to end in November. I would have to quit a few weeks early, maybe in September, and fly home to London to have the baby. Screw Shinichi. If he really cared, he would do as Carl did. Carl followed Shiori back to Tottori after she had given birth; he was now a devoted dad to his twin girls. If Shinichi gave even the slightest damn about Kami, he would chase me across the world to London.

But first things first. I needed to be brave. I needed to go in and request the check-up.

I reached into my canvas shoulder bag and lifted out the Kami doll. How strange that only a short few months ago, she had frightened the life out of me when I had found her sitting on my doorstep. I had thought of her as creepy. Haunted. Sinister. Now her presence was a comfort. I cuddled Kami close to me and marched up to the reception desk.

"Erm, I'm pregnant, er... watashi wa nimpu desu. Er, I need to see a doctor. Um, how do I say that in Japanese? Eto, isha sensei ni ai ni ikitai. Wakarimasu ka."

"O namae wa. What is your name," said the receptionist.

"Kimberly Thatcher." I jotted my name in katakana and in English on a notepad page from my bag, ripped it off and passed it to her. She typed it into the computer.

"Sho sho o machi kudasai. Please wait. The doctor will see you soon."

I took a seat, feeling proud of myself. I had successfully communicated my needs in Japanese. My functional Japanese was improving, even if my conversational skills remained rudimentary. Kami and I didn't need Shinichi; we could manage by ourselves.

I lost track of time while I waited to be called. Soon, a nurse arrived to lead me through to the sonographer's room. I recognised the same medic who had seen me before, at my twelve-week scan. Luck was on my side, it seemed. He would hopefully remember me from the last scan, and therefore would be better placed to advise me on what was best for Kami going forwards. I perched on the edge of the gurney with a smile, clutching my bag with Kami in it close to my stomach.

The sonographer kept a neutral, but enquiring expression as he scrutinised me over the top of his glasses. He spoke to me in a soft voice, but didn't slow his Japanese, or use simple words for my benefit. Was it a sign of respect that he used the same vocabulary that he would if he were speaking to another native Japanese speaker; did he assume I was proficient? Among the torrent of vocabulary, I caught the word 'nimpu'.

"Yes, hai, nimpu desu. Eto, ju roku shukan wa seiri ga nai, desu. Em, it's been about sixteen weeks that I haven't had my period. Wakarimasu ka. Erm,

The Wabi-sabi Doll

yokagetsu wa seiri ga nai. Four months," I said, holding up four fingers.

The sonographer pressed his lips together and exhaled through his nose, before he spoke in clear, but staccato English. "Kimberly san. I saw you before. You come here with boyfriend."

"Yes, I came for my twelve-week scan," I answered, pointing to my stomach to make sure he followed.

He interlaced his fingers, holding his hands across his middle, and turned to face me squarely. "No baby in your stomach at last scan. You understand?"

I blinked at him, processing his words. He must've been mistaking me for someone else. "*Yes*, there was a baby in my stomach. My boyfriend Shinichi was with me. He translated what you said."

The sonographer continued staring at me, with the Zenlike repose of a monk. "No pregnancy at your last scan. Stomach was empty. No baby in there. I told to your guardian at the time."

His clipped English juxtaposed with his calm demeanour made his words hit harder. How could he be so calm?

"I'm sorry to be rude, but I think you're mistaking me for someone else," I breathed. "Erm, chotto chigaimasu. Mae no yoyaku no atode de, tabun hokano gaikokujin no yoyaku o shimashita ka. Tabun, kanoko wa nimpu ja nagatta ka. Demo, watashi wa nimpu desu."

I gulped, trying to translate what I thought I had said: that he was wrong; that maybe at my last appointment another foreigner had seen him afterwards; that maybe she hadn't been pregnant. But, I was most *definitely* pregnant.

He took off his glasses, slipped them into his breast pocket and observed me with his own eyes. Was there a hint of sadness in his eyes? Or maybe tiredness.

"Kimberly san, you have no baby in your stomach at last appointment. Perhaps if pregnant after last appointment, I can do one more scan and check?"

His words hit me like a tonne of bricks, numbing my body, sedating my mind. No baby in there. It had to be a mistake. I had missed my last three periods. My once flat stomach had become round.

I had to be rational. Calm, and rational. He would do the scan and I would see my Kami, my little girl, floating around in there, quite content.

I nodded my consent. "Yes, I think that would be for the best."

I set my bag with Kami on the floor and lay back on the gurney. The nurse attendant gave me tissue paper; I pulled up my top and tucked the tissue into the hem of my trousers in preparation for the gel, which she applied liberally all over my stomach. I was well used to the preparation since I had been through it three times, the first time being when I had suffered a miscarriage, and the second time only one month previously at my recent twelve-week scan. My bladder was full too, as I knew it helped to show the best results.

There was nothing wrong with my Kami; I was sure. The scan would tell me what I already knew. I glanced at my handbag on the floor. How I wished I had taken the doll out of my bag for a comforting hug while I waited for the sonographer to do my scan.

As soon as the probe touched my stomach, the familiar black triangle on the screen showed moving grey blobs and white lines, none of which looked

The Wabi-sabi Doll

anything like a baby. I watched the screen, hopeful to see sweet Kami's face swim into view soon. Any minute and she would pop onto the screen; then I would get my first glimpse of my beautiful, soon-to-be daughter.

Any minute now.

The sonographer spoke to me in Japanese. He waved his hand. His words were a blur. He shook his head. All of it was a blur.

Any minute now, my Kami would show up on the screen.

More Japanese, the nurse too, speaking in a soft, soothing tone.

Any minute now. My hands jumped to my belly, feeling the cold, slippery gel. I wiped both hands on the tissue.

Another person came into the room. Not the doctor, or the sonographer, or the nurse.

"Miss Thatcher, I'm a translator from the International Centre working with the hospital." Perfect English to match her perfect teeth, and perfect blue-framed glasses, and perfect hair, and perfect shoes, and perfect manner and–

Why was everything so perfect, but none of it made sense?

I looked at the perfect translator, standing over me and appearing so spartan, and clinical, and immaculate, and I blinked, and looked and blinked.

"I am afraid to give you bad news."

No. It wasn't possible. It was nonsense. Not about my Kami. My Kami wasn't dead. It wasn't possible. I shook my head.

"It isn't what you think."

I shook my head with more vigour. "No. This can't be happening a second time. She isn't dead. You're wrong."

"The baby isn't dead. I'm afraid there isn't any baby in your uterus to begin with," she said, in a soft, but curt manner.

I didn't like her standing over me, looking down on me. I swung my legs over the edge of the gurney and sat bolt upright. "That doesn't make any sense. I haven't had my period in close to four months. And I've started to get a bump. My ex boyfriend came with me to my twelve week scan and translated for me. He even gave me a scan photo that the sonographer gave him."

The sonographer spoke to the translator in rapid Japanese. The only words I understood were Shinichi Sanbonmatsu. The translator listened without interrupting before turning to me. Her eyes swept closed, her chin lowered for a moment, like a person about to recite a eulogy, and then she spoke.

"I am afraid to inform you that Mr. Sanbonmatsu took a scan photo that was left behind by another patient. Sometimes an expectant mother does not want—"

A strange, choked sound rattled out of my chest. It was an octave or two deeper than my own voice, sounding more like the bellow of a cow than a noise a woman would make.

Shinichi had lied to me.

Shinichi had tricked me.

No. My brain wouldn't – couldn't – accept it. I steadied my breathing, which was quickening.

"If there's no baby, how am I having the symptoms of pregnancy? I know how it feels. I was pregnant last year before I lost the foetus."

"You are experiencing a false pregnancy. It often happens when a mother has suffered loss." She paused, her eyebrows upturned in pity. "I could refer you to a counsellor to discuss your loss, if you like?"

Ugh, how I hated that look of pity. I wasn't a misery case, a broken woman. Was I?

Carl's voice popped into my head, like a little demon sitting on the left side of my brain: *You have a baby bump because you're a fat cow. Who ate all the ramen? You greedy bitch!*

First, a seven year relationship with my devious ex from London, Carl, and now a four month liaison with another devious ex, Shinichi. Why did I break up with the one man who could've been so good for me – Naoki?

It was like a floodgate opening in my head. A waterfall splashed down my face unabated. I was a mess. I wasn't falling apart. I hadn't been whole in the first place – ever.

May madness. I had wasted so much of the past five months by making bad choices. I needed time to reflect about why, and a practical solution to what I would do about it. I would make myself whole – by myself – and then be ready for whatever lay ahead.

Chapter thirty-two

Phantoms of the mind

My legs dangled over the end of the concrete pier at Tottori beach. The wind blowing around my bare legs and feet felt so liberating. If only I could have taken off everything and splashed straight into the Sea of Japan, deep in the water with my baby, Akari, all would be well.

Akari, my first baby.

No, Akari my *only* baby. Kami wasn't real. She was simply a figment of my imagination.

Phantom pregnancy.

Phantom.

A figment of my imagination.

I clamped both hands over the round curve of my stomach, then pinched the roll between both forefingers and thumbs and squeezed until it hurt. Nothing in there but fat and gristle.

The Wabi-sabi Doll

Why did my head try to make meaning out of nothing? Wasn't that what this was all about? My brain still trying to process the rape, and miscarriage I had suffered ten months before.

I lay back on the pier and spread my arms wide, then looked at the sky. Random tufts of cloud swirled by going here and there, or nowhere all at once.

"Random. Meaningless," I mouthed to the sky.

Akari. Light. Akari. Bright.

"Akari, light bright. A mother's delight."

Mad. I was going mad. Going crazy with the weight of the pain, and the trauma, and the guilt.

"Random! Meaningless!"

I shouted the words into the blue sky. Not so much as a bird acknowledged what I had to say, or even my presence.

No, not random or meaningless. My traumatised brain had tried to create meaning through the phantom pregnancy. I had attributed it all to the porcelain doll, Kami.

"Kami."

The doll that was in my bag.

I brought her out and stood her beside me on the pier, propping myself onto one elbow to look at her. Her wide, dark eyes peered out from under her heavy black fringe. Her red lipped smile was fixed in place and her pink kimono immaculate. She wasn't creepy, or scary, or sweet or anything. She wasn't alive. She was only as much as what I attributed to her. Even her name: Kami.

"Kami means god. Kami means hair. Kami means paper," I said to her.

She didn't answer me back.

"You weren't in here. You were never in here." I lifted my top and pummelled my flabby stomach with both fists, hearing the sound of my knuckles on the bare skin.

Phantom Carl's voice resurfaced: *You have a baby bump because you're a fat cow. Who ate all the ramen, you greedy bitch?*

Phantom Carl, in my head was right. I needed to lay off the ramen.

"I dyed my hair black. I wanted to fit in. Carl cheated on me with Shiori, a beautiful Japanese woman, just like you." I addressed the Kami doll. "I thought I could be beautiful too, just what any man would want. Beautiful and fertile."

Miscarriage. Phantom pregnancy.

Real Carl's words now popped into my mind: *Hope you don't turn out as barren as this beach you love so much.*

The words he had said to me on Tottori Sakyu beach, while he had paraded his beautiful, fertile partner, Shiori along with their twin girls Naomi and Karen.

Tears dropped onto my bulging, bare stomach. I rubbed them in with my flat palms.

Was that what this was all about? I feared that Carl had dumped me because I couldn't have children? Even if that were true, what did it matter? A woman was more – far much more – than the sum of her loins. Worth far, far much more than her ability to have children or not. What did that matter? A person's character, and what they could bring to the world, mattered so much more.

"Kami," I said to the doll. "Where did you come from? Did Shinichi give you to me? Did he do it to control me? You appeared at so many places where I went. Was it Shinichi moving you all that time, to make me believe you were real?"

But no; that couldn't be. He wasn't there all the times the doll appeared to move. Like when I had thrown it off my balcony, and then found it inside my flat later on.

"You aren't *really* possessed by a child spirit, are you?"

Even saying it out loud made me feel stupid. No, there had to be a rational explanation for it all. There had to be. Because, if there wasn't, then it meant I was going mad.

May madness. Mad as a hatter. Without the mercury.

Why did men have such a hold over me? I channelled my Clinical Psychology training. I didn't think of myself as the kind of person with a Daddy complex; but then why was I acting out so much? Why was I handing over my power, and my self-esteem, to the control of men? Not just any men, but abusive ones?

Carl. Vince. Shinichi.

But hadn't I dumped them all in turn too? Hadn't I told each of them no, and walked away? That had to mean something to my own fragile psyche, didn't it? I had *some* degree of autonomy over my life; I had a *smidgen* of control over my destiny. Didn't I?

Didn't I?
DIDN'T I?
"Didn't I?!"

I looked over my left shoulder, then right. If anyone was nearby, they'd think I was mad.

"Mad and sad. And after men who are bad!" I shouted to the waves.

I looked back to the Kami doll. She had turned, as I was, facing the waves.

Everything in my body stopped at that moment: my breath, my nerves, the blood pulsing through my veins. My whole body paused in time. Kami had really moved her position without any outside influence.

Was that proof? Was she really haunted by a child spirit?

Whether she was or not, it had to be a benign spirit. It hadn't caused any harm, not really. In fact, it had been a source of comfort through my non-existent pregnancy and pointless love affair.

I sighed. What a summary of my year so far. A slow clap for my delicate ego, indeed.

"Kami, I need to take a leaf out of your book. You don't look for any outside validation at all. You even move by yourself!"

I stood up and turned on my heel, leaving Kami, and the pier behind. If she really was possessed by a spirit, then she would make her way back to my flat by herself, if that was where she was supposed to be.

Chapter thirty-three

Revelations on Kyushu

I combed my fingers through my newly stripped, white-blonde hair and turned to inspect it. The hairdresser had done a fine job. It was a shade lighter than my natural baby-blonde colour, but I liked it. In the June sunshine, it shimmered with a silvery hue. My body cut a slimmer angle in the reflection too. After three weeks of tuna salads and pounding the treadmill, I was back to my former size ten figure.

No Kami for three weeks either. Guess she hadn't been possessed by a spirit after all. Kind of silly of me, really, to be worrying about a haunted doll. How I had got myself so worked up about such a notion too.

What a lovely June day. The rainy season would be coming soon, but for now the sky over Tottori was cerulean. What to do with such a great day?

My phone pinged just then. What a weird coincidence, just as I had been wondering what to do. Naoki's number popped up on the screen.

Weirder still. I hadn't heard from him for two months, since he had found me crying in the Jusco carpark in the rain and had given me a lift home.

Has been a while. How r u?

I blinked at the screen. Was the universe trying to tell me something?

I tapped my reply. *I'm good. What about u?*

Fine, thanks. Are you free today?

I hesitated. What could it be about?

I'm free. What's up?

Want to climb Kyushu mountain?

Intriguing. My curiosity was piqued, to epic proportions. What on earth did he want to talk to me about all the way up Kyushu mountain?

I punched in my reply. *Yeah, sure. What time?*

How about one hour? Would that suit?

Wow, he was proper keen. *OK. I'm just out of the hairdresser, so I'll leave now.*

My legs pedalled like the wind across Tottori towards Kyushu mountain and I parked my bike in a rack near the entrance to the park.

"Kimberly. You changed your hair."

Naoki's voice behind me made me spin. He was looking great, wearing a dark grey leather jacket over a flannel shirt, and light grey slacks.

"Yeah, I thought it was about time I got the last of the hair dye stripped out." I smoothed it flat.

"I prefer it blonde. Although this shade is lighter than your natural colour?"

His focus on my hair was making me lose my composure; heat started to spread in my cheeks. "Er, yeah I guess. It'll take a bit of getting used to, but I like the change."

"Well, you always look great," he smiled.

The Wabi-sabi Doll

I returned his grin. "Thanks. Same to you. New haircut?"

He nodded. His hair was closely cropped on the sides and floppy on the front, falling forwards over his brow, making him look like a J-pop star.

"You want to go for a walk?" he suggested.

"We could climb up to the Tottori castle ruins? I haven't been there for a while."

"Sounds good to me," he said.

We walked along the path leading into the park, and climbed in a comfortable silence. Once we had reached the castle, we leaned over the edge of one of the ruined walls and stared out across Tottori. Staring out over the urban expanse was easier than looking at Naoki. I had so much to say to him, but I didn't know where to start.

"You look really healthy," he said, breaking the silence.

I cast a sideways glance at him, enough to see that he was looking downwards at my slimline physique. Was he referring to my lack of baby bump? Time to clarify, without getting too personal.

"I went on a diet and I hit the gym."

Quite a curt response, but I said it in a soft tone. I could see from the corner of my eye that Naoki was watching me, a thoughtful expression playing on his face.

"When I last saw you, I thought you were, you know." His words trailed off as he pointed at my stomach.

I inhaled through my nose and exhaled with a puff through my mouth. "So did I."

"Did something happen to—" he faltered, searching for the words. "What I mean is, did you lose the baby?"

I exhaled again through my nostrils. "There was no baby to begin with."

"No baby?"

"It's a long story. I don't think I'm ready to talk about it." My retort was quick, and maybe a notch too sharp.

A pause. "Sorry. It's not my business."

"No, I'm the one who should be sorry. I don't mean to be such a bitch." I reached for his hand.

My gesture was meant only as an apology, but Naoki took my hand in his and linked his fingers through mine. We stood for a moment, again in silence, looking out over Tottori.

"I really feel bad for the way things ended between us. I feel bad that I wasn't there for you when you needed me and that I put the family business first," he said, his voice weary.

"It's okay. You had to help your parents. How is your mum anyway?"

Naoki sniffed. "She's okay. She was able to recover properly after her hip replacement while I took over running the business with dad. It's for the best, as dad wants me to take over soon when he retires, especially as mum can't quite do what she used to either, and Mitsuko is now helping out too."

"I'm glad things are going well for your family."

"Thanks. Things were a bit tough, sort of, right before you and I first got together," Naoki continued.

I turned and looked at him squarely. "In what way?"

He looked upwards to the sky, inhaling through his nostrils, then composed himself by exhaling through his mouth.

"It's complicated. I don't want to bore you."

The Wabi-sabi Doll

I squeezed his hand. "Well, I'm always here if you ever want to offload."

Best not to pressure him, though I had to admit, I was curious. I thought back to the awkward conversations we'd had at my flat back in January about me wanting to meet his parents, and what sounded like excuses, added to my jealousy at seeing Carl and Shiori playing happy family with her parents and the twin babies.

"It hasn't been an easy year for my family – apart from mum's hip replacement operation, that is," he started.

"Oh?" I said, hoping to goad him along.

"I know you were so keen to meet my parents, and it was a bad time, back at the start of the New Year," he continued.

I remained silent, watching him, but giving him the space to keep talking; willing him, to keep talking.

"The thing is, Mitsuko and her husband actually separated back in September."

His words dropped like a lead balloon. I let my brain absorb them while I scrambled to think back over dates and times. I had met Mitsuko back in January, while she was home for the New Year holiday. That meant she was already separated when I met her. I recalled her pretty, happy face. If she been sad at all, she had masked it well.

"Is that why she was back visiting Tottori alone? You said her husband was spending it with his family in Nagoya?"

Naoki nodded. He looked down at the grass momentarily, as though gathering his thoughts. "She found out that his parents had hired a private investigator to look into the origin of our family name before they allowed them to get married two years ago and he kept that a secret from her. She found the paperwork in his mum and dad's house and confronted him."

"What's wrong with your family name?"

"Nothing," he said quickly. "Yasuda means expensive rice paddy in Japanese."

"Why did her husband keep that a secret from her?"

"I think he was ashamed that his parents had hired a P.I. Yasuda is unusual. I suppose they wanted to check it wasn't a Burakumin name."

I tucked my hair behind my ear. "What's Burakumin?"

"Somebody considered an untouchable in Japan. They're people considered to be from the lowest class," Naoki explained.

"Oh, so like the caste system in India, you mean?"

"Yeah, basically. It's a form of prejudice," he went on.

"I had no idea there was such a thing in Japan. I always thought it was a pretty harmonious place here."

"Mitsuko was furious at his parents when she found out they hired a private investigator to check out her background, before they would let the marriage go ahead. She got into a big fight with them – and with him – and threw the papers in the air. I mean, we're not from a samurai family – we're not elite – but our family name isn't a common one."

"I can't blame her for that. I'd be pretty furious. I'm sure it eroded all her trust in him that he kept such a thing a secret from her." I shook my head.

"I feel a bit sorry for him too. From what she told me, he sided with her and stood up against his parents for hiring a P.I. But they obviously found out what they wanted to hear anyway, which is why they allowed the marriage to go ahead. I guess that's maybe why he didn't tell her – to save her the heartache," Naoki said.

"Well, it clearly made things worse in the long run. He should've just come clean," I scoffed.

"Would you have, though? I mean, think about when I met your parents at Christmas last year. Just imagine they had told you they didn't want you to marry a Japanese guy, but then they changed their mind at the last minute and let the wedding go ahead. Would you have told me, knowing it would have hurt me?"

"Yes," I said defiantly. "Yes, I would've told you. Something that important? Absolutely. I think that honesty is the best policy for a happy marriage."

Naoki faltered. He looked down at his hands and I knew he was thinking fast.

"Your parents didn't say something to you about you dating a foreigner, did they? That wasn't why you kept delaying me meeting them – at New Year, and so on, was it?" I studied his face, for any trace of an answer, but his expression was stoic.

"Not exactly. It came up that they hoped I would settle with a nice local girl so that we could run the family business together." His voice was low and cautious.

"And they knew you were dating me?" I ventured.

He nodded, his lips tight.

"Even after what Mitsuko had been through with her husband, and they knew how that felt?"

He nodded again, still not looking me in the eye, still looking down at his hands.

"Did you say anything to them?"

He spun around and fixed me with his large, warm eyes. "You know I did. Kimberly, you know I love–"

He trailed off, biting his lip, as though to stop the flow of words.

I don't know what happened then. It was like a dormant volcano that had been simmering slowly for thousands of years suddenly erupted. I launched myself at Naoki, his warm lips against mine, his arms around my back and mine around his shoulders, intertwined; two slithering octopi knowing they were both about to get tossed onto the sushi chopping board. No wonder our romance had been ill-fated. I didn't care for that. I didn't care for his parents, or their restaurant, or Carl, or Shinichi, or the phantom pregnancy and Kami, or anything; only our passion.

Finally, we pulled apart.

"You told me before that you love me. At the time, I never said I love you too. But now, I need you to know that I do. I loved you then and I still love you now." I breathed into his mouth, gasping to steady the intake of air, the oxygen flow halting the dizziness of my love-starved brain.

He stared into my eyes and a soft smile spread over his face. "I love to hear it. I've missed you, Kimberly. My feelings for you haven't changed. In fact, they've grown stronger."

We kissed again, but this time, it was controlled. Gentle. Measured. I savoured the delicate touch of his lips, and without our faces smeared over one another, I smelled the natural scent of his skin, and ran my fingertips over his face and through his hair.

"I don't care what other people think. All I know is that I want to be with you. I won't let that go again," I said, and I meant it.

"We'll make it work. I promise, we'll make it work," he said.

We bumped our foreheads together, our eyes so close that his blurred into one large cyclops eye. Mine must have looked the same to him. We linked fingers on both hands, and we laughed.

Chapter thirty-four

Winter worm

Naoki wanted to drive me home, but I didn't want to leave my bike at Kyushu mountain. As a compromise, he gave me a head-start, so that by the time I reached my flat, he pulled into the driveway outside my apartment block.

Victoria was working on the early shift at Voyce, so that meant I would have the place to myself for three more hours. What to do with Naoki for the afternoon? I allowed myself a sneaky smile.

"I hear you have a new roommate," he said, as he stepped out of his car.

"How did you know?"

"Remember Zoe's ex, Ryuji? He stayed friends with her and she told him."

My stomach twisted into an unexpected knot. It hadn't occurred to me that Zoe might be passing titbits of information about her life to an ex. A new colleague in the school was certainly a bit of benign gossip; but what else? She and I spent a significant amount of time together as we had overlapping days off; was Zoe the reason why Naoki knew I had been seeing Shinichi?

I cringed at the thought. Hopefully she had the sense to keep my personal information secret. She wasn't someone who struck me as the type to indulge in idle gossip, but it wasn't as though I had specifically told her *not* to spread my personal business. I just hadn't thought that there was a need to tell her to be quiet about it.

While Naoki was locking his car, I unlocked my front door, my mind still on the new information, when giggles and murmuring voices distracted me.

Victoria's bedroom door swung open at speed and ricocheted off the wall. My eyes must have bulged out of their sockets at the sight of Shinichi stumbling out of her room, wearing only his boxers. I composed myself, setting my mouth in a taut line as he let his laughter settle into a cheeky grin, which he fixed on me.

"Kim, how's it going?"

So blasé. The *audacity*. He tried to pull the bedroom door closed behind him, but it was too late; I caught a glimpse of Victoria on her futon with the duvet pulled up to her bare shoulders, her dark blonde hair tousled.

"You two look cosy." I ignored Shinichi and leaned around him to peer through the gap in Victoria's bedroom doorway. "Aren't you meant to be working an early shift?"

She let out a nervous giggle. "I called in sick."

With Victoria put firmly in her place, I rounded on my sleazy ex.

His eyes roved me; down then up the length of my body before settling on my newly bleached hair. "Nice dye job. Did you go blonde for me? You weren't trying to get me back, were you?"

I paused, allowing myself the space to gather my thoughts. "For your information, I'm naturally blonde. I just got the dark dye that was in my hair stripped out. As for wanting to get back with you? Don't flatter yourself."

The hallway fell into shadow as Naoki appeared behind me in the doorway, blocking the sunlight.

Shinichi's face fell as he saw him. He turned to me with a teasing grin. "Maybe your new friend might want to see how glamorous you can be. You're rather famous in Tottori these days."

He grabbed his phone off Victoria's dresser. I cringed, averting my eyes as he thrust the photo of me dressed like a geisha, with boobs bared, in Naoki's face.

"I don't care about that." Naoki swiped the phone aside. "All I know is, Kimberly deserves better."

Better wasn't enough. Anger surged through me in an unquenchable flow. I snatched Shinichi's phone out of his hand and ducked under Naoki's arm, leaving semi-nude Shinichi flailing in the hallway while I slipped outside to scroll through his photo gallery.

Girls. So many scantily clad girls. Some posed on poles and from their glittery outfits and outlandish makeup, I knew they were pole dancers. Others posed in candid shots on beds or sofas, their clothing askew, or artfully pulled down to expose their bare chests. Some lay sprawled on their fronts wearing only thongs and giving bedroom eyes to the camera. I stopped on one of Victoria. It was taken outside at night. She had pulled down her low-cut, black satin top to flash the camera, showing her large, braless bust. I recognised her clothing as the outfit she had worn on the evening of our double date; the night I had broken up with Shinichi and stormed home. Curious, I tapped the information button in the top right-hand corner. Indeed, it was taken on the same day of our double date. I clicked on another photo of Victoria, this time flashing her round backside as she winked at the camera. It had been taken a few days earlier than the night of our double date; in other words, when I had still been seeing Shinichi.

Shinichi bumbled out of the flat wearing his unlaced shoes and with a dressing gown covering his boxers and bare chest.

"What's this, huh? Explain this." I shoved the phone in Shinichi's face, the same way he had done to Naoki moments before.

Shinichi snatched his phone back, a sly smirk in place, but didn't answer. I suppose I didn't expect him to. What could he have said to that?

I stomped back inside the flat and glared at Victoria, still in her bedroom. "You have some explaining to do too."

She at least had the good grace to blush.

"Shinichi and I were still together when those photos were taken," I elaborated.

That was all I could manage. My anger, close to boiling, might have exploded in a way I couldn't control if I continued. There was only one thing I could do. I marched into my bedroom and started throwing my possessions into my suitcase, and once it was full, began loading the rest of my things into the fold-up travel holdall I had bought for my Christmas visit back home.

Naoki didn't talk, but he stood close by as I packed. I appreciated his presence as it was a comfort. Once I had finished, Naoki carried my suitcase outside and I took the holdall, glad to see that Victoria's door was shut, saving me the need to avert my eyes.

Once I was outside my flat, I breathed a sigh of relief. A weight had been lifted off my shoulders, allowing the tightness in my chest to ease. But as I stood at the top of the stairs watching Naoki load my suitcase into his car, the gravity of what I had done hit me. I had nowhere to go.

Naoki came back up the stairs and reached for my holdall while I stood, numb, reeling from the aftermath of my impulsivity. He gestured behind me. "Are you bringing that too?"

I spun, following the line of his finger, and saw Kami propped up against the door jamb.

The tightness in my chest flooded back on a tsunami of fear. The doll was dressed in a different kimono than the pink one I had left her in on the pier at Tottori Sakyu beach. This one was pale lilac. Her wide eyes and red lips were the only features that made her recognisable.

I faced her, paralysed. Not a breath in, or a breath out. Was my heart even beating? My thoughts alone seemed to function, like I was suffering from locked-in syndrome.

My voice returned in a gasp. "That wasn't there when we arrived."

That was proof. It couldn't have been Shinichi. He had been inside my flat the whole time. If he had slipped out of Victoria's bedroom while Naoki and I were leaving, I would have heard the door clicking open.

The doll was moving by herself. It was the only explanation. She had found her way back home to me from the pier, and as a reflection of my own emotional journey, had even changed her appearance to resemble me.

My legs began to buckle. I steadied myself on the handrail at the top of the stairs.

"What's wrong?" Naoki dropped the holdall and grabbed me under the armpits.

"I don't feel very well. So much has happened, especially over the past few weeks. I'll tell you later, but first I need to get out of here. I don't even know where I'm going to stay."

He picked up the holdall and slung it over his shoulder, keeping both hands under my arms. "Don't worry about that. Are you upset by the doll? We can leave it."

I nodded. "She can manage by herself. She's good at finding me, even if I don't want her to."

A puzzled expression clouded Naoki's face for an instant, then disappeared. The last thing I needed was for him to think of me as mentally unstable. But it was too much to summarise, especially on my doorstep, where my vindictive ex was still lingering. There were certainly worms in my brain, feeding on the detritus, but I would clear them soon. Winter worms, summer grass for a brain. One of my students in class had told me about parasites invading the larvae of Ghost moths. They infested their bodies in winter, but by summer, produced a fruiting body that was a popular aphrodisiac used in Chinese medicine. It certainly was a fitting analogy for how events in my life had turned out since Christmas.

"Then let's go. My sister just got an apartment near Tottori station. I'm sure she'd be glad for some company until I can help you to get your own place."

Those were the words I needed. Leaning against the handrail, and supported under my armpit by Naoki, I made my way to his car.

Chapter thirty-five

Summer Grass

"You're blonde."

Mitsuko smiled, but I noted that unlike when we had first met at the Italian restaurant in January, her smile didn't reach her eyes.

What had Naoki told her about me, after we broke up? Hopefully nothing *too* bad. Not that I didn't deserve any of it, mind.

I swept both palms down over my hair from the centre parting, smoothing it as if it wasn't already bone-straight. "Erm, yeah, it's just a shade lighter than my natural colour. I had the black dye stripped out."

"Suits you better."

I kneeled on her dragonfly print *igusa* feeling the pins and needles in my legs. Misuko seemed very stiff as she kneeled, her hands placed on her lap in a rather formal manner. Maybe staying with her wasn't a good idea. Then again, where else would I go?

From the corner of my eye, I could see Naoki shifting on his knees, like a ref in a boxing match. I wanted to look at him, give him a glance that would let him know I needed out of there, but I dared not make the awkwardness any worse.

Mitsuko beat me to it. "Why did you dump my brother anyway?"

Awkward! I forced the gears in my head to turn.

Naoki rescued me. "She didn't *dump* me. I was working too much at the restaurant, and I stood her up one too many times."

Mitsuko's expression changed like the sun passing out from behind a cloud. "You didn't tell me that, little brother. You just said she called it off. In other words, dumped you."

She spun round to me and jerked a thumb towards her brother. "He acted like a puppy that had been tossed to the side of a road. I thought you'd done something horrible to him."

My mind jumped to conclusions. "I'd never cheat on Naoki. I'm not that sort of person."

Her eyes were marbles. "I wasn't implying that. Listen, I'm in the middle of a nasty divorce so feel free to ignore me about relationship stuff. I get a bit snippy when it comes to romance at the moment. Sorry if it sounded like I was accusing you of something."

I flapped my hand. "I'm sorry too. My last couple of exes cheated on me, so I suppose, being unfaithful is a sensitive spot for me."

We smiled, and this time, I saw the warm, gentle expression that she had given me before. I was back in her good books. The look of relief on Naoki's face couldn't have been clearer.

"Well, I was about to make something for dinner. You're welcome to join me, if you two don't have other plans."

Would it be an intrusion? I couldn't read her at all. Family dinner sounded lovely, but her offer had been so clipped, it was hard to tell. Probably best if I made a grand gesture, so smooth things over.

"I could cook, if you like? How about pasta carbonara, if you have the ingredients?"

She tilted her head. "Aww, you remembered my favourite food!"

I could see her from the side of my eye, leaning against the kitchen cupboards as I mixed the raw egg and cream, ready for when the pasta was cooked. My peripheral vision revealed things I wouldn't have caught if I was watching her directly. Like the fact that she had her arms folded and was twitching one leg. What was with the jitters? Still guarded too; maybe her trust would never fully extend to me after breaking up with her brother. Or maybe it wasn't even about me in the first place. Mitsuko had been honest about feeling snippy when it came to anything romantic.

"What happened with your roommate that you had to move out of your flat?"

I switched the cooker off and glanced at Naoki. I'd have to let her know in a way that would spare Naoki the details of my tryst with Shinichi.

"I started seeing this guy, Shinichi, and I found sexy photos of Victoria on his phone that were taken on the night that I broke up with him. So I had a bust up with both of them earlier at my flat."

I drained the boiling pasta and tossed it together with the egg and cream. My finger touched the hot pan, bringing tears to my eyes.

"I've heard of Shinichi. That guy's bad news."

Hadn't Naoki tried to warn me of something similar? I dished the pasta carbonara onto three plates and garnished it with ham and parsley. Naoki helped me to carry the food to the kitchen table.

"In what way bad?" I asked.

"He's a club promoter, and from what I've heard, involved with some nasty types. You know, mob types," said Mitsuko.

"You must be thinking of the wrong person. The Shinichi I was seeing was a fireman."

Her eyebrows practically hit the roof. "Is that what he told you?"

"It's definitely the same Shinichi. He has dyed blonde hair and a kind of scary-looking face," Naoki cut in.

I looked between brother and sister, searching their faces.

"He also owns a snack bar in Yayoicho. A rather sleazy one, too. I think it's called Bar Nightfall," Naoki went on.

Bar Nightfall, the one that I had spent so much of the year getting hammered in. I didn't want to believe them, but after all that I had learned about Shinichi's character over the past few weeks, I knew they were right. Everyone except me seemed to know the truth. Had I been walking around town with Shinichi on my arm and making a fool of myself the whole time?

Why? So much time had passed since I had broken up with my abusive ex, Carl, and yet I hadn't learned anything. I was still chasing after bad boy types; that was how I had wasted seven years in a dysfunctional relationship, and then got myself involved with a sleazy character like Shinichi.

I dared to raise my eyes from my pasta and let them meet Naoki's. His warm gaze was full of compassion and understanding. What had I been expecting? Disgust? Pity? Maybe I felt those things for myself, but he clearly saw me in a different light; and I was thankful for that. I didn't deserve his compassion, but I was grateful to have it.

"Well, if Shinichi's as bad as all that, then I suppose I have to let Victoria know. We might not be flatmates anymore, but she's still my colleague, and I guess I should warn her. I'd hate for anything bad to happen to her – just in case," I said.

Just in case. Cases of crimes against foreign women by Japanese men were rare, but they did still happen. There had been two famous cases against English women in the early noughties: one a hostess in Tokyo, and another an English teacher at a school, also in Tokyo, and both women had been murdered.

I allowed an involuntary shudder to wrack my body, and after it passed, made a mental note to focus on positives. There were many things to be grateful for:

Carl was no longer part of my life.

Vince was no longer part of my life.

Shinichi was no longer part of my life.

Naoki and I were back together.

Love life aside, I lived in a beautiful part of the world. Tottori had stunning natural scenery, like the Sakyu sand dunes, Kyushu mountain, Tottori and Karo beaches, as well as fascinating tourist attractions such as Kawahara Castle and the Inaba Manyo museum.

I had my health back, both mental and physical.

Winter worm: I had shed the darkness of the past few months.

Summer grass: I was ready for a fresh start in the second half of the year.

Chapter thirty-six

Rainy season

We were at an impasse. Something had to change. Something had to give. The head-turns the other way. The cold shoulders. The air, heavy with the presence of so many words that needed to be spoken – or shouted – but instead lingered, turning sour within mouths, festering in pools of bitter saliva.

For once, it wasn't a romantic relationship that had broken down. It wasn't even a friendship. My work relationship with Victoria had stagnated before it had got started. As June neared July, the rainy season in Japan was a metaphor for my mood.

Things couldn't go on as they were.

But now it was the day of reckoning. We were both due to work together on the late shift.

Victoria had worked at Voyce school for two months, but it had only been the past five days that we hadn't been on speaking terms at all, ever since I had left my apartment and moved in with Mitsuko. That was about to change, however. Naoki had found me my own flat, and I would be moving in the following week. Thinking of a place all to myself had mellowed my mood – marginally – and I was ready for a do-over with Victoria. If she would allow it, naturally.

My student files for the late shift were spread out on the table before me, but my mind was elsewhere. Any moment now, Victoria would wander into reception, and then we'd be forced to talk.

I heard her greet Akemi at the front desk and braced myself. Her normally chirpy voice sounded downbeat. Was that because she knew we would be working together?

Victoria walked in, without even a glance at me, and hung up her denim jacket on the coat stand. She set her bag on a table behind me. I turned, leaning one elbow over the back of my chair, in an effort to keep things casual.

"Hi," I said.

"Hey," came her terse response.

Well, that was that. No conversation starters, no ice breakers. I laughed inwardly, thinking of what I would make my students do in such a situation, if they were stuck on a topic in the free conversation *Chat* classes. Better not laugh *outwardly* lest I torpedo any chance of reconciliation with Victoria permanently.

"Looks like you have a lesson with Yoichiro at seven. He hasn't been in ages," I said.

She glowered at me. "You can save it, Kimberly."

Such sarcasm, the way she said Kimberly, enunciating each of the three syllables with such venom.

The Wabi-sabi Doll

"Oh-kay," I muttered. Hmm. Maybe not the most mature response, but better than giving her an eye roll.

She huffed, throwing her shoulders up and down dramatically. At first, I thought she was putting on a theatrical act, trying to rebuff my efforts at small talk, but then I realised she was crying. She hiccoughed in between sobs and stood with her chin on her chest letting the tears flow.

"Are you alright?"

Such a pointless question, but I didn't know what else to say.

"What's wrong?"

She turned to me then, wiping her tear-streaked face with her sleeves. Her cheeks were blotchy and her nose red.

"I'm okay."

Clearly she wasn't, but it wasn't up to me to say so.

"Actually, I'm not. I'm a mess."

"Are you alright to teach?"

She sniffed and shook her head.

I looked at her timetable. Twenty minutes before both of us were due to start teaching. Maybe if I gave her a free therapy session, she might be able to get herself into the right head space.

"What happened?"

She sat down. "I want to go home."

"You're homesick?"

She shook her head again. I needed to stop interrupting, to let her words flow.

"Something bad happened a couple of days ago."

Shinichi. It had to be something to do with the notorious bad boy. I opened my mouth, his name on the tip of my tongue, but couldn't say it. Part of me wanted to know, but part of me didn't.

In spite of my feelings, I reached out anyway. It wasn't about me, it was about her. At least, that's what my inner counsellor, the trained psychologist in me, told me. "Do you want to talk about it?"

"I'm finished with Shinichi."

I pressed my lips together, swallowing my judgement.

"He could be quite manipulative. I didn't notice at first, but I see that now," Victoria sniffed.

"What did he do?"

She wiped the corners of her eyes. "He got me to do things, that normally I wouldn't have done."

Like dressing as a geisha, showing my bare boobs. I closed my eyes, feeling the shame of the *Fresh Fridays* posters all over again.

"It was little things at first, but then it got kind of wild, kind of out of hand."

I tilted my head. "Like – what sort of wild things?"

Why was I giving free therapy to the woman who had caused my ex-boyfriend to cheat on me behind my back?

"Well," she started, with a sniff. She raised her eyes in a puppy dog manner. "You'll think I'm crazy."

I put up both hands. "I won't. Trust me, I know what Shinichi is capable of."

She gave a weak smile and took a deep breath. "Like, he convinced me to pole dance at a snack bar."

"You stripped off?"

"Just my top half, though don't ask why. I've never exposed myself in public before."

I folded my arms. "I think he owns that snack bar, or so I've heard. Was it Bar Nightfall, by any chance?"

The Wabi-sabi Doll

Victoria slumped down in a chair, her defences lowered, and gave a single, solemn nod. "It got worse after that."

Did I want to hear? Maybe I was enjoying her pain; maybe a small, sadistic part of me was enjoying that karma was paying her back. Was I a sadist?

"He convinced me to take on a *modelling* job, telling me I was beautiful, the sexiest blonde he'd ever dated," she said, with a dismissive flap of one hand. "But the modelling job was – well, I'm so ashamed. My parents would be disgusted–"

A floodgate of the worst thoughts opened in my head. Had she done porn? Become a prostitute for him?

"It was this thing called Nyotaimori," she said in hushed voice, glancing towards reception. "Naked sushi. I had to lie on a table and my privates were only covered by a plastic leaf. There were two maki rolls on each of my nipples."

I conjured an image of Victoria, lying naked on a table, covered by an array of sushi. I pictured Shinichi directing men to take whatever selection they wanted off her body, using chopsticks.

That was when I did the worst thing possible; it was as if I had become temporarily possessed by a demon. A horrible, saliva-splattering, wide-open mouthed guttural laughter burst out of the bowels of my belly and flooded the small staffroom.

Victoria's face crumpled in outrage. "Oh my gosh, laugh it up, why don't you? Why did I even bother telling you? You don't need to be such a bitch about it."

I covered my mouth with one hand, using my forefinger and thumb on the other hand to wipe tears away. "I'm so sorry. I don't know what came over me. I laugh when I'm nervous."

V for Victoria, in a compromising position, with only sushi on her tits, laid bare like *Eve* with a fig leaf over her fanny. Too funny. Too fucking funny.

God, I was a bitch.

Karma was a bitch.

"I'm sorry." I put up one appeasing hand, letting my laughter subside and forcing my face to be stoic once more. Was I trying too hard? Was I enjoying the comeuppance on the woman who had made my boyfriend complicit in cheating on me? "It's just that — well, it's not that bad. I was expecting you to say something worse. I mean, it's *bad,* but not *bad-bad.* After all, you consented to be his sushi model, didn't you?"

Victoria's face was beetroot, her eyes icy with their hatred of me in that moment. A moment I probably deserved.

"What I'm saying is, you shouldn't beat yourself up about it," I continued. "You trusted him. He's the one who should be ashamed."

"It doesn't stop there," she said, her eyes on the floor.

I fell silent. What next? Porn? Prostitution?

She took a long, deep inhale. "A couple of days ago, we went to the beach. He said he wanted to be kinky, like, in a sex-on-the-beach type way, you know? He said that because it's the Rainy Season here in Japan, there wouldn't be any onlookers, so we could have fun."

I fought to keep my face neutral. Part of me was happy to hear her shame, and I didn't want even a hint of a smile to show on my face.

"He said it was a fantasy of his to get sucked off in the sea. So, I started doing that, you know, on my knees with the water up to below my bare chest." Victoria closed her eyes and pain clouded her expression. "But the tide was coming in, and the rain was lashing down. The waves were getting bigger. At one point, I was underwater. When I tried to pull away, he grabbed the back of my head and forced me to do it, kind of pushed my head, and thrust himself forward at the same time, so that it made me gag."

Assault. Sexual assault. That was worse than porn, or prostitution. Her story had veered beyond the point of no return. It had gone into the worst territory. No laughter from me now.

"He tried to say he got carried away in the moment, but he was so pleased with himself, I knew he was lying. He wanted me at the edge of death as it gave him a thrill. Even worse, when I looked back up towards the main road, there was a man watching us in a grey van, holding a camera up. He was one of Shinichi's friends, filming it."

Grey van. Had the stalker in the grey van who had turned up near my apartment block in January been Shinichi, or an associate of his, all along? The person who had pushed a note through my door?

I sat back in my chair, letting my arms drop so that my hands lay in my lap. Victoria had been seeing Shinichi longer than I had. Would all that have happened to me, if I had let him continue his games after the bare-boob geisha cosplay that ended up on a promotion for *Fresh Fridays* at Club Passion? Would he have sexually assaulted me, or worse – let one of his seedy grey van friends assault me instead?

My lower lip quivered as I tried to think of something – anything – to sooth Victoria. Instead, words failed me. I went to her, wrapped my arms around her, and hugged her. A tsunami of tears poured onto my shoulder, but it was okay.

Was that me, a natural counsellor? Back in London, with my Masters in Clinical Psychology, I had my career mapped out in my head, before it had been upended by my need to escape from Carl. Carl, a verbally abusive, manipulative, possessive, controlling narcissist. He had followed me to Japan, leeching my time and my money, living on top of me in his last-ditch, desperate bid to control my newfound freedom after seven years of our smothering, stagnant relationship in London. During those three months, while I had been slaving at work on probationary teacher wage, he had been cheating on me with Shiori, the sales assistant from *Classy Girl*, clubwear shop downstairs from my workplace in Jusco. After seething looks, and petty female rivalry for months between Shiori and I that was more akin to adolescent drama than anything befitting fully grown women, she had turned up at my workplace revealing her heavily pregnant stomach, only to inform me that Carl had ditched her. I had counselled her then, empathised with her mistreatment at Carl's hands. And now?

Déjà vu. There I was counselling Victoria, consoling her amidst tears, sharing in the mistreatment we had both suffered, this time at the hands of a different man: Shinichi.

Why was I being a counsellor to these women who had both been complicit in my then-partners, now-exes, cheating on me behind my back? Was I a sap? Too nice? Too much of an emotional sponge that people could see a mile away? Was that why men with bad intentions gravitated to me in the first place, because they saw me as vulnerable; an easy target? Was that why the women they had hurt came to me for shared commiseration despite hurting me themselves?

What was I anyway?

As I hugged V for Victoria, I listened to the rain drumming down on Jusco's roof above us. One tiny drop seeped its way through the laminate roof of Voyce school and plopped onto my forehead, right in the centre of my brow, between my eyes. I smiled to myself: my third eye. My third Eye chakra, splashed wet with rain. Another droplet, fatter this time. One splattered Victoria's shoulder and she peeled back from me in surprise.

"Is it leaking?"

Akemi's voice, calling from reception.

"Is the roof leaking?"

Voyce school's artificial lights flickered and died, and then we were in blackness. I sat still, letting the fat raindrops assault the middle of my forehead.

"Yes, it's leaking," I answered. My voice sounded distant in my own ears, as though through a badly tuned radio, though I couldn't say why.

Rainy season. Rain on my head. Rain in my heart. Raindrops on the sea smothering V for Victoria performing fellatio on a felon. It was leaking, yes, it was flooding. My brain, my thoughts, my cells. The cell membranes had ruptured, the cytoplasm leaking downwards through my body starting from my crown chakra. This was an awakening. And in the darkness, I let myself dissolve.

Chapter thirty-seven

Friends, and amends

Inhale through the nostrils for one – two – three. Exhale through an open mouth for one – two – three – four.

Four. The number representing death in Japan. Death. Of me. Of my persona. Of me, as a physical person. But not of my soul.

In for three, out for four.

In and out, for three then four.

Seven. A lucky number in England, as well as Japan.

Seven. Associated in Buddhism with growth and overcoming challenges.

Three in, four out; a cyclical activity. Repetition. Me getting involved with men who treated me badly: Carl, and now Shinichi. Me counselling Shiori and Victoria because of the same men who had also treated them badly.

Me, back in a relationship with a man who was good for me. Naoki. Where did he fit in the cycle?

The Wabi-sabi Doll

What came between Death and Rebirth? Reincarnation?

A part of my persona had died the previous summer. Carl had cheated on me, I had broken up with him, and predatory Vince had sensed weakness, raping me at my own party, and leaving me broken. I had burned their names on a piece of paper on Tottori Sakyu beach and my hair had caught fire, singeing my fringe. Broken and burned. Cremated. Then reborn, a phoenix from the ashes. Last year's phoenix had chopped her long, blonde hair into a bob with a blunt-cut fringe and entered a new, healthy relationship with Naoki.

A relationship that had also run its course in winter. Dying in winter, soon after new year.

This year, another cycle, another death of my persona. Not a haircut this time: my shoulder-length blonde hair dyed black.

Then stripped brown.

Now bleached blonde.

Why was it that women tended to change their hair after a relationship breakdown? Did men do such a thing too? Maybe. Maybe it was human nature to want to shed the 'old' us and usher in the new.

Rainy season, washing me clean. Cleansing my soul.

I watched the rain drumming down on the windscreen of Naoki's Toyota Prius. The sound brought me back to reality, alerted me to my surroundings, grounding me again in the present. Occasional sniffs from Victoria, huddled in the backseat with her arms around herself for comfort. Had a higher power intervened to save her from having to teach in such a distressed state? Voyce school had closed for the evening due to the leaking roof and electrical blackout. Victoria had suffered enough humiliation. She and I were back to neutral territory. Square one. Blank canvas. My heart went out to her.

Did I have a heart? Maybe. Maybe underneath my selfish exterior, the façade that was all about me, me, me resided a caring soul. One that could see the good in those who had wronged me. Was there good in narcissists like Carl, and Shinichi? Yes. Maybe. Otherwise, I wouldn't have been in relationships with them in the first place. Would I? Was I so foolish to get myself involved with bad men? Did I think I could save them, somehow?

No, some people were just bad. Fundamentally bad, rotten eggs. Vince was most definitely in that category. There wasn't much that was redeemable in Carl, or Shinichi either; but maybe by saving the women they had wronged, I could redeem myself in some way, even if I couldn't save myself.

I rubbed my forehead, massaged the bridge of my nose. Was that what it came down to? That I had to be saved? From who, then? Myself?

Was Naoki my knight in shining armour, on his white Toyota Prius horse? Rescuing both Victoria and I from the torrential rain. His car followed a familiar route back to my old flat, Maison Libido, where Victoria now lived alone.

I didn't need a saviour. I *was* the saviour. "Will you be alright? We could stay with you for a few hours?"

She gave a single nod of confirmation, her eyelashes clumped and wet.

I had spoken for Naoki without asking if he was okay with us keeping Victoria company. Why? To prove to myself that I was the knight in shining armour, not him?

The Wabi-sabi Doll

We started to get out of the car. I swung my feet out into the rain. I focused on my cute, black and white patent lace-up shoes, perfect for work, perfect for the image of a teacher, a role-model, the epitome of a professional, businesslike woman. Was that me? Under those black and white patent shoes lay feet that mere weeks before had kicked Shinichi on his shinbone when he had plastered nude photos of me all over his *Fresh Fridays* flyers.

Would a respectable teacher get herself into a compromising position, enticed to pose for topless photos dressed as a geisha? Why not? I had trusted Shinichi, my boyfriend, who I thought was the father of my child. He had manipulated me into all of it; posing nude, thinking my phantom pregnancy was real.

I glanced at Victoria, hurrying up the steps to her flat. She had trusted him too, and why shouldn't she? It was human nature to trust others. To see the good in others.

Was there good in men like Carl, Vince, and Shinichi?

Back to the same old question. A cycle, repeating. Good? Bad? What was good, or bad? Who decided what was good, and what was bad? Society? Me?

I watched Naoki follow Victoria up the stairs.

Naoki was good. Why was he good? Because he didn't cheat on anyone? Because he didn't manipulate people into posing nude? Because he didn't sexually assault anyone? What made him good, and Carl, Vince and Shinichi bad?

A flash of colour at the side of my eye drew my attention to the front window of the ground floor flat below Victoria's. The bamboo blind had been drawn aside and a little girl peeped out.

"Kawaii-chan," I mouthed.

I hadn't seen her for several months; not since the end of January, in fact. Kawaii-chan made no pretence about watching me, unaware, or uncaring of social norms, like not staring. Was she too young to care? How old was she anyway; four years old?

I stopped and waved at her, and she waved back.

And then I surprised myself. Instead of dashing up the stairs Behind Victoria and Naoki, I stood in the rain, at the bottom of the steps, and put my palms together, pressing my forearms against the other to make a tree.

"ōkina kuri no kinou shita day," I began to sing.

Kawaii-chan copied my actions through the glass, and together, yet separated by a windowpane, we sang the lyrics of 'Under the spreading chestnut tree', the Japanese nursery song she had taught me.

Kawaii-chan made a motion as though she was going to come outside and join me, but I flapped my hands and shook my head.

"It's raining. We can't play together right now, but we will soon," I said, giving my brain time to translate. "Erm, sugu, kimi tou nakayoku asobimashou ka."

I gave one last wave goodbye, then dashed upstairs to Victoria's flat. I was drenched, but the moment with Kawaii-chan was worth it. She saw me as a friend. Was she lonely? I had only ever seen her playing outside by herself; there didn't seem to be any other kids her age in the vicinity. No other kids at all, for that matter.

Friends. Amends. I had much to learn from a preschooler. Victoria and I were friends again. Naoki and I would keep her company for a few hours, even if just to get her through the rainstorm. After the rain, the sun would come again. I hoped.

Chapter thirty-eight

Kawaii-chan

There she was. In the pouring rain, under the shadow of grim, grey clouds. There she was. Just as Naoki and I had got Victoria settled, just as we were about to leave and go back to Mitsuko's flat for my last night staying with his sister, there she was.

Kami.

She stood on Victoria's doormat, all thirty centimetres of her, wearing her pristine pink silk kimono, her shiny red lips and wide dark eyes unblinking as they stared at me. No emotions, yet all the feeling in the world. Mocking me, taunting me, making fun of me. Saying, what are you doing, Kimberly? Why are you consoling someone who helped your ex-boyfriend to cheat? Are you such a doormat that you would allow yourself to get used like that?

Yes, that was it. That was why she stood on the doormat, taunting me. She was there, a physical manifestation of a metaphor for me, and my life.

Doormat Kimberly.

Not a saviour of broken women, not a saviour of my broken self-worth, but a doormat.

I felt the air leave my chest, replaced by boa-constrictor tightness, and draining blood, and surging adrenaline. I couldn't think. I couldn't feel. I certainly couldn't breathe.

"Naoki." My hoarse voice trickled out, a pathetic croak.

Stars swum before my eyes as dizziness beset me. I knew the signs. If I didn't control my breathing, my fully fledged panic attack would cause me to pass out.

I felt Naoki's hands on my shoulders, giving a comforting squeeze. "What's wrong?"

"She found me. She wasn't there when we came in and now she's back. She came for me."

I looked at him, looking down at the doll. His eyes narrowed by a sliver and his lips pressed into a thin, taut line.

"Dolls aren't alive. She didn't find you. It's simple though, I think I've figured it out. She always appears on your doorstep, right? So, it's obvious. The girl downstairs gave her to you."

So plain, so simple. So obvious? Occam's razor giving me a smack to reset my irrational mind.

I chewed my lip. "She appeared in other places though. She was in a restaurant, Cafe Throwback, that Shinichi took me to for a date. I saw her in the hospital too, when I went with Shinichi for an appointment. I didn't bring her to either of those places, and I doubt Kawaii-chan went there either."

The Wabi-sabi Doll

"Kawaii-chan? That's so cute, Kimberly."

I scooped up Kami and walked down the steps, lingering in front of the downstairs flat where Kawaii-chan lived. Now that the panic attack had subsided, thanks to Naoki's TLC, my logical brain had kicked back into full gear.

"If you're right, and Kawaii-chan gave Kami to me, then let's find out. You've no idea how this has taken control of my life for months."

I appreciated the fact that he didn't smile. No condescension, only confirmation; one solemn nod of approval at my plan.

I knocked on the downstairs door.

Kawaii-chan's mum opened the door. I let Naoki do the talking, my brain still deescalating from the panic attack. His smile told me the answer before he even translated.

"She said that Nana chan put the doll on your doorstep."

Nana chan. All along, sweet little Nana, Kawaii-chan, had done it. I needed to process Naoki's words. Kawaii chan had put the doll on the doormat.

Nana's mum continued talking, and I waited for Naoki to translate. "Nana's mum made the doll for her. It's her job. She said she has a business making crafts and teaching ikebana, flower arranging. She didn't know Nana gave it to you."

As if on cue, Nana appeared behind her mother, clinging to her leg. She saw the doll in my hand then raised her eyes to me and spoke in cute colloquial preschooler words, none of which appeared in my Business Japanese book.

"She says Nana gave it to you as a present because you are her friend," said Naoki.

Under the spreading chestnut tree
You and me,
playing nicely
Under the spreading chestnut tree.

The song she had taught me floated to mind once more. I wanted to grab Nana in my arms and give her a big hug, but it wouldn't have been appropriate.

It all made sense. When I had thrown the doll out, dirty and askew in the rain and dirt, Nana had washed it and given it back pristine. When I had thrown it off the balcony, she had found it in the grass below and returned it, clean once more.

What about when I had seen it move in my room? Overactive imagination? Trick of the light?

"What about at the snack bar, Bar Nightfall? It was there among the memorabilia. At Cafe Throwback too? Nana couldn't have brought the doll there."

I heard the words *Shinichi, Bar Nightfall* and *Cafe Throwback* amidst the conversation as Naoki explained to Nana's mum. Though, a part of me didn't need any translation. Deep down I–

"Eri said she gave a doll as a gift to him. She said they had a brief fling a few months back."

Eri. It was like a lightbulb switching on in my head. When I had thrown the doll off my balcony, I had seen Nana's mum talking to a man who looked like Shinichi. That man hadn't only *looked* like Shinichi, it had actually *been* him.

He had been cheating on me with Nana's mum, Eri.

Eri. Sexy photo texts sent from Shinichi to Eri.

Eri had given him a doll as a gift.

The Wabi-sabi Doll

"Naoki, can you ask Eri if the doll she gave him as a present had a blue dress?"

Her single word response was a block of concrete in the pit of my stomach.

Then that explained it. Shinichi had put a doll she had given him in Bar Nightfall. He had seen my reaction to it on a drunken night with Zoe, Shinichi and his friend Keitaro, and had compartmentalised that titbit of weakness on my part, to use for later. He had placed a doll – the same doll, another doll, it mattered not – at Café Throwback, a restaurant he either owned or worked at as a club promoter. He had done that, knowing that I thought the doll was possessed, knowing that I thought it was the doll that had arrived on my doorstep. He knew I had been vulnerable at the time, knew I thought the spirit of my lost baby Akari lived in it, like a stone Jizo. Yet he had sat us at a table with the doll overlooking us.

I felt sick.

Gaslighting. Crazy-making. That was what Shinichi had done to me. He had intentionally fucked with my head, making me even more paranoid, even more vulnerable. A vulnerable person could be manipulated. That was why he had done it.

Anger began to bubble in the pool of sickness.

"Did Eri know that Shinichi was my boyfriend, at the same time he was seeing her?"

"She said he told her he was getting English lessons from you when he saw you with her at Jusco one time."

Naoki's face was tinged red. Amidst my desire to get to the bottom of the mystery with Eri and the doll, I hadn't thought of the pain this was causing Naoki, caught in the middle. Not only did he have to translate about his girlfriend's former boyfriend during the period when she had broken up with him, but had to listen to how the love-rat had cheated on multiple women.

"Eri feels really bad about the whole thing. She had no idea you were both being played off each other by Shinichi."

An inner calm flowed out of me, chasing away the nausea and the anger that had bubbled mere moments before.

"It's okay. I don't care about any of that now. I'm just happy I got to the bottom of things."

Nana, still clinging to her mum's leg, peered out at me with her wide brown eyes. I found myself dropping down onto one knee and opening my arms wide. The little girl's face broke into a smile and she rushed forward to embrace me in a hug, burying her face in my shoulder.

"Ningyo wo arigatou." *Thank you for the doll.* Knowing the truth about how my Kami doll had come to me had hit a reset switch in my brain. I definitely felt like I had learned a big lesson, and some mistakes that I wouldn't repeat again.

Chapter thirty-nine

The Wabi-sabi doll

The wooden floors of my new flat felt soothing on my bare arms and legs. I wore only shorts and a t-shirt in the sweltering July heat as I lay, spread-eagled, in the middle of the living room. I extended one arm, and pointed my finger at the white, painted ceiling. From there, I traced a straight line and stopped at a random point to the right, on an imaginary dot.

Randomness. Attributing meaning when there was none.

Attentive melancholy.

Impermanence.

From the random point I had selected, I brought my finger down at a right angle and stopped on the immobile, immaculate face that smiled back at me.

This time, Kami, as I had named her, had shoulder-length, blonde hair like mine. She wore a lilac kimono, and her lips were pink instead of red. She was a doll-version of me, an immaculate shrine to the phantom baby that I had yearned for so badly, that had taken root in my heart and in my head. Eri had made her for me specially.

I still had Kami too, of course, gifted to me by Eri's lovely daughter, Nana. With her black hair, red lips and pink kimono, she looked like a twin sister of the Akari doll. Akari my water baby. My two personal Jizos to keep me safe. I inhaled in one long, slow deep breath. Time for a poem.

Title: Jizo

Stone baby,
a permanent etching on my heart
of an impermanent moment,
when my water baby was washed away
but pain passes too; I remain melancholy.

Jelly baby;
but the doll is no longer haunted,
I'm no longer tormented.

Mystery doll,
Drunken doll,
Haunted doll.

Jelly fish bobbing,
making me aware, now,
of the transient nature of all things
on earth.

Come to me, keep me safe,
protect me, *mamoru,*

The Wabi-sabi Doll

And I'll protect you both too,
My Akari,
sweet Jizo,
My Kami,

My wabi-sabi doll.

Was my handwriting getting messy? Maybe so. I shrugged to myself. There was beauty in imperfection, why not?

Beauty in imperfection. Wabi-sabi.

What was the strange laughter? High-pitched like a screeching, warbling bird. Throaty and spluttering, and demented.

Me. It was me.

What on earth? Had I cracked up? Finally lost it, after all these years? Eight years. Seven with Carl, lucky seven for some but not for me. Eight, a lucky number in Japan. A symbol of growing prosperity. The kanji symbol, widening, spreading at the base, like Mount Fuji. Stability. Was I widening at the base? After eight years, yes. Sorting out my head, and my heart, and even my physical self, which had been neglected through obsession over a child that wasn't even inside it in the first place. A wabi-sabi doll, implanted in my brain, and in my belly.

More laughter. Cleansing my soul and my physical self was more cathartic than I realised. Long overdue too.

Another poem manifested in my mind, materialised in my midriff:

Title: The wabi-sabi doll

Beauty in impermanence
A mantra for a tormented soul,
Taking root, in the mind, black-haired doll,
Becoming whatever I projected onto it,
But not living or breathing in my arms.
Wabi-sabi, attentive melancholy,
Manifesting in my midriff,
A longing that grew bloated, curved,
Through my own warped desire.
Better now, expanding, widening at the base,
Blonde-haired doll watching over me,
Overseeing the detritus leaving my head.

Mystery doll,
Drunken doll,
Haunted doll.
Wabi-sabi doll.

My new ground floor apartment, near Tottori Station, didn't have the stunning view of Kyushu Mountain that my former first floor flat in Akisato had, but I didn't need a view as a projection of the idealised life I wanted to have. The image of my life as I wanted it to be was internal, not external.

Chapter forty

Funeral for a death doll

2AM. Under the cover of darkness, even in the middle of Tottori's thriving nightlife district, Yayoicho, I glided, silent as a ghost in my white, satin ballet pumps. My platinum blonde hair gleamed in the lamppost glow, ghost-bright. It hung, bone straight, down over my shoulders and my thick fringe skirted the tops of my brows in one heavy line. The cotton fabric of my white *yukata* summer kimono swished as I walked, the *kanzan* double cherry-blossom print unnoticeable in the dark. But not for long. Soon, my carefully planned appearance would have a dramatic impact. A memorable impact. I hoped. I certainly *looked* very dramatic. A lady in white, head to toe. I was thankful for the hot, humid air of early August, as it meant I didn't have to wear a coat – my entrance would be more dramatic without one - and with *Obon* so close, the festival of the dead, when many women wore traditional clothing such as *happis* or *yukatas*, I didn't look out of place, even as a foreigner.

Bar Nightfall lay ahead. The unobtrusive sign gave the air of a cafe, but I knew it was much seedier than that. It was a snack bar, owned by my ex, Shinichi.

I hadn't been to Bar Nightfall since January, when I had been out drinking with Zoe. That night, I had met Shinichi. The birth of an ill-fated relationship. Tonight would be a fitting ceremony to honour the death of that relationship.

I pushed both of the swinging doors open and entered in a mini-tempest that materialised the moment my foot crossed the threshold. The pathetic fallacy couldn't have been more on point; a self-actualising whirlwind as though my very thoughts were manifesting into a physical reality. In that moment I felt invincible. Dressing up, almost as a character, exacerbated my feeling of invincibility. My sleek hair, perfectly pressed clothing, immaculate makeup; all of it made me feel very doll-like.

A doll. A wabi-sabi doll.

Beauty in imperfection. Me, imperfect. Tonight, a perfect moment in an impermanent phase of my life.

Two AM; closing time for Bar Nightfall. Indeed, only one customer remained, one drunk, middle-aged man slumped over his empty glass on the counter. All of the booths with their tacky memorabilia, that decorated the interior of Shinichi's bar, were empty.

Shinichi, counting the cash at the register, looked up as the swinging doors opened. His eyes widened and his face froze, horrorstruck, as his gaze rested on me.

Me, an apparition in white, on a dark night.

The Wabi-sabi Doll

I shuffled my feet, in tiny, dainty steps, seemingly gliding along the aisle between the booths towards the counter.

Did it help that I knew Shinichi enjoyed patronising his own bar, loading up on too much liquor, while he worked? Maybe so. Did it help that I had made sure to wear my yukata with the right side crossed over the left, like a corpse? Maybe so. Did it help that I looked as ghost-white as *yuki-onna*, the snow woman demon of Japanese mythology? Maybe so. Did it help that I knew how superstitious Shinichi was, since he had taken me to a temple to buy a Jizo stone baby for my miscarried Water Child? Maybe so. Did it help that I knew the onset of August was also the onset of Obon, the festival of the dead in Japan? Maybe so.

Was it mean-spirited of me to take advantage of Shinichi's beliefs and use them against him?

Maybe so.

Karma was a bitch. I stretched my red lipsticked mouth into a wide smile, keeping my black highlighted eyes wide and staring as I swept towards the counter, backlit by the ambient mood-lighting in the snack bar. I knew my brightly painted features, offset by a white talcum-powdered face, would look stark and ghostly.

Shinichi gulped. "Kim?"

I caught sight of my reflection in the mirrored wall behind the bar. A spectral sight. If I had seen a vision of myself a few months before looking as I did in that white, kanzan yukata, I might have had palpitations.

I said nothing. Shinichi's face began to relax as the realisation set in that a hideous, doll-like apparition didn't stand before him; but rather, I did.

"The bar is closed. Did you want to see me?"

A flicker of a smile, his usual, cheeky, sexy smile dared to materialise at the corner of his mouth. Time to ramp up the fear factor.

I spoke, in a soft, sweet croon. "Am I beautiful?"

If only I could have captured the look on Shinichi's face. His mouth zigzagged in a downward slope to the left. His eyes, normally dancing with mischief, sagged with the weight of fear on his soul. I made sure to trace the lines of his features with my eyes, permanently etching the grooves of sheer terror indelibly into my brain.

Am I beautiful? An urban legend in Japan, a tale of the slit-mouthed woman, asking the question of lone men on dark nights. My one-time nemesis, Shiori, had asked something similar of Carl through her question "Do I look sexy?" when she had seen us together in Jusco, many moons before, and that had helped to formulate my devious revenge on superstitious, ghost-believing, Shinichi.

It was a delightful moment. Payback was a bitch.

Without saying a word, without changing the pace of my soft creeping footsteps, I veered to the right, away from the bar, and padded towards the booths along the side. The booth where Zoe and I had joined Shinichi and Keitaro for drinks at the start of the year still had its tacky memorabilia. I spotted the Hina doll that Eri had given him, clad in its blue kimono, and stretched my left arm out towards it. In my hand, I had hidden the twenty-four carat yellow gold diamond tennis bracelet that Shinichi had given me for Valentine's Day. Under the cover of my drooping yukata sleeve, I discreetly looped the bracelet over the doll's head, letting it fall like a necklace around her neck. Another part of my meticulous plan. A devious plan, the perfect revenge, even if I said so myself.

Out I glided through the double swinging doors into the darkness beyond. A sense of smug satisfaction, of wicked accomplishment, descended over me. Karma comeuppance for a lying, cheating bastard whose disdain for women could have earned him a chauvinist of the year trophy – even surpassing that of my abusive ex, Carl. Shame I'd never had the chance to exact revenge on Carl. But payback to Shinichi sure felt good.

Chapter forty-one

Shan Shan festival

"Do you want to participate in the Shan Shan umbrella dance?"

I stared at Naoki's smiling expectant face. An image of myself dressed in a yukata, twirling a colourful umbrella in the parade, like the dancing women I had seen at Tottori's annual festival the previous year, popped into my head. The Shan Shan Matsuri was a Tottori-specific festival with an onomatopoeic name based on the sound of the hot springs bubbling below the city centre, combined with the 'Inaba Umbrella Dance', based on a tradition passed down through the eastern part of Tottori prefecture.

"What would I have to do? I can't dance."

His grin stretched wider. "I have something else in mind."

What could that be? An intrusive image replaced the one of dancing, umbrella twirler. Courtesy of my recent embarrassment, an eyesore image of me as a bare-breasted geisha on a colourful float before a crowd of thousands in Tottori city centre usurped any other picture that came to mind.

Fresh Fridays were still too fresh in my brain.

Naoki tilted his head, contemplating me at an angle. He knew I had heavy things in my head, I could tell.

"I thought you could carry a 'Matsuri' festival sign. It's just a thought though, you don't have to do anything you're uncomfortable with."

The notion of carrying the festival sign presented a much more palatable image in my head. I imagined myself dressed all in white, like a ghost bride, carrying the sign to honour the festival of the dead.

Naoki cut across my musings when he stuck his phone under my nose. "We can wear these matching happis."

The Japanese shirts looked much like the kind that restaurant staff wore. They were navy blue, with a black and white checked lapel and a red Japanese character on the left breast and enlarged on the back.

"What does the kanji writing say?"

"It's the name of my family restaurant, Yasuda Ramen."

Warmth flooded me then. Was this a suggestion, in as many words, that I had been welcomed into Naoki's family?

"Mitsuko and I will be wearing them. It might be the first year that Mum and Dad can't take part in the festival, so it would be great to have you as part of our team, but only if you want to."

I threw my arms around him, almost knocking his phone flying. "I'd love to. I'm honoured you would ask me. Are your parents okay with it? I mean, I still haven't met them."

A dusting of red appeared at his cheeks. "They'll be watching in the crowd. They want you to come to our house afterwards for takoyaki. Do you like takoyaki?"

I nodded, beaming. "I'm so looking forward to meeting your parents."

Happy families at last. I imagined the three of us – Mitsuko, Naoki and I – wearing our matching festival shirts and eating takoyaki with his parents.

With only two days until the Shan Shan Matsuri, on the fourteenth of August, I was glad I didn't need to do any rehearsals. Carrying a festival sign seemed straightforward enough physically, but the emotional significance for me was huge. I was officially a part of Naoki's family. Such a thought kept me walking practically on air for the next two days. Work, which had been much better since Victoria and I had made amends, breezed by without event. With over a year of teaching experience under my belt, I could whip up a lesson plan in mere minutes, and felt confident delivering even the trickiest of subjects to students with little to no knowledge of English. Tangentially, it was pleasant to not have to see Shiori working at Cover Girl, the shop near Voyce Language school, since it appeared she no longer worked there as a sales assistant. Even though my seven-year relationship with Carl was relegated to history, any reminder of how he had cheated on me with Shiori, who he had met while waiting on me to finish my shifts at Voyce school, would have been enough to dampen my mood, and so I was thankful not to have any reminders of this on my daily commute.

The Wabi-sabi Doll

Yes, I was happy. Happy and settled for the first time in a long time. Feeling that I had been welcomed into Naoki's family felt like the first step towards us maybe getting engaged. Would I feel any happier if he were to pop the question? Maybe. It was hard to imagine; could be I was jumping the gun. It wasn't too much of a stretch for me to imagine us engaged; though after my long and disastrous engagement to Carl that was achieved nothing other than keeping me under his control, I wanted to take my time with any future engagement and make sure I was truly committing myself to the right man for me.

Mitsuko collected our tailor-made matching happis, with the Yasuda Ramen logo emblazoned on the left next to the lapel, and enlarged on the back. As I pulled my happi on over my white vest top, and fastened the tie at the waist, I couldn't help but spin, looking myself over in the full-length mirror near my front door. The navy-blue happi with red embroidered logo, along with the black and white checked lapel suited me, the colours standing out bold against my stripped white hair. Mitsuko stood shoulder to shoulder with me, we exchanged smiles in the mirror. Behind us in the reflection, I could see into my living room through the open sliding door. Both of my dolls, Akari and Kami, stood next to the TV. Blonde and brunette, just like Mitsuko and me. I grinned back wider at her in the mirror, and we slung our arms around the back of each other's waists, bumping hip against hip.

My new flat had the closest proximity to Tottori Station, where the Shan Shan festival would be starting, and so the three of us: Naoki, Mitsuko and I, got ready at my place. Having them in my flat made it feel more like home; in a way, I had begun to feel as if Naoki was indeed, already, my family.

Was that wrong? No. Why would anything that made my heart swell so much be wrong?

Mitsuko busied herself with the fuchsia-coloured Matsuri sign, checking that it was secured to the pole for me to hold, while Naoki fastened his own jimbe at the waist, identical to the happis that Mitsuko and I wore. He joined me at the mirror.

"It's a good look on you." Naoki looped his arms around me, linking his hands at my stomach and resting his chin on my shoulder.

"Maybe someday I could work with you in Yasuda Ramen? I don't see myself being an English teacher for my whole life."

Naoki unlinked his hands from my waist, a placid smile in place. "I thought you wanted to be a Clinical Psychologist?"

"I do. Back in London, but not here. I'd have to learn Japanese fluently to compete with native speakers for such a job."

He gave a casual shrug. "You'd have to speak Japanese fluently to work as a waitress in a restaurant too."

A casual shrug, or a brush-off? My comment in jest suddenly seemed to hold so much more weight. Albatross on my shoulder weight? I brushed off such a thought too; no point having negativity and insecurity before a family occasion. Naoki had done nothing to make me feel unwelcome in his family. He was right, of course. Being an English teacher didn't require fluent Japanese; being a waitress in a family-run restaurant did.

The Wabi-sabi Doll

Takoyaki and meeting the parents. Such things wouldn't be on offer if I were to be brushed off.

Deep breath. I smoothed my happi, smoothed my hair, and smoothed my mindset.

We walked together to Tottori Station, me in the middle, all three arm in arm. I loved Naoki, and I loved Mitsuko too, like a sister.

The previous year when I had watched the Shan Shan festival, it had been a spectacle of colour and dance; but it was an altogether different experience being a part of the parade instead of a passive tourist enjoying it. My job was easy; holding the Matsuri sign with Naoki and Mitsuko stepping in rhythm to the drums on either side of me. The drumbeat, from the taiko drums, resounded through my chest, helping to get me in the spirit of the festivities. Thousands of people lined Route 53, the main road stretching from Tottori Station towards Kyushu Mountain at the northern end, a long straight main road of restaurants, department stores and shops. As we walked, I spun, waving the Matsuri sign, getting into the groove of the traditional music played. My eyes scanned the faces in the crowd. Occasionally I spotted a western face among the numerous heads and my gaze lingered for a moment longer, searching for familiarity, before moving on.

What was I looking for, among the faces? Validation among the crowd? Validation for what? A chance to show off? To who?

My eyes settled on the target I had been seeking. He stood, with his petite, beautiful wife, outside Tottori Cinema.

Carl spotted me immediately. His smiling face, which moments before had been enjoying the colour and revelry, turned to a glower as he saw me approaching with the Matsuri sign. His eyes roved my happi, then darted to one side observing Mitsuko. Gone were his heavy eyelids and taut, downturned mouth as his eyebrows rose in approval at Naoki's sister.

My head twitched sideways towards Mitsuko myself. Even though I knew from the moment I first met Mitsuko, that Carl would find her attractive; and even though it had been over a year since I had split up with my narcissistic ex, nothing could have prepared me for the pang of jealousy that seared like a lightning rod right through my core. Why did I *still* want Carl's attention? I didn't love him, didn't even like him. In fact, I *loathed* him.

Another lightning rod struck me. *That* was the problem. I still cared. Even in a dysfunctional sense, loathing him still meant giving him my attention and energy – and power. What I wanted was to *not* care; for Carl to evoke no reaction, or emotion, in me. I wanted *not* to care; for Carl to merely be another face in the crowd. It seemed that seven years could not be undone so easily. What I wanted and what I felt, were two entirely different things.

Apparently my body responded differently from my brain too.

A drinks promoter of Kirin beer handed out cans in the crowd. Now I understood why Carl had chosen to stand where he was; he held a free can of beer in each hand. I weaved towards the promotion man through the procession, and grabbed a can. Shaking it, I yanked the ring pull and watched froth spray across Carl's face, splattering down his t-shirt.

"Ah, chotto gomen yo!" I called, in my best, sing-song pantomime voice. Sorry, but not sorry. I couldn't help smiling to myself as I turned on my heel and walked back to my place in the parade, ignoring the gasps from the crowd, the puzzled awkwardness on Naoki's face and the surprise on Mitsuko's.

As the taiko drums kept beating, and the music kept playing, I danced in a dizzy whirlwind, weaving figure eights around Naoki and Mitsuko as we moved with the procession. Giddiness beset me. Was I proud of myself for exacting petty revenge on Carl, soon after my petty revenge on Shinichi? Yes. Was it the mature thing to do? No. Was I happy that I had paid both of them back? Yes.

Was this the culmination of my inner journey triggered by the wabi-sabi doll this year? Hmm. I needed to ponder that notion for longer. It seemed on the surface that I was hellbent on pursuing karma payback. But for what?

Justice for the women who had been wronged, myself included? Shiori, Victoria, me.

Justice? Maybe revenge was nearer the mark. Justice, revenge, same difference. Who cared. All I knew was that petty payback, and exacting my own brand of karma comeuppance, felt good.

Chapter forty-two

Takoyaki

When was the last time I had been to Kawahara? The village south of Tottori was a short train ride away, but an even quicker drive. The last time I had been for a visit was when I had been new to Tottori prefecture, as a novice teacher still within her three-month teaching probation period at Voyce language school. One of my students in the casual conversation *Chat* class, in between structured lessons, had given me tickets to visit Kawahara castle. It was a small museum near Kawahara station, where she worked as a Tour Guide. I had enjoyed my trip to the castle museum on a day when I knew she would be there, and she had enjoyed a chance to brush up her English conversational skills in a real-world setting. A mutual day of enjoyment for us both.

The Wabi-sabi Doll

This time, I was driving south with Naoki and Mitsuko, ready to meet his parents at their house for takoyaki. I twisted my hands together in my lap.

"What should I call your mum and dad? I mean, I know they're called Reiko and Hajime, but you don't address people by their first names here. So, what should I say?"

Naoki smiled and reached across to stroke my hand with his thumb, before returning it to the steering wheel. "Don't worry so much. They know you're a Londoner, it's fine."

I knew he intended his response to relax me, but it didn't answer my question, so I felt even more anxious. As we turned off the main road into winding rice paddies, I decided that letting them take the lead with the introductions would be for the best. By the time the Shan Shan festival had finished, less than an hour before, Naoki's parents had already driven back to Kawahara, to get set up to host the takoyaki meal. It was a shame I hadn't been able to meet them more casually at the Matsuri, as it would have taken the pressure off. Meeting them in their home seemed much more formal – and scary.

As we pulled into the driveway of a house, I realised it wasn't as I had expected. What *had* I expected? For the Yasuda family to live in an apartment block, like I did; like half of Japan did? The house was made of brown wood with a sloping roof that resembled the ones I had seen on temples. Very traditional looking and old-fashioned; not to mention *large*. Next to it, looking diminutive in comparison, was Yasuda Ramen, a small rectangular building with red and black logo. Business must have been successful to pay for such a grand looking house. Now I could understand why

Naoki had to work so much. Would he inherit the house someday? I imagined myself in a Japanese housecoat, making passing conversation with the neighbours from the front door. Getting ahead of myself, again.

Speaking of the front door; it opened as Naoki parked his Toyota Prius and a large, grey and white husky padded out. The dog ambled towards the car, tongue hanging out, and Naoki stooped to ruffle its shaggy hair as soon as he got out.

"Aww, who is this?" I swooped down upon the dog and scratched its chin.

"This is Momo," Naoki beamed.

"Momo? As in, peach?"

He nodded.

"That's so cute. Who named her?"

"Mitsuko did," he smiled.

Mitsuko stepped out of the car and petted Momo. "I got her when I was fifteen. It seemed like a good name at the time. Now I've had her so long, she wouldn't suit anything else."

"Well, I love it. It's so cute – and unique." I threw my arms around the dog's thick, shaggy neck and buried my face in her fur.

Emotional support dog. It certainly made me feel much calmer than even Naoki's words of reassurance.

"Hello Kimberly. It's so nice to meet you."

I let go of Momo and stood to see Naoki's mum's smiling face. Reiko was wearing a traditional house jacket over slack trousers, and her short grey hair was threaded with white. She had a long, slim face, and I could see much of Naoki in her, rather than Mitsuko.

Mitsuko, on the other hand favoured their dad. Hajime was not quite as tall as Naoki, standing at

The Wabi-sabi Doll

around five foot nine with a slight stoop. He had thinning hair, and soulful eyes, as Mitsuko did. He wore a dark blue jimbe with silver threading, which I knew was for the Matsuri, but I couldn't help wondering; had he picked a smarter one to make a first impression on me too?

"Bannarimashita," said Reiko with a bow.

Bannarimashita? I looked to Naoki for help.

"It's a Tottori way of saying 'Konbanwa'," he explained.

"It means good evening," said Reiko, in perfectly smooth English.

I relaxed, allowing air to enter my lungs. Had I been holding my breath? Trepidation wasn't good for my body.

"We've heard so much about you," said Hajime, also in perfect English.

I bowed to both of them. "It's lovely to meet you both at last."

Though I had mentally rehearsed what I would otherwise have said in Japanese, it certainly took the pressure off to be speaking my own language. I appreciated it a lot. From the sounds of their accents, neither spoke English as fluently as Naoki or Mitsuko, though had clearly practised what they intended to say, which made me feel even more grateful, and welcome in their home.

"Do you eat takoyaki?" Reiko paused. "Octopus balls?"

"Yes, I love it."

She beamed, even wider.

Reiko and Hajime led the way inside. A sliding screen separated the living room from the hallway. I took off my shoes and slid my feet into a pair of white cotton slippers. Cool air from the air conditioning unit in the living room blew over me, a welcome retreat from the evening heat. My eyes were immediately drawn to a shrine that looked like a miniature altar. It seemed to be a black and gold lacquered chest to my eye, with the doors wide open and an array of ceremonial objects: a golden cup, a gold vase with flowers, a white candle in a gold holder and a plate with what looked like a nectarine on it.

"It's our family *butsudan*, where we honour our ancestors," Naoki explained.

I understood; a Buddhist altar.

The delicious smell of cooking batter distracted me from the altar. Reiko appeared through a door leading to the kitchen.

"Have you seen a takoyaki grill?" she said.

I let Momo lead me towards the appetising smell. The takoyaki grill was a large square grill with two handles on either side. It was divided into twenty round compartments in which cooked the battered balls with small slices of octopus tentacles inside. It was a summer festival food, and a street-food staple. Hajime turned the balls with a skewer, making sure they were cooked on all sides. The smell made my mouth water.

"I really think Londoners would *love* takoyaki. Same with okonomiyaki," I said.

"Dozo. Please help yourself," said Reiko.

I took the small plate she offered me and held it out as she served a steaming hot takoyaki ball. Hajime squirted it with Japanese mayonnaise and takoyaki sauce, and I bit in. I winced as the steaming hot ball burned my tongue and my eyes watered. Just as I worried I had done a faux pas, Naoki's parents

The Wabi-sabi Doll

apologised. I fanned my mouth with one hand and swallowed my mouthful to apologise myself.

"It's delicious, just very hot!" I wiped the tears away with a finger. "Sugoku oishii!"

For a moment, the scene in Naoki's family house seemed very surreal. I had momentary detachment, almost like I was within a movie, not real life. There we were, playing happy families, all smiles. Even Momo the dog seemed to smile as her tongue protruded while she waited for a titbit.

I looked around at each family member in turn, still feeling a sense of derealisation. I had wanted this moment for the whole year so far, ever since Naoki and I had flown back to Kansai airport after visiting my family for Christmas in Southampton. But now? Now what? I felt strangely numb. Was that because of the derealisation, or something more?

I couldn't be unsatisfied, could I? I had finally got what I wanted: to meet Naoki's parents and have them accept me as his girlfriend and they had welcomed me into the Yasuda family in a way I had dreamed of for eight months. As I munched on takoyaki, I realised that now I had got what I wanted, I felt deflated.

Guilty. And ashamed. But nonetheless, deflated.

Chapter forty-three

Obon

After dinner at the Yasuda family house the evening before, Naoki had stayed over at my apartment, and we had enjoyed a lovely intimate evening, enjoying each other in a sweet, wholesome, way. Sex with Naoki had always been tender and full of caresses, but after meeting his parents, it seemed to reach an even more delicate and gentle level. He treated me like a fragile flower. I wasn't sure what I thought of that, but I knew how I felt about Naoki, so that was alright.

We woke together, on Obon morning, entwined in each other's arms. I spent a lazy afternoon eating oden and ramen from a nearby Lawson convenience store and watching Japanese TV while Naoki attended family business in the afternoon. The solitude was a welcome time for reflection. Was it really mid-August already? The year had simply *flown* in. Less than a fortnight until my best friends, Sasha, Ronnie and

The Wabi-sabi Doll

Aaron, would fly in from Heathrow. I had saved some of my annual leave to travel with them across Japan. Naoki planned to take three days off from his family's restaurant to join us all in Tokyo, and then my friends would jet off to Thailand before going back to London. After that, Mum, Dad and Zac were planning to visit in September, so I had to spread my annual leave around sparingly, in order to play tour guide to them in Himeji, Nara and Kyoto. So much travelling would keep me away from Naoki, and our relationship already revolved around his restaurant schedule.

But for now, I needed to bring my mind back to the present. Ironic that the present was a celebration of the past. Obon, on the fifteenth of August, was a day to honour the dead, focusing on life and death matters. For me, that meant one thing: honouring Akari.

Naoki arrived at my flat late in the afternoon, and we walked in silence towards the temple holding the stone Jizo that Shinichi had purchased for Akari's memorial. The avenue leading to the temple was lined with hundreds of stone Jizos, all decorated in their red knitted hats and bibs. It had been busier earlier in the day, but with the Obon fireworks festival soon to take place, the late afternoon had quietened down. Still, I averted my eyes from other grieving parents, allowing them their privacy and solitude. Naoki held my hand, but didn't try to start up a conversation. Was he allowing me the space for my own sanctuary, even in my head? I could only guess. His presence nearby, but unspoken, meant a lot. It meant the world. Though solitary in my grief, I didn't want to be physically alone.

Sunset. The creamy haze, overlaid with dusky pink, added a salubrious glow to the temple grounds. Akari, as I approached her, looked the picture of health in her red hat like the others. One or two *hotaro*, the first of the evening fireflies, weaved around her, engaging in a magical dance. Moisture appeared at the corners of my eyes. I dabbed my pinky finger into each in turn, stemming the flow.

"Akari," I said, my voice solemn in the still air.

I reached into my *kinchaku* pouch, my yukata accessory bag, and brought out the incense stick that I had purchased from the temple earlier in the day. I lit the stick and attached it to the base of my stone Jizo.

"Be brave, my girl, and I'll see you again someday."

An image of a four month old baby, gurgling and grabbing her own feet with chubby fists, popped into my head. She had blue eyes like mine, and dark hair like Vince's. If Akari had lived, she would have been born in April. Had that been at the back of my mind, bubbling in my subconscious, when I had been in the throes of my phantom pregnancy – and phantom haunting by the Kami doll?

Honouring the dead. For me, that meant letting go of some mental habits that no longer served me either.

A deep breath. What a year it had been so far, and only two thirds over.

I stepped back from the lit incense, and the wind whipped the scent over me. It felt, for a moment, like basking in Akari's spirit, like she was embracing me in a loving hug.

Naoki stood a few feet behind, facing the other way. He watched the growing twilight, a pensive look on his face.

"You can come closer, if you want," I said, to reassure him.

Momentary embarrassment flitted across his face, before he composed himself with a placid smile.

"That's okay. Are you ready for the fireworks? They should be starting soon."

A misunderstanding. Hurt seized my heart. What did that mean? Did Naoki not care about Akari, or the pain I felt through my loss? I wanted to say something, to ask him, but no words would form. He seemed eager to leave the temple, walking away as soon as the words had left his mouth. I doubted he was as excited as all that for the fireworks display. My head raced with thoughts:

Was it because he had guessed that Shinichi had bought me the Jizo?

Or was it because Akari was a baby conceived by a man who had raped me?

Or did he not care for unborn children, maybe only valuing life once it was born to the world?

So many thoughts that flooded my brain, but wouldn't transpire on my tongue. Like a gentle evening of being treated like a delicate flower, and now cold indifference. At least, to me it was a one-hundred-and eighty degree swing.

We walked side by side along the main road back towards Tottori Station. At some point, his hand found mine and our fingers interlaced, but loosely so on my part. Despite the August heat, my hands were cold. It was as though all the blood in my body had rushed away from my extremities in order to try and heal my broken heart.

Yes, broken. Naoki's small gesture, a simple act of turning away from my grief, had broken my heart. On Obon, no less. It seemed extra cruel that he had acted in such an offhand way on the day when Japan honoured the dead. Akari was as much a real person I was, or Naoki was. Again, the words wouldn't come out of my mouth to say so, to protest against the injustice of his nonchalance towards my loss.

I hung my head as we walked. My heart felt full of lead. It was incomprehensible to me. Was it a misunderstanding? Surely he knew how much I loved and wanted Akari, despite the circumstances of her conception?

Hanabi. Fireworks. Literally, fire-flowers. The Obon Hanabi was as impressive as it was beautiful, with displays I hadn't seen before, like heart-shaped patterns with arrows through them, but I felt numb. Drained and numb. Everything in the past twenty-four hours had sent me reeling: my sense that something was missing after meeting Naoki's parents, feeling deflated after our sensual intimacy, and now, Naoki's indifference to Akari's Jizo.

What was wrong with my head? I had a perfectly decent man, a good life, and yet–?

There was rot in my brain, that was it. It had to be. Being with Carl for seven years had rendered me as damaged goods. On some inexplicable level, I had not got over my ex, and it was affecting my ability to be happy, or to move forward.

Obon. Death. A celebration of a part of my brain that was dead and could not be mended.

Chapter forty-four

Wabi-sabi wedding

My pen flew across the next blank page in my green poetry journal.

Title: Wabi-sabi brain
The Japanese concept of wabi-sabi encourages us to appreciate that nothing is truly perfect or permanent.
It is the Japanese art of finding beauty in life's imperfections.
Since I am in Japan, therefore I am subject to this rule.
It has permeated my skin, infiltrated my brain.
I am far from perfect. I am imperfect.
I will never be perfect. But I do not feel guilty for being this way.
I am trying my best. That is all I can do.

I stopped writing, and sat back on my haunches, gasping as if I had just run a marathon. My writing looked long and looping, sloping towards the left. The ink had barely made any indent on the page. What did all that say about me? Optimistic, or a psychopath?

I laughed aloud, clapping a hand over my mouth to staunch the effluence that poured out of my diseased brain. This was not a laughing matter.

"What's so funny, hun?"

Sasha, my best friend from London, burst into my bedroom and found me kneeling on my tatami mat, hunched over my poetry journal. I had met her while we were both working at Topshop on Oxford Street, and she had been the only one of my female colleagues on the team who hadn't hated me with a passion. Apparently a rumour had gone around that I had been sleeping with the other girls' boyfriends. Not true, and not my fault that they had fancied me to cause such petty jealousy in the first place. Sasha had stuck up for me at the time; she always had my back. We were thick as thieves, she and I.

I shrugged, in the offhand, petulant-teen manner that I always reverted to when in Sasha's company. "Something stupid, nothing important."

She stood, framed in the gap between my sliding screen doors, wearing a cute floral crop top and shorts combo, with an oversized floppy wicker hat. Very summery – and very Sasha. She suited anything, of course, with her thick black hair, hazel eyes and olive skin. Sasha's heritage was Persian. She was easily beautiful, though always insisted I was the more attractive one between us. Not true; and often ended up in one of those, *No, you're so skinny and hot, and I'm fat and ugly*, sort of conversations that girl-friends *sometimes* succumbed too.

Hmph. Easy ego boost.

The Wabi-sabi Doll

"Show me!" Sasha flopped down beside me and sat cross-legged on the floor. She snatched up my green poetry book and scoured it.

A year ago and I would have hated anyone reading my poetry journal. But, not only was this Sasha, my soul-sister and someone who was likely my conjoined twin in another lifetime, but I had become more confident in my poetic abilities since journalling so frequently about my travails in Japan.

After devouring my poem, Sasha flipped with her thumb and read another page, then another, and stopped. Her eyes widened, two suns arcing across the sky until they set on the horizon that was my face.

"What is the meaning of this, pray-tell?" She held my green journal up like it was an incriminating article.

When it was clear I had no clue about what the big deal was, Sasha flipped the book around to show the page that her thumb wedged open. I practically felt my eyeballs grow crimson as I re-read the poem I had written several days before.

<u>Title: Yearning</u>
First you got inside my loins,
sending a fire inside my belly,
blowing the top of my volcanic mind
but when the lava settled,
it formed dust and ash, that got under my skin,
making me feel wrong. So dirty,
though, you didn't stop there. I cut you free.
Scrubbed the filth from my skin,
started anew. But here you are,
back inside my mind, burrowing your way
from my brain, to my heart,

*even when my heart has been given
to another.*

"What?" I said, in mock indifference.

She puckered her mouth. "I've gotta meet this hottie, if he's all *that*."

I tucked a strand behind my ear, this time faking my nonchalance. "You've already met him. It's about Naoki."

Sasha made a derisive puff, blowing her hair off her forehead. "Don't bullshit me. It's about your little *Yakuza boy*, don't lie!"

That caused sweat to prickle across my hairline. I stretched upwards on my haunches, like a prairie dog looking for danger, then with no sign of interest from Aaron or Ronnie in my living room, ducked back down. I snatched the journal away from her and gave her a playful smack on the arm with it.

"Okay, fine. Shinichi has been on my mind – once or twice."

"On your mind?" She scoffed, theatrically. "Making you cream yourself, you sket!"

We both shrieked as I pushed her over and we wrestled on the tatami mat. Definitely reverted to my teenage self; Sasha was guilty of bringing out my inner Peter-Pan syndrome.

"Woah, what's this? You should've let us know there was going to be some girl-on-girl action and I'd have brought some popcorn," Ronnie joked, appearing in the doorway.

We were a crass bunch, really. It flung my dusty brain straight back to a memory of Carl the previous year. He had been visiting me at the time, over on a three-month tourist visa. I had arrived home from a shift, only to find photos of me and Ronnie pulled from one of my photo albums. He had laid them out on my futon, and I had found him, glowering in the bath, waiting for an explanation. Innocent photos of me and Ronnie on nights out, hugging, or me sitting drunk on Ronnie's lap. It didn't matter that my friendship with Ronnie was purely platonic, or that he was engaged to his very lovely fiancée back in London, Clara. It didn't matter that I had shown similar photos of me sitting on Aaron's lap, or on Sasha's. Aaron was gay, Carl had argued, and Sasha a woman, so it was different with them than with Ronnie. What it came down to was that Carl didn't trust me. First nail in the coffin for our doomed seven-year relationship.

I jumped to my feet and tucked my green poetry journal into my handbag. "Come on, you lot. Let's get out of here. I've so much planned for your Tottori tour."

Sasha gave me side-eye. "You're just trying to get off the hook."

I ignored her comment and headed for the front door, where I slipped on a pair of plastic clogs; my most suitable shoes for a walking tour. We started out towards Tottori Station, then veered right towards Yayoicho. Lunch was the first thing on my mind, and I knew that a Japanese bento meal might be a good way to introduce them to Japanese food with a slight western twist; burgers and tempura, along with a selection of pickles and egg. One of my favourites and palatable to unseasoned Londoners on their first expedition to rural Japan.

The restaurant and club district of Tottori looked quite different during the daytime. So much so, that even though my feet followed a familiar path, I allowed my brain the leeway to blame my surroundings, rather than my muscle memory, for the mistake. Nevertheless, my scuffed blue clogs landed us right on the doorstep of Café Throwback.

Shinichi's restaurant wasn't what I had in mind for brunch, but my friends had already sensed my hesitation, and had started inside the restaurant.

Kimberly Thatcher, I chided myself, in my most derogatory, schoolmarm tone I could conjure inside my own head. *Kimberly Thatcher, you are a glutton for punishment!*

Before I could chivvy us out, one of the waiting staff showed us to a table. What on earth was I thinking? Nope, scratch that; clearly I *wasn't* thinking. Was I expecting to bump into Shinichi? If so, then what? The chances of that happening were slim. If Shinichi was the owner, he wouldn't be there for the day-to-day running of the place. *Was* he the owner? I knew he owned Bar Nightfall, the snack bar where we had met, but not Café Throwback. Didn't he work as a club promoter, alongside dodgy Yakuza types, according to Mitsuko.

Maybe I could relax after all.

Another waiter approached our table to get our drinks order. His face was composed in a hospitality smile, but stretched with more reverence as his eyes lighted on me.

"You are Shinichi San's friend, aren't you? Are you here to see him?" he said, in competent English.

Or maybe not. Relaxation wasn't in my vocabulary, apparently.

"Iie, Shinichi tou issho ni yotei ga nai." *I have no plans with Shinichi.* Why did I answer in Japanese? To impress him? Impress my friends? I peered up at the man. "Why, is he working today?"

Ronnie, Sasha and Aaron sat still, apparently on tenterhooks; or was that just my imagination?

"He's not here today, I'm sorry," said the man with a slight, apologetic bow. "He is at a wedding."

Wedding. Why did that information make my heart quake? To who? I wanted to ask, but didn't. Instead, I thanked the waiter for the information and ordered our drinks. After the waiter left our table, my friends rounded on me.

"What's going on, you naughty little devil," Aaron teased. "You brought us to your ex's restaurant? Go on then, *explain*."

I swept my eyes across each of them, then turned my head away in a vain attempt to conceal my smile. "Swear down, guys, it was entirely by accident. Must have been a subconscious thing on my part."

"You liar!" Sasha teased. "It's not like you took us to Yasuda Ramen to try and see Naoki, you brought us here to Café Throwback because it's your ex's. *You* still have feelings for Shinichi, admit it!"

Luckily our waiter returned, just in time to save me from having to rustle up a half-assed answer. He served our drinks with a rather sheepish smile flashed in my direction; or at least one that seemed that way to me.

Sasha, a wicked grin on her face, turned to the waiter. "Where is the wedding?"

I think the world must have collapsed in on my head at that moment; I aimed a kick at Sasha under the table, missed, and had to sit fully awash with my embarrassment, searing my cheeks.

The waiter gave her a surreptitious grin. "At the Tottori City Guesthouse. It's a Ryokan near Kyushu Park."

A wedding at a Ryokan, a traditional Japanese hotel? Seemed odd. Japanese weddings were normally held at Temples, or Shrines, since the country was mainly Buddhist or Shinto. What sort of wedding was Shinichi attending in a hotel?

Not to worry; I had been planning to take my friends to see Tottori Castle ruins in Kyushu Park as one of the first stops on our walking tour. A small detour to the Tottori City Guesthouse would be a fun addition to our excursion.

☙

As we approached the Tottori City Guesthouse, the crowd in the traditional Japanese garden alerted me to the wedding taking place. Sasha, Ronnie, Aaron and I stood by the gate, watching the throng of black suited men and women wearing western-style skirt-suits facing towards a makeshift chapel. The chapel had been constructed out of latticed wood in a pale shade; maybe pine or oak. I wasn't an expert on trees. It looked like a summer house more than a formal chapel, but was very attractive in the Zen garden. Red carpet had been placed across the lawn leading up to the chapel. I craned my head and could see the black-suited groom and white-dressed bride facing an altar where a Christian priest, wearing a white cassock, officiated the wedding. As my gaze landed on the priest and recognition set in, I did a double-take.

Carl.

My ex was officiating the Christian wedding.

The Wabi-sabi Doll

"What? Oh my God…"

It had to be a joke. Carl wasn't even religious, never mind Catholic. How could he be working as a priest?

My feet led me to gatecrash the wedding, my curiosity beyond control. Apparently my friends felt the same way, as they followed me along the stonework path among bonsai trees towards the gathering. What on *earth* was Carl doing, officiating a wedding for a Japanese couple? The ceremony had to be fake. Yes, Carl had to be moonlighting as a fake priest. Not the worst thing he could have been doing for money in Japan, but still – how?

"By the authority festered in me…vested in me, I now pronounce you husband and wife," Carl stumbled.

I turned away, stifling my laughter with both hands. What a *fuck-up* my ex was. He couldn't even *pretend* to be a convincing priest. The couple deserved a better fake clergyman than Carl.

A familiar, bleached-blonde head stood out among the dark-haired wedding guests, and my laughter faded. I recognised my other ex, Shinichi, from a distance. As I sidled up beside him, Shinichi turned his head and glanced at me. His stoic expression broke into a rather sexy lopsided smile, one that I had missed for many months, sending my heart pell-mell into my stomach.

Ugh, why did I have to fall apart like a teenage girl with a crush? Luckily, Sasha, Ronnie and Aaron were too intrigued by the wedding to notice and had wandered closer to the chapel.

"Long time no see." Shinichi whispered, so as not to interrupt the ceremony. "What brings you here? You aren't stalking me, are you?"

"Don't flatter yourself." I took a deep breath through my nose and exhaled slowly, composing myself. "I'm showing my friends around Tottori. We were on our way to Kyushu Park, when we saw this wedding and thought we'd watch."

"Oh?" One eyebrow twitched upwards. "Are you sure it isn't because of the priest? You seemed to know him when we were going into Café Throwback a few months ago, remember?"

I folded my arms. "And apparently you seem to know him too. Why else would you be at this wedding?"

He slung his hands in both pockets, cool and casual – and hot – as ever. "I'm here for the bride. She's a friend. Used to work at the snack bar I – where we met."

His recovery wasn't so smooth that time, though he kept his face neutral to cover the slip. I wasn't about to let him off the hook.

"You were going to say 'at the snack bar I own' weren't you? Don't think I don't know that you aren't a fireman like you told me."

Shinichi flashed a flirtatious grin. "You got me there, but I got you too. Carl is your ex, isn't he?"

He *certainly* got me back. "Yes, but he wasn't a Priest. What's he doing officiating a wedding? Carl isn't even Catholic, his family are Church of England."

"They're called *nisei bokushi,* fake priests. It's a job. Some Japanese couples like to get married in a pretend Christian ceremony before their real wedding with a *Kannushi,* a Shinto priest in a temple. The fake wedding is just for fun."

I felt my upper lip curl. "And how much is he getting paid for this fake ceremony?"

"About go man en for a one hour slot."

What was that, like, one hundred and fifty quid? "And how many of these ceremonies does he do?"

Shinichi leaned closer to me, as our whispers were beginning to disrupt the wedding guests. "Shiori said he's doing at least five or six a week, even as far out as Sakaiminato. Shiori drives him."

I watched him with side-eye. "How do you know Shiori?"

He turned and grinned full in my face. "I know everyone in this town."

Hmph; women, at any rate. "You weren't fucking her behind my back too, were you?"

I couldn't help myself; it rolled off my tongue, slippery as a snake. Worth it too, for the look in Shinichi's eyes, which went momentarily wide.

The fake ceremony cut the conversation, as the bride threw her bouquet of white roses into the crowd, and Carl watched, his hands pressed together in a faux-regal pose, his chin raised.

Moonlighting as a nisei bokushi. For nine hundred quid a week, maybe more.

If what Shinichi said was true, then Carl was making more money than I was as an English teacher working full time. Carl, with no higher qualifications beyond high school, and no knowledge of Japan. I seethed.

"Wait a minute," I spluttered. "Carl's not allowed to work. He's over here on a three-month tourist visa."

"Not according to Shiori. He switched to a working holiday visa a few months ago. They're planning to get married in November, to celebrate their twin girls' first birthdays."

Carl. Getting married in November.

November. When his daughters would turn one.

November. My second year anniversary in Japan.

What had I achieved during my time in Japan? I had broken up with a racist, verbally abusive cheater that was Carl, only to get raped by a sleazy, predatory scumbag that was Vince, then had broken up with a kind, sweet man that was Naoki, only to get involved with a sleazy, manipulative liar that was Shinichi. What had Carl achieved during his time in Japan? He had got another woman pregnant behind my back, and now was planning to marry her and play happy family with their twin girls.

My stomach bottomed out. Shinichi's words floated in my ear and sank down through my hollowed-out insides.

My abusive, controlling ex Carl was doing better at life than me. He had gotten his shit together more than I had.

I shook my head, like a mutt shaking water off its shaggy fur. I wanted to slap my cheeks, but it wasn't the time for self-denigration; I needed to get my own shit together too, before my shit got the better of me.

Chapter forty-five

Wabi-sabi brain

What on earth was I doing?

I felt I was on a slippery slope over a rocky crevasse, leading to certain doom. There we were, the five of us: Sasha, Ronnie, Aaron, Shinichi and I, sitting in a booth in Bar Nightfall. Shinichi sat between me and Sasha with his arms spread along the backrests, so that if he wanted to, he could have draped his arms over each of us. From the sleazy glint in his eye at Sasha's legs in her short-shorts, I could tell he would have *loved* to do that.

Sitting in Shinichi's bar made me feel dirty, like I was cheating on Naoki. In a way I was; he was slaving away in Yasuda Ramen, and trusting that I was taking my Londoner friends on an innocent walking tour of Tottori. Instead, we were drinking shots of Shinichi's own family shochu, brewed by his grandfather who lived in Iwami. Or so he said.

The shochu was certainly going straight to my head.

"Tell me again, Kimberly, why *did* you break up with this fine specimen?" Sasha put on her most sultry voice, and I noticed that she leaned closer to Shinichi as she said it, sweeping her seductive hazel eyes over his taut form.

Sheesh. I was going to kill Sasha for that – if I didn't die of embarrassment first.

"I wasn't very good for her," Shinichi replied. He moved his arm from behind me and dropped his elbow on the table, curving his body towards my bestie and freezing me out. Shinichi on the pull. I rolled my eyes. *So* predictable.

"I told you when we face-timed. He cheated on me with my flatmate Victoria, remember?" I added.

Aaron cut in. "Don't forget plastering your tits all over Tottori. You never *did* show us those Fresh Fridays posters."

"And I never will!" I jabbed Shinichi in the shoulder with a finger. "And you better not show them either."

Shinichi leaned back again, arm resuming its position behind me. "I stand by what I said, you looked hot in that Geisha get-up. But anyway, she's seeing Mr. Straight-laced now, she doesn't need a bad-boy like me."

"*I'm* free, though," Sasha purred.

Oh – my – days! If ever I wanted to *proper* smack Sasha, it was for flirting so brazenly with my, admittedly sexy, ex.

Poor Naoki. He deserved better than that. I swigged the last of my shochu, winced, slammed the shot glad down and stood up. "Thanks for the hospitality, Shinichi, but we have to go. So much to do, so little time."

He grabbed my sleeve. "Wait."

The Wabi-sabi Doll

I sat down like a sack of potatoes, purposely jutting my chin out in what I hoped was a disdainful manner.

"A few weeks ago, I was visited by a beautiful apparition in white. A ghostly lady with silvery hair, pale skin and a startling white kimono came into this very bar and asked me, did I think she was beautiful." The hint of a smirk started at the corners of his mouth.

I kept straight-faced. "Oh? And what?"

I could see the delighted faces of my friends, grinning at the free entertainment.

"It was you, wasn't it?" Shinichi went on.

I glared at him. "What makes you think that? Are you saying I'm an apparition, like the slit-mouthed woman?"

Shinichi licked his lips and continued. "At first I thought I was seeing a ghost. It was nearly Obon, after all. But then when I was sober the next day, I thought to myself, that ghost looked rather like Kimberly. Like Kimberly, only whiter."

Talcum powder. I tried not to laugh.

He leaned back, one elbow on the table to feign nonchalance. "You played a trick on me, you sly little minx. Why?"

The jig was up. "Why not? You deserved it for all you did to me – and to Victoria."

"I'm impressed. I didn't think you had it in you." He surveyed me with a lustful smile; one that was borne of his admiration at my trick, rather than desire to have our relationship back. After a pause, contemplating what I had said, he went on. "Though I don't know what you mean about Victoria."

I gawped at him, not even needing to exaggerate my incredulous, open mouth. Was he for real?

"She told me about what you did – the sushi platter – the pole-dancing – and even what happened at the beach."

Shinichi's smug grin, which had remained in place at mention of the sushi and pole-dancing, crumpled into a frown of confusion. "What about the beach?"

"Do I need to spell it out?" I glowered.

He blinked at me. "What did she say happened at the beach?"

"You – and her – in the water. She said you asked her to do something sexual to you in the sea and then you held her head underwater so that she nearly drowned – and all the while you even had a friend in a grey van film all of that."

Shinichi's narrow eyes were as wide as I had ever seen them.

"Are you saying it didn't happen like that?"

"It didn't happen at all. The only time I've done anything at the beach was with you—" He paused as my friends exchanged sly grins. "Not with Victoria. We did it in other places, like at the top of Kyushu Mountain, but we never did it at the beach."

I searched his face, ignoring the secretive glances between Ronnie, Aaron and Sasha. He was telling the truth.

"What about the other stuff then? Tricking her into doing a naked sushi job, and pole dancing at this very bar." I pointed to the metal pole that extended between the bar counter and ceiling at the left side.

Shinichi's grin returned, confirming his answer. "Yeah, that stuff happened, but she was up for it. She loved the attention she got when she swung round the pole and as for the *nyotaimori*, I told her what the job would be, and she said she would do it but only for *ichi man en* above the asking salary."

Hmm. I studied his face. His handsome face. His attractiveness worked, somehow, to focus my mind, to remind me that he was a master manipulator. I couldn't let him warp my head into thinking that he was innocent and Victoria was a liar.

"Why would Victoria say you sexually assaulted her if you didn't do it?" I said.

His face stayed neutral. "I don't know. Maybe you should ask *her*."

I ignored him and went on. "Because it seems like a strange thing to make up about someone – especially if it didn't happen."

Shinichi shrugged. "Victoria didn't even want to go to the beach. She hated the beach."

What a pathetic excuse. I wasn't buying it. Shinichi had to be lying; after all, this was the man who had cheated on me with multiple women, lied to me during an ultrasound leading me to suffer a phantom pregnancy, and now expected me to believe my ex-roommate would fabricate a sexual assault.

He sniffed. "If you don't believe me, I'll show you."

He scrolled through his phone, then handed it to me. I looked at the screen, showing text messages. A thumbnail of Victoria appeared beside each of her messages.

Victoria: *Thanks for understanding. I need more time before I can go near a beach again after what happened.*

Shinichi: *It's OK. I'm here for you.*

Victoria: *You're the best. At least I know I'm in good hands. And I'm in Japan, not home!*

I looked up at Shinichi, confused. "This doesn't explain anything."

He jabbed a finger at her message mentioning the beach. "She told me something bad happened to her at a beach back where she's from in Canada. She wouldn't say what, but it was why she refused to go with me for a beach barbecue at Karo beach."

My head swirled in a cloud of thought. Who was lying: Shinichi, or Victoria? Was Shinichi akin to rapist Vince? Or was Victoria making dangerous false accusations against a sleazy, but innocent man? Yes, Shinichi was a cheater, and sleazy too, pushing the boundaries of consent; like tricking me into posing topless for photos which then appeared on posters. But sleazy was different from being a sexual predator. Had he sexually assaulted Victoria, or had she lied to me? Had she fabricated a story, which had changed the narrative about Shinichi in my own mind?

I stood up, slower this time and with less lustre. "I gotta go. Thanks for the shochu – and for letting me see those...messages."

Not that the messages were unequivocal, of course. I had much to reflect on.

I turned and walked out of Shinichi's bar, without saying a further word. The rustle of clothing and clatter of footsteps announced that my friends were following me. Their visit came at a good time; the perfect time. Whether the liar was Shinichi, or Victoria, someone had betrayed me, so I needed people I could trust more than ever. How would I disentangle the knots of thought and emotion in my head? I felt exhausted. Tired and fed up with all the players in a rigged game who had deceived me, and manipulated me, for reasons that remained inexplicable.

Wabi-sabi brain. Was Voyce school a cesspit of gaijin who came to Japan because they had to escape their lives? Vince… Victoria. Hmm. Maybe it was just the teachers whose names started with V. Either way, my colleague relationships – both romantic and platonic – were dysfunctional.

I had much to ponder. Wabi-sabi; life was constantly changing. Moments were fleeting and full of imperfections. I needed to accept the life I had created for myself in Tottori, keeping mindful of all its flaws, for it was the only way I would be able to achieve contentment with how things were, rather than striving for unattainable perfection.

Chapter forty-six

Outside perspective

"Can we *not* do this right now? I mean, can we talk about this later?"

Naoki sat, stony-faced at my dining room table, his arms folded across his chest like a huffy child.

Seemed he wasn't going to say anything, which left it up to me to try and keep the discourse going. "My friends feel so awkward listening to us that they went outside."

"Your friends didn't even try to stop you from going to *his* bar. That man is trouble, Kimberly. I tried to tell you that before. Mitsuko tried to tell you that too."

I sighed. "You know, Shinichi isn't perfect, but I can't help but think he's getting blamed for a lot of bad things lately – and I don't think he deserves all of it, to be fair."

The Wabi-sabi Doll

Naoki shot me a stern look. "He associates with Yakuza. I'd be surprised if he didn't have a tattoo himself."

"Well, he doesn't," I retorted. "I would know."

I had spent the morning coming clean to my boyfriend about all of it: dressing like a creepy, white phantom in a kimono to frighten Shinichi, taking my friends to Café Throwback, followed by attending the wedding where Carl was acting as a fake priest, and then drinking Shinichi's family shochu at his snack bar. I had expected understanding from Naoki; not hostility. He was normally so sweet and placid. The change in his demeanour was alarming.

"You have nothing to be jealous of," I added.

He glared at me. "Is that really what you think?"

"Well, is it that you don't trust me then?"

He shook his head; not to refute what I was saying, but a shake of incredulity at my assumptions.

"You drank his unlabelled shochu, in his bar, and believed his version of events instead of your coworker Victoria," Naoki said, his voice raised.

"He was telling the truth," I cut in.

"He's not to be trusted," he shouted.

"So you keep saying," I huffed, folding my arms and turning my head away.

Naoki gawped at me. "I don't know how you can prove that he was telling the truth anyway. Have you even spoken to Victoria?"

"I've been off on my annual leave, so – *no*," I said, mustering as much sarcasm as I could.

It wasn't the first fight that Naoki and I'd had, but it was one of the ugliest. I dropped my arms. "Look, I don't want Shinichi to come between us."

"Too late for that." Naoki stood up, sending the dining room chair skidding backwards. "I have to go. Dad needs me at the restaurant as Mitsuko can't work tonight."

He turned, without trying to offer a kiss, and left the room. I heard him fumbling with his shoes at the door, then muffled voices as he chatted to my friends outside, before the conversation outside stopped. The momentary silence in my apartment was deafening, as it allowed my brain to scream inwardly to itself.

Aaron came in first. "He didn't take that too well, did he, hun?"

I welcomed the hug from him. Aaron cradled my head in the crook of his arm and kissed my forehead.

"We didn't try to stop him leaving," Ronnie said, hands up. "We're staying out of it."

"That's probably for the best. His mind is made up about things anyway," I said, with a shrug.

"But is yours?" Ronnie added.

I paused. *Was* my mind made up?

"I don't think so. A lot will be decided when I go back to work and hear Victoria's version of events."

Sasha contemplated me with narrowed eyes, a look I knew only too well that meant she was concocting a plan.

"Do you love Naoki?" she blurted out.

I pursed my lips. "What's that supposed to mean? Of course I do."

"Of course you do, or you *think* you do?"

Why did my friends' eyes feel like spotlights on my soul? "He's kind, and caring – and gorgeous too. He's a good man. What's not to love?"

The Wabi-sabi Doll

"But he spends more time at his restaurant than with you, and look how long it took for him to introduce you to his parents," said Ronnie.

I hadn't told them the drama about Mitsuko's husband's family and the private investigator; it was too personal. It made sense that Naoki's parents were cagey about any potential love interest after that. But how could I tell that to my friends without telling the Yasuda family secrets?

"Naoki's going to be running the restaurant when his parents retire so he has to work long hours there. It doesn't mean he doesn't love me."

Sasha grabbed my hands. "You know we think Naoki is a great guy – and you two are so cute together. But it's our job to protect you from more heartache, especially after that bastard, Carl."

"What are you saying?"

She pressed her lips together in a way that I knew meant she was preparing for a serious topic. "If the choice came between you and the restaurant, what do you think Naoki would pick?"

I scoffed. "What do you *think* he would pick? The same that Shinichi would pick. They both run restaurants. If love got in the way of business, and you were a business owner, what would *you* pick?"

I expected Sasha to tell me I'd got her there, but she didn't. "You didn't answer my question. I'm not letting you off the hook that easily."

I turned away from her, like a stubborn toddler. "It's a stupid question. It doesn't make me think less of Naoki's character. You're being a bit too overprotective. He's not a bad guy."

"I didn't say he was a bad guy. He cares about you a lot and he treats you well. But come on, hun, you're my bestie. What about all those drunken voice notes you left me in, like, January and February just before you two broke up? That he wasn't there for you when you needed him emotionally because he was at his family's restaurant all the time?"

I huffed. "So you're saying Shinichi is better – a man who cheated on me and used my topless photos without consent?"

She rolled her eyes. "Oh my days, Kimberly, you can be so *dense* sometimes! Of course not. Both of them are hot, but neither of them is *The One*."

Aaron and Ronnie nodded in agreement. "You sly bastards have been talking about this behind my back?"

Three nods of unison confirmed what I thought.

The One.

Was I looking for The One, that unicorn in the stars, a soulmate? Did such a thing even exist? Truth be told, I had thought ahead enough to imagine how things would look, long-term, with Naoki. I had ventured a fleeting long-term view with Shinichi too, when I thought I was pregnant with his child, Kami, imagining our life together as a trio. But marriage?

Carl and Shiori were planning to get married.

Hmm. My friends gave me an outside perspective, daring to encroach on areas I hadn't considered. What would happen if I pushed forward, with baby steps of course, and considered asking Naoki to move in with me. Would he do it? It would show he was committed – and prove to myself that I was committed too. I could use myself as a guinea pig to see if Naoki really was The One – and prove my friends wrong.

A challenge. Yes, I was up for a challenge. But, just to rule out any other possibilities, any room for doubt in my heart, I had other business to contend with too

— Victoria. If Shinichi was lying, then I could rule out that *tiny* little part of my heart that reserved a space for him. If Victoria was lying, then I would press ahead with Naoki, taking our relationship up to the next level, without any interference.

Chapter forty-seven

V for vindictive

"It's on me."

I pushed the slice of strawberry cream cake towards Victoria with a smile. It was in my best interests to sweeten her up, so that she would give me the information I was looking for: that Shinichi was lying.

Yes. That was the answer I was looking for. The answer I was sure I would get, so that I could shut down that *particular* sneaky little avenue that my heart was trying to trick me with: Shinichi. Then, my heart would be entirely free for Naoki.

"Wowee zowee, you didn't have to," she answered, sugary-sweet.

Could sugary-sweet Victoria have a bitter aftertaste? I studied her cheerleader perfection as she sat opposite me, but couldn't imagine her lying about something as serious as sexual assault. Then again, she had been the

The Wabi-sabi Doll

reason why my then-boyfriend had cheated on me. *That* certainly wasn't so sugary-sweet.

"I wanted to check how you are. How things have been."

Did a faint blush appear on her cheeks? It wasn't a particularly leading question. I was deliberately trying to start casual and see if she would volunteer information without me having to be more direct.

"Aww, you know. Same old." Was it just me, or did her shrug seem more pronounced than her offhanded manner would imply? A little bit too tight, with shoulders bunching close to her ears.

Sheesh, she wasn't making it easy; like pulling teeth in fact. "Are you enjoying having the flat to yourself?"

"Oh, I'm not alone. My boyfriend stays over."

My mind worked quickly. "I'm glad you've found someone new – and better than Shinichi. You know, I bumped into him recently."

Her sugary smile faltered and her gaze dropped to the cake, which she munched without looking at me. "Oh? What did he say?"

"Well, I hope you don't mind, but I wanted to grill him about what he did to you – you know – to make him sweat a bit, for what he put you through. Just to let him know that I knew what happened."

Victoria licked cream off her lips without looking up, keeping her head lowered over the dessert.

I continued. "You won't believe what he said. Can you imagine the creep said it didn't happen?"

There was a splodge of cream at the corner of Victoria's mouth. Her tongue darted out and it disappeared. A small, pointed, pink tongue. A tongue that was capable of telling lies? A tongue that darted out like a viper's, for the purposes of causing harm.

V for viper.

I tucked my hair behind my ear. "Like really, can you imagine the gall of him to lie about something so serious? He was suggesting you made that up, right?"

Patchy redness broke out across Victoria's forehead and across the bridge of her nose; crimson, like the sky before a thunderstorm.

"I mean, it *did* happen, didn't it?" I went on.

She finally looked up, fixing me with an unblinking stare. Wasn't that something that liars did when they were trying to convince someone that they were telling the truth?

"Yeah, *sure* it happened."

Without her mega-watt smile, Victoria's mouth turned down naturally at the corners, giving her a rather sour look that I hadn't noticed before.

"At the beach, here in Tottori?" I prompted.

The patchy redness on her cheeks and forehead became a speckled haze, like a sunset.

She forced a wide grin, her eyes crinkling to slits. "Why's Shinichi trying to stir up trouble? I mean, like, the guy was so horrible to both of us."

I kept pressing. "It's quite simple, really, did it happen, or not?"

Victoria made an exaggerated huff. "Why are you grilling me, I mean, I already told you."

"I'm not grilling you, I'm just asking a basic question. If you already told me, then why can't you say it again?"

"Because I shouldn't have to." Her retort was quick, her blotchy face crumpled in outrage. "I told you some deeply personal stuff, and now you're making me relive some of that trauma, just because you don't believe me?"

Momentary guilt swamped me, before I mentally shook myself to my senses. She was laying it on thick. Was she being defensive to cover her tracks, or evasive because she was genuinely upset?

All of my clinical psychology training told me that she was covering her tracks. I had to keep pressing to get to the truth.

Time to get direct. "You told me a very serious accusation against Shinichi, that he forced you to suck him off in the sea while he held your head under water and you nearly drowned. Did that, or did it not, happen?"

She tilted her chin upwards, so that she was looking at me down her nose. "Not exactly."

I felt my forehead tighten. "What does that mean? It either happened or it didn't?"

"It *did* happen, just not here in Japan." Victoria gave a small toss of her head, making her blonde curls dance like Medusa's snakes.

"So, how could it have happened outside of Japan? With Shinichi?"

She hunched forward, putting a dramatic hand against her brow. "*Alright*, so I got confused. I was upset that day at work when I was telling you what happened. I might have mixed up my facts a bit."

"What are you saying? Did Shinichi force you to suck him off underwater, and almost drown you, while his friend was watching – or not?"

She flicked her head left, then right, casting a surreptitious glance over each shoulder for any eavesdroppers. "No. It was my ex, Mike, who did that to me back in Vancouver. It's part of the reason why I decided to come to Japan."

Ah-ha. Another broken person escaping her hometown. I was right. V for vindicated.

I sat back in my chair, resting my hands with fingers interlaced in my lap, like a detective. "Why did you blame it on Shinichi then?"

She twitched her nose, a momentary hesitation, that I guessed was to buy her some time. "Maybe he reminded me of Mike a bit. You know, all looks and charm. Maybe I thought he deserved it."

"What, a false accusation of sexual assault? You thought he deserved that?"

Her eyes bulged, in outrage. "I didn't do any harm. It's not like I went running to the police. I only told you."

"You did a *lot* of harm! You accused an innocent man of a horrible crime. It totally influenced what I thought of him – and how I treated him – after. Come on, Shinichi is a cheating bastard, and he's sleazy, but he isn't a sexual predator."

Victoria pressed her eyes shut in an exaggerated blink. She didn't look proud of herself; nor did she look remorseful. Her face was blank, with an edge of hardness around her jaw.

"Can I at least know why you lied to me?"

She pressed her lips together, her chin wrinkling. "I caught him coming out of the apartment of the woman living downstairs, so I dumped his ass. Maybe I wanted to get back at him for cheating on me. I didn't think there'd be any chance of you ever getting back with him if you thought he was *that* kind of man."

V for vindictive Victoria, from Vancouver.

My own slice of strawberry cream cake remained uneaten on the table in front of me. My unfocused gaze rested on it as my mind whirled. I stood up. "I feel sorry for whoever you're seeing now. He could do better. And by the way, I take it back. The cake is definitely *not* on me."

Chapter forty-eight

Whirlwind

Back to work while Sasha, Ronnie and Aaron visited Okayama and Himeji, and then we would be taking the *shinkansen* bullet train east towards Tokyo. I distracted myself, thinking of soon-to-be adventures with my friends, to get me through my first shift back at Voyce after my café bust-up with V for vindictive Victoria.

Work + Victoria = Disaster

Work + Ben + Victoria = ?

Hmm. Ben wasn't always there. He had recently been promoted and now managed both the Tottori and Misasa Voyce schools and tended to split his time between them. All I could do was keep my fingers crossed and hope he was there before the vindictive bitch arrived on shift. Or else things might get ugly.

Could I be professional? I wasn't sure; not after what she had told me.

The Wabi-sabi Doll

As I approached the front desk, Ben's bald head showed above the computer screen at reception. Thank goodness; I was saved.

"Ben, can I have a minute, please?"

He looked up from the computer, and after a second's hesitation, a reluctant smile materialised. Odd. Ben was usually so friendly and approachable. Maybe he was overworked.

We walked into the only private place there was; the stationery room behind the quasi-public staffroom.

"What's up, Kimberly?" he said, his voice still cool and professional.

Very odd. Had Victoria already spoken to him? She *could* have, since her shift had started at nine o'clock, whereas I was on a late shift starting at one in the afternoon. Would she have gone running to the boss about something so private, though; especially when she was the one in the wrong?

"It's about a personal matter."

"Is it about you moving into your own flat?"

Good guess. "Kind of. It's related to that. Actually, yeah. It's about Victoria."

"I know she started seeing your ex-boyfriend and that caused conflict, which is why you moved out." Ben peered at me over the tops of his glasses, giving his expression a judgemental aspect.

"How did you know?"

"Because Zoe got into a fight with her last week while you were off on your annual leave, and I had to tell both of them to cool it."

Zoe. I owed her one. It was lovely to hear of her loyalty to me against my treacherous ex-flatmate. Still…

"Wait, Shinichi wasn't my ex at the time, I was still seeing him. Is that what Victoria said?"

Ben jerked his head backward, in a sudden, birdlike manner. "That's odd. Victoria made out like you guys had broken up when she started going out with him."

The *audacity* of that girl. "No, he was my boyfriend and Victoria slept with him behind my back. I wanted to talk to you because I found out yesterday that Victoria was lying to me about more personal stuff to do with Shinichi, and the thing is, I don't know if I'll be able to work with her anymore after what she's done. I can't trust her."

Ben pressed his lips into a smile that looked to me more mocking than appeasing. "Lying is a strong word, is it not? Go easy on her. She's been through a lot."

I snorted. "And I haven't?"

His nostrils flared as he sucked in a deep breath. "I know what you went through last year with Vince. You know I helped to get him transferred after what he did."

Blood rushed to my brain. "Then I don't understand why you're siding with Victoria now. She accused Shinichi of something like what Vince did to me, and it was a lie. So, when I say that I'm not sure how I can work with her after that, and that my trust in her is broken, I thought you would be a bit more sympathetic, at least."

Ben wiped his forehead with his thumb and forefinger. "Listen, I don't know exactly what has been going on, or what she told you. But, like I said, I was able to transfer Vince to Osaka easily enough last year. I'm the joint manager of this branch and another school in Misasa. It's a lovely town with hotsprings. Very relaxing."

The Wabi-sabi Doll

I opened my mouth to talk, then shut it, as the words wouldn't come out. Was Ben suggesting that I was the one who should transfer, not Victoria?

"Are you saying you want *me* to go? I've been here for nearly two years. I'm settled in Tottori. This is my home from home. Victoria has barely been here for five months. And what's with the patronising tone about Misasa being 'very relaxing'? I'm not a mental patient."

Ben put both hands up. "Woah there, now, I *did not* imply that, let's be clear."

Our chat was done; Ben had clearly picked a side. What was so appealing about Victoria? Sure, she had 'cheerleader' charm, but I thought a family man like Ben would have been above such rudimentary lust.

I turned and pushed the stationery room door open. I didn't want to make any rash decision, but Ben was making things very difficult.

Nah, fuck it.

I spun back around on my heel, and paused halfway through the door. "You know, you used to be so supportive. You used to be the kind of boss who understood things, someone I could have spoken to about anything. I don't know what has changed. Don't worry about transferring me. I don't want to work here, or for any other school that you are in charge of. I'm going to do my shift today because I care about the students – not to make your life easier – but after that, I'll be taking the rest of my annual leave, and then unpaid leave for the rest of my one month's notice."

His eyes were marbles. "What're you saying, Kimberly?"

"I'm saying, I'm handing in my resignation. I quit."

Chapter forty-nine

The fiasco of Fresh Fridays

My first lesson of my final shift at Voyce school was not going to plan.

"Kimberly. There are some posters. Is it you in them?"

Very not to plan.

Forty minutes. Forty of the longest minutes of my life. The longest lesson for my soul.

How could I command enough teacher-student respect to lead a Business English class with four professionally dressed men and women, all peering at me expectantly, awaiting an answer? I probably didn't even have to speak. The heat in my face said it all.

How did they know? The Fresh Fridays posters had appeared in clubs and bars in Tottori *months* ago.

My frazzled brain, already pushed to the edge with fallout from my disastrous fling with Shinichi, fought

The Wabi-sabi Doll

to fabricate a response. I tucked my hair behind my ear, getting myself battle-ready.

"I don't know what posters you're talking about."

Four pairs of scrutinising eyes stared, unblinking in their assessment of me. To my right sat the speaker, a young woman in a black business suit, who contemplated me over her textbook. Next to her, a thirty-something man watched me with a steely gaze behind his glasses. To my left, an older man in a grey business suit gave out equally grey judgement in his gaze. Beside him, a fortyish woman wearing a pinafore dress stared at me with a no-nonsense disposition.

"There are posters in the corridor going into the toilets. Geisha gaijin presents Fresh Fridays." Was there judgement in the young woman, Tomoka's voice, or simply my imagination?

I could feel my blood freezing as though liquid nitrogen had been poured over my head. Time to play dumb. "What toilets? Here at Voyce?"

A succession of tacit nods.

Thirty-nine minutes.

I had to keep playing dumb. "I don't know about any posters, and it doesn't interest me either."

"The thing is, she looks like you. The girl in the posters. She wears a black wig like a Maiko, but she looks like you," Kenji, the thirty-something businessman, explained.

Ugh! Time for a sharp tone, and my best poker face. "Well, it *isn't* me. I'd really like to get our lesson started now."

I allowed my fingers to lead me, aimlessly, back and forth through the pages of my teacher copy of the Business English textbook.

This was torture.

What page was the lesson I had planned for today? Thirty-eight minutes.

My students had no respect for me. They were watching me, reassessing their view of me. If they respected me, they wouldn't have pinned me to the spot, demanding answers about whether it was me who appeared in the Fresh Friday posters.

Finally, oxygen seemed to have reached my brain, for the culprit popped to mind. This was Victoria's doing. It had to be.

"If it is you, then you look good as a *maiko*," said Tomoka.

Enough. It was as much as I could tolerate.

Without a word, I stood up and marched out of the classroom, leaving my four bewildered adult students reeling, surprise written all over their faces. Victoria had pushed me too far this time.

My feet slapped along the corridor between the eight classrooms and out into the foyer beside reception. I turned left towards the toilets and witnessed an assault on my eyeballs. No less than ten Fresh Fridays posters had been taped up in a row along the corridor leading into the toilets.

This was, by far, the worst humiliation I had endured in any job I had ever worked in. How long had the posters been up? More to the point, why was Victoria so vindictive?

I snatched each poster off the wall and crumpled them, one by one, in my fist. Huffing, I then turned and strode back to the classrooms.

Victoria was teaching a lesson in classroom two. I was about to teach her a lesson of a different nature.

The Wabi-sabi Doll

I pushed the door open with force, causing it to rebound on its hinges, and brandished the crumpled posters in my fist. "What's the meaning of this?"

Victoria's professional smile melted into one of amusement as her eyes rested on the crumpled posters. "I don't know. I've been teaching all morning."

"Why would you do this? Is it because I spoke to Ben?"

She continued to smile, giving a look like butter wouldn't melt in her mouth. Such a cow, giving me cow eyes, the picture of innocence in front of the students. I could see through her lies. She made me *seethe* with anger. She made me see *red*.

"I'm afraid I really don't know what you're talking about," she continued, in a tone that could barely conceal her enjoyment of torturing me.

"I don't know what your game is, or why you would want to hurt me like this." I thrust the crumpled posters under her nose at the word 'hurt'. "But you have serious problems. Go see a psychiatrist, you'll be doing everyone a favour."

Enough was enough. Despite wanting to stay to the end of my final shift, it was clear I wouldn't last the duration of my first lesson. Twenty minutes left of the forty-minute class, but the curtain had fallen on my time at Voyce.

I went back to classroom seven. My bewildered students peered out the door, listening to the discourse between Victoria and me. "I'm really sorry. Something has come up and I have to go. Please feel free to go and see Akemi at reception to get a refund for your lesson."

Freedom. My career as an English teacher had lasted almost two years, and now it was over. I was no longer Kimberly the Voyce school teacher. Now I was Kimberly the jobless. No confinement, no borders, formless, boundless and free to take a leap into the unknown. One thing I knew for sure was that for every door that closed, another one would surely open. I closed the door to the staffroom at Voyce school for the final time, descended the escalator and stepped out into the afternoon sun to phone my friends.

For the first time in a long time my heart felt lighter.

There was no void in my chest, no hole in my soul. The air of adventure filled my body, and I let excitement lead me onwards.

Chapter fifty

Out with the old

The sunset over the Sea of Japan was stunning. It skimmed the horizon, an orange ball, casting a serene yellow haze across the blue sky. Such a moment was so beautiful that it should have been profound, but my mind halted, as though time had stopped. I couldn't even evoke any philosophical musings; I sat merely in the moment.

Yes, this was what it was all about. This was why I was in Japan. For moments like watching the sun setting over Tottori.

"What are you doing there, hun, sitting like a sad-sack? It's your *Leaving Party*, come and dance!" Sasha grabbed both of my hands and pulled me up off the sand. It had been their idea – Sasha, Ronnie and Aaron – to contact my favourite students and organise a *Farewell to Voyce* party. Of my colleagues, only Zoe was invited. Not Ben, and certainly not Victoria.

My friends really brought out the best in me. They fought the part of me that was self-defeating and helped me to have my best interests in mind. After walking off the job earlier in the day, instead of hanging my head in defeat over my disastrous last shift, I was able to raise my chin and socialise with my friends – and friendly students – with pride.

We had spread several picnic blankets on San-in beach, a curved bay with sandy shore, surrounded by tree covered hills. Located further west along the coastline from Karo beach, it gave us the seclusion I craved after work-burnout. We had brought bento boxes from a convenience store, along with snacks and beer. One of my students had brought bongo drums. I found the rhythm soothing, alongside the ebb and flow of the waves. Only one person that I had invited was yet to come: Naoki.

I was about to text him, when I saw him strolling across the sand from the direction of the car park. He wore a Hawaiian style shirt and beige slacks, his hands slung in his pockets. His sandals kicked up sand behind him, a shower of fine grains like confetti in his wake. A slow smile spread across my face as he neared. It was a relief to see him, one less thing for my mind to worry about, after Victoria and the death of Voyce.

"Hey." His voice was casual, with an edge of weariness. "I got your text. Did you really quit your job?"

I handed Naoki a beer and took a swig of my own. "Sure did. Best thing I've done in ages. Apart from getting back with you. That was the best thing I've done all year."

His mouth twitched into a smile, but it seemed forced. "It's too bad that Shinichi was the reason why your career as an English teacher had to come to an end."

"It *wasn't* because of him. It was because of Victoria." Was my rebuttal a bit too quick, and too defensive? Maybe, but all that mattered was that he forgave me. I hooked my arm through his elbow. "Let's go for a walk and I'll fill you in on everything."

We left the party and walked parallel to the water's edge along the beach. My flipflops dangled between us, held in the hand that was hooked through Naoki's arm, while I supped from my beer bottle with the other. The cool waves felt refreshing as they lapped around my ankles, and I imagined them reaching my head, massaging my mind. Ebb and flow, crest and trough; catharsis.

I was centred, I was safe. No worries about how quickly my savings would run out without a job. I was happy in the moment, back with Naoki.

He was silent for a few minutes after I finished talking. He looked upwards as a seabird swooped overhead, his eyes following it until it disappeared inland.

"What are you going to do for your last three months in Japan? How will you pay the rent on your apartment?" he said, as though reading my thoughts.

A fair question. "How about if I was to help you at Yasuda Ramen? I could be a waitress."

He inhaled, long and slow. "We talked about this before, though Kimberly. You don't know enough Japanese."

"Would I really need to speak a lot of Japanese? I mean, how much would I need to say to bring bowls of noodle soup out to customers?"

He hesitated. "I'm really surprised you quit because of Victoria. Couldn't you have asked Ben to put you on different shifts than her?"

"He took her side, that was the problem. I can't work in a place if I don't trust a colleague – and don't have the support of my boss."

Naoki cast his eyes to the water as he waded, dragging his toes in the wet sand. "I'll speak to Mum and Dad and see what I can do. But it's not a promise, though."

I squeezed his arm. "Thanks, Naoki. I mean, I looked good in the Yasuda family happi at the Obon Matsuri after all, didn't I?"

He gave a closed-lip smile, and I seized the opportunity to land a quick peck on his lips. He placed his hands lightly on my hips and let me give him the kiss, though I noticed he didn't respond.

Hmm. Was he still mad at me for our argument about Shinichi in my flat? How would I get him to stop being such a cold fish? We had walked so far along the beach that the curve in the coastline concealed us from the party. A tree-covered rocky outcrop lay ahead. An idea popped to mind.

"You *know*," I made my voice sultry, "There are lots of secret little nooks along here, and we're alone, if you get what I mean?"

I dropped my sandals and beer and reached my arms around him, slipping my hands into the back pockets of his slacks and giving his ass a firm squeeze with both hands.

Naoki looked bashful. He squirmed out of my grip. "Not here, Kimberly. It's broad daylight."

"Not for long. The sun has already set."

The Wabi-sabi Doll

Nothing like make-up sex on the beach to heal a lover's tiff.

"Don't you *want* me?" I said, adding a dash of pleading to my voice. "I want *you*."

He looked left, then right, his eyes roving the beach, his face beetroot. "It's not the right place. Not now. I'm not in the mood."

"Then, why don't you let me *get* you in the mood." I unzipped his fly.

Naoki's brow dipped downwards. "Kimberly, stop. Are you crazy?" He stepped back, and half-turned away to zip up his fly.

"I just wanted to have some fun. Don't you want to live a little?"

Call it a moment of madness; a sudden thrill of excitement beset me and I pulled my t-shirt up over my head, and whipped off my bra. Naoki stared at my bare breasts for a second, as I tossed my top half onto the sand. Instead of arousal, I saw surprise and a note of panic cross his face.

"Someone will see you," he gasped.

"Nobody's about." I whipped down my trousers and stepped out of them in my thong.

His brow bunched upwards. "Would you do this in London?"

"Of course not. London isn't by the beach. But I did it in Southampton. Come *on*. Skinny dipping is fun. Don't you get a kick from doing something risqué?"

His upper lip twitched with disapproval. "No, I can't say that I do."

I turned and splashed into the sea. It was tepid in the growing twilight, but I enjoyed the sting on my bare thighs and stomach, and the tingle in my boobs; both from the coldness and excitement at getting caught.

After a lap one way and then the other, I decided to reign in my hedonistic urges, lest I push the spoilsport too far.

"That was amazing. So refreshing. You really should have joined me."

"I prefer swimming in a pool," he said, his voice flat.

Swimming in a pool, sex in the confines of the home. Where was the adventure in that? Such a stick in the mud. Silence fell between us as I pulled my clothes back on.

As we walked back to the rest of the party, I cast a sideways glance at Naoki. "I love you."

My intonation rose at the end; it was almost a question, almost a test. Did he still love me too? Would he reciprocate?

He sighed. "I love you too, Kimberly, you know that."

I gave him a playful nudge with my elbow. "Would you still love me just as much if you had to see me every day at work in your restaurant?"

The orange sunset reflected in his eyes as he turned to me, and I saw sadness in his gaze too. "Actually, I don't know if it would be the best idea for you to work at Yasuda Ramen. It's a bit too soon."

My lower lip quivered. "But – but then, what will I do?"

"How about, don't quit your job?" His abrupt tone caught me by surprise.

What was going on? Why was Naoki suddenly being so cold? "Are you still mad at me about going to Shinichi's bar? I don't still have feelings for him, if that's what you're thinking."

The Wabi-sabi Doll

"It's not that." He stopped walking and faced me. "You met up with him and went drinking. If you want to be friends with him, that's fine. This isn't about me being jealous. You know I love you, and trust you not to cheat. But–"

"But what, Naoki?"

"I don't think you make good decisions. If you were to work at my family restaurant, while you're associating with someone like Shinichi – dodgy, as you English would say – then that puts my family business and the reputation of Yasuda Ramen at stake."

"I'm not associating with him! We met as a one-off thing to settle the score about what Victoria had told me – which turned out to be lies," I argued.

He looked sad. "It doesn't matter if it's a one-off thing, or if you want to be his friend. You can do what you want, I'm not stopping you."

"Are you…" I paused. "Is this a break-up?"

He still looked sad, but there was a notch of defiance in his stare. "Do you want it to be?"

"Of course not. In fact, I was hoping for things to be more serious between us. You know, like, us moving in together."

"Your visa runs out in November, Kimberly, and it's August. You can't renew your visa if you aren't an English teacher anymore. So, how could we move in together if you have to leave?"

The truth of his words hit me. He was right. Technically, Voyce had sponsored my visa. Unlike a working holiday visa, where foreigners could come to Japan for six months and work in any jobs while travelling around, my work visa was a sponsored one for the company I was working at.

Unless, of course, I changed jobs, and my new job sponsored me. Naoki had made it clear that he didn't want to risk the reputation of his family business though.

I jutted my chin out at him. "That's fine. I'll get another job. I'm sure I can find something in three months."

"Maybe. It's a small place, Tottori. There aren't too many other English schools you could work at."

Hmph; quite the pessimist. "If I get another job, and can stay in Japan, would you move in with me then?"

Another sigh; more like a huff than a sigh. "I don't know. Honestly, I have a lot to think about. It's all a bit much too soon, Kimberly."

As we neared the party, Naoki began to veer off towards the car park, rather than keep parallel to the sea, wading in the water with me.

So that was that, I supposed. He wanted his space. I wasn't sure how long I could wait for him.

Chapter fifty-one

Payback

When life gives you lemons...

...You squirt the juice in the eyes of those who wrong you.

I scoffed to myself. What a cynical mood I was in. And why not? I had most certainly been wronged, and I was allowed to feel bitter. Feeling bitter was the first step to working through my feelings; to gaining closure, and then hopefully being able to move on with my life.

I was wrestling with the best way to pay Victoria back for the nasty stunt she had pulled by plastering the Fresh Fridays posters all over the Voyce toilet corridor. Not to mention being given the cold shoulder by my on-again, off-again boyfriend of the past ten months. Somehow I had ended up in a negative cycle, through no fault of my own. What better way to get myself out of a rut than by some payback.

Tomorrow, Sasha, Ronnie, Aaron and I would escape Tottori for adventures on the bullet train across Japan, in Tokyo. That made tonight the perfect time for vigilante justice.

My leaving party on San-in beach had ended a few hours ago, and in the moonlit early hours, after a few too many beers, I staggered out of the taxi at the bottom of the flight of stairs leading up to my former flat in Akisato. I held the crumpled Fresh Fridays posters in one hand as I stomped up the steps to Victoria's apartment, then squatted to shove them through the letterbox slot at the base of the door. If she was home, I was prepared to give her a piece of my mind. If she was out, then hopefully she'd slip on them when she got home and fall in the dark, preferably giving herself a big cut or bruise.

The bolt clicking to unlock startled me, and I stood as the door swung back. Instead of Victoria's confused face in the hallway, I was confronted with Ben's angry face.

"Ben! What're you doing here?"

His angry face transitioned to puzzlement before landing on fear. Two things were clear. First, he had been expecting someone else to be coming to the door. Second, considering how he was dressed I was the last person he wanted turning up at Victoria's flat. Or rather, his *lack* of dress. Ben was wearing a bath towel tied around his waist – and nothing else.

My eyes travelled up from the towel, over his protruding stomach and podgy chest to his rounded shoulders, which were covered in black hairs. Not a sight I ever wanted to see. I quickly tried to imagine my boss in his suit and tie at work; anything to get the nauseating image of his portly, semi-nude torso out of my tormented brain.

I averted my eyes. "I see. I understand perfectly now why you were on Victoria's side and wanted me to transfer to Misasa."

"Kimberly, it's not how it looks," he said, his hands outstretched in appeasement.

"Oh, I'm sure it's all perfectly innocent," I chortled, backing away more, lest his grubby paws should try their luck on me too. "Aren't you married?"

"I needed somewhere to stay in Tottori tonight, and Victoria was the only one who has a spare room at the moment."

I snorted. "A likely story. Where is she anyway? Don't tell me she isn't home."

"No, she's home. She's just chilling in the living room watching movies while I had a shower. It really *is* innocent – you caught me at the wrong moment, is all."

"Why can't you go to your own house? Or is it because you wanted to fuck Victoria first, and then go home to your wife?" I shouted.

My loud voice had done the trick. Victoria's blonde head appeared behind Ben. Her bewildered face studied the crumpled posters and then rose to glare at me.

"What do you want, K? Go home. You aren't welcome here."

"Alright, I get it. You've turned yourself into the Tottori town bike, it seems. First you fuck my boyfriend, and now the married boss. Who hasn't had a ride?"

An ear-splitting shriek deafened me and then next thing I knew, Victoria had me pinned against the stairway railing, both hands grabbing bunches of my hair. She let go of one handful of hair and started raining thumps on my cheek and temple with her free hand. I had no choice but to defend myself. Victoria was an inch shorter than me, but at least a stone heavier. Doing the only thing I could, I struck her on the chin with an uppercut and watched as blood glistened over her pearly whites.

Momentarily stunned, Victoria wiped her mouth with the back of her hand and when she saw the blood she gasped. "You bitch! I'll kill you!"

I struck her with a short jab, just a pop to her nose, my self-defence evening classes in London paying off. Her blonde curls bounced back as her head jerked backwards, creating space between us – which was promptly filled by Ben. He stretched both of his arms outwards, putting six feet of distance between Victoria and I.

"Ladies, please, come on. Can we be adult about this?"

"I'll kill you, you fucking whore," Victoria screamed, clawing the air in a desperate attempt to reach me.

"Alright, calm yourself, psycho bitch," I gasped.

Amidst the struggle, of Ben holding both of us back, his towel slipped revealing his nudity in the moonlight.

From the side of my eye, I could see my friends at the bottom of the stairs with their phones out, recording the commotion.

"Put those phones away, I mean it," Ben shouted. "You have no right recording this."

"It's a public place – you're outside," Ronnie laughed.

Ben snatched his towel back into place and held Victoria back with one arm wrapped around her in a bear hug, sticking his hand out like a traffic warden at me. "What is it you want, Kimberly? You quit, remember? If you want your job back, I can do that."

"As if I'd want to my job back with both of you still working there, don't make me laugh."

"Then what?" he shouted.

"Why were you so angry when you answered the door? Who were you expecting?"

"Shinichi, since you told that boyfriend of yours what Victoria said," Ben spat.

"He's not my boyfriend," I corrected. "Why would you care anyway, if you're only staying here as a place to crash, like you said?"

He blinked, hesitating, and said nothing.

"I thought so. I take it your wife doesn't know you're fucking that little tart. Where is Chiaki anyway?"

He blanched at mention of his wife's name. Probably didn't realise I had remembered what she was called. Of course I had. I had cared for Ben, a sort of big-brotherly affection, and had admired him for being a role model of what good men should be like, amidst my disastrous break-up with Carl the previous year, and sexual assault by Vince.

Hmph. Some role model. Were were all the good men in the world?

"We live in Misasa now, not Tottori," he said, his anger deflating. He had no fight left.

"Why would you cheat on Chiaki with *her*?" I pointed at Victoria. I wanted to add, *better get yourself checked for STIs*, but thought better of it; round one of her catfighting had been bad enough.

In the absence of Ben's anger, his voice was weak and flat. "If you don't want your job back, what *do* you want? You didn't come here just to shove all these posters through Victoria's letterbox, did you?"

"I did, but now, since all this has happened, I'll just add something else to my list. How about you give me my last three months of pay on top of my holiday pay," I said.

"Done," he said. "And your friends will delete the videos?"

"Once the money is in my account," I added.

He took a deep breath. "It'll be in your account in five business days."

"Good." I turned away. "Nice doing business with you."

Chapter fifty-two

Hostess

I leaned forward to offer a forkful of Victoria sponge to the drunk businessman who was laughing at all my terrible jokes. He clamped his sluglike lips around the morsel, slid the bite off the fork and made yummy noises while he chomped, giving me time to dust cake crumbs off my satin dress. Luckily no cream had smeared on the fabric; the dress was sentimental to me. A recent purchase, but an important one, nonetheless. I had bought the abstract print garment at a street stall in Korea, while mum, dad, Zac and I were on a weekend trip to Seoul, courtesy of my Voyce employee discount. Seeing my boss half-nude and cheating on his wife had its perks.

My family had gone back to London, and a new month had rolled in: October. Only two months left of my visa in Japan, and I intended to make the most of it.

Not that feeding cake to patrons of Bar Nightfall was what I wanted to do with my time, but working as a hostess in Shinichi's bar certainly paid more than teaching English, and I intended to go back to London in November with enough money to start my PhD in Clinical Psychology. As the sozzled businessman opened his gaping maw for another slice of cake, I ran through my mental checklist:

Get my PhD at UCL.

Set up my own practise as a qualified Clinical Psychologist.

Get a dog.

Hell, a dog seemed much more reliable than a man. All the affection and commitment with none of the blandness and abandonment, aka Naoki, or any of the sleaziness or cheating, aka Shinichi and Carl.

Speaking of sleaziness.

I leaned forward, allowing my ample cleavage to bulge over the top of the abstract-print dress. The businessman's eyes bulged in response, almost popping out of his ruddy face.

"Koibito imasu ka," the businessman slurred. Do you have a lover. Not *kareshi*, the word for boyfriend, but *koibito*, the word for lover.

My normal response would have been *kankei nai deshou*, none of your business, but he was a patron in Shinichi's bar that I was being paid to flirt with, and not a random stranger in a pub or club.

"Dou deshou," I purred, in my sexiest voice. *What do you think?*

Sheesh, it was hard to flirt with an aging businessman that I didn't find remotely attractive. I flicked my eyes across to Shinichi, gabbing away with

The Wabi-sabi Doll

the bartender, and tried to transplant his gorgeous face onto the man.

Did that mean I still had feelings for Shinichi?

The man puckered his sluglike lips, ready for a kiss.

Ugh! I was under no obligation to kiss any patrons; Shinichi had confirmed this himself. Instead, I offered another bite of cake.

"Karaoke wo shimashou ka." I grabbed his sweaty hand and pulled him up to sing karaoke. The man obliged me, curling his arm around my waist. Phew; saved for now.

Did I like being a hostess? If I was honest with myself, the validation was nice. Dressing in skimpy garments and having men fawn over me was an easy ego-boost that I didn't think I needed. Plus, I felt much more confident in my Japanese ability, since I could make small talk and be understood, which propelled my ego even further into stratospheric levels.

The rest of the night whittled away, and the customers with it. Shinichi cashed up the register while I kicked off my shoes and massaged my feet.

"Tired?" he said, with his usual sexy smirk.

"A bit. Why? Did you have something in mind?"

The sexy smirk twitched a fraction higher. "Not unless you do?"

Waves swept to mind, and sandy shores. Clothing stripped off, and inhibitions with it. Recent images of the same attempt with Naoki, diffused by frigid meanderings, dumped, right there on the beach.

I was single, wasn't I? What did I have to lose?

"Nothing like a midnight skinny dip to wash away a bit of tiredness, wouldn't you say?"

Both his eyebrows shot up in mock surprise. "You really want to strip naked with a scoundrel who splashed posters of your tits all over Tottori?"

I pulled myself into a pose of coy affectation, my pinky finger at the corner of my mouth. "I'm a naughty hostess now, not a respectable teacher anymore."

"Alright then, you're on." He gave a nod, and I jumped to my feet.

‌   ଓ

And just like that, quick as a flash, we drove to the beach and fucked on the shore. Me on top, friction burns on my knees from the coarse sand. Him behind me, doggy style, bending me over jutting rocks that cut small slices into my stomach and breasts. Hedonism and masochism, sending me spinning into a heatwave that I didn't think I had in me. Kimberly the sleaze, getting fucked, not by Mr. Right, but by Mr. Right Now.

He wasn't marriage material, but then again, neither was I.

Chapter fifty-three

Five years later

He wasn't marriage material, but then again, neither was I.

I stared down at the piece of paper in my hand. Two years of marriage had degenerated into a crumpled bill of divorce. I opened my fingers and watched it float, with only one measly spin, and land on the carpet at my feet.

Not to Shinichi. Not even to Naoki. My life in Japan was a distant memory, now half a decade old.

Divorced from my ex-husband, Chris. Oh well, at least I had the dogs. For now. No way I would let him take Millie, my sweet pug, and Minnie, my golden boxer, off me. The one thing we had managed to compromise on was that he could take half of the house, so long as he let me have our babies.

My babies.

Face it, they were the only babies I wanted or needed. My reluctance to try for a family in the first place was why Chris had left. He wanted human babies more than fur babies. To me, fur babies were the real deal. The only deal.

So much for getting it on with a patient. A mistake. I would never mix business with pleasure again.

Was that why business had taken a nosedive of late anyway? Had word got round among my clients that my husband, who had once been a client, was now my ex-husband? Didn't paint a very professional image of me, I supposed.

I sighed. Why was my life a mess?

Five years after my Zen retreat in Japan, time spent sorting out my head, going through Death-Cremation-Rebirth of my soul. Death: I had broken free of my dysfunctional relationship with Carl. Cremation: I had burned the names of toxic Carl, and rapist Vince, on Tottori beach. Rebirth: I had found a charred fragment of paper among the ashes that was shaped like a buddha, and kept it as my own 'Buddha's Bone' in a locket to remind me of my journey.

I twisted my head to the right, to look at the locket, which now hung around Akari's neck. The doll, with her perfect black hair, pristine red lips and immaculate stance gave me her usual benign smile as we locked eyes for the first time in several months. I needed her now.

"Water baby, you were the reason I was too afraid to try for a family. What if I had suffered another miscarriage? Wouldn't it have been easier for Chris to think that I *don't* want kids than for us to try and find out I *can't*? What if Carl cursed me that day, on Tottori beach, five years ago by calling me barren?"

The Wabi-sabi Doll

I swallowed a lump in my throat that became a mass in my chest.

What age would Carl's twin girls, Karen and Naomi be now? Five. A few months older than my Akari, had she lived.

Instead, I had my Akari doll. She would never die, and I would never get hurt, as a result.

Warm wetness on my left hand alerted me to Minnie, my beautiful boxer dog, licking my hand. A living, walking contradiction to my own thoughts. One day Minnie would die, and I would get hurt. The hurt might be comparable to losing a child. I had lost Akari, at almost twelve weeks of gestation. I had never lost a pet thus far, but Millie and Minnie were my children. I didn't want to think of what kind of pain that might bring.

Worrying about my ability to have children was a different kind of pain. Was it fear? Fear of the unknown, an untested hypothesis? Shinichi had caused me to have a phantom pregnancy; my eyes slid sideways to my perfect Kami doll. I had believed myself to be pregnant based on a falsehood. Maybe that had been when my desire to *really* have kids had died, and the fear had crept in.

Fear. What could I do to swamp the fear. I needed to fill my time, so that there wouldn't be static in my head; white noise. How to do that, though? I could go for a walk with Minnie and Millie along Southampton beach, a mere ten-minute stroll from the flat I was currently renting near my parents. Maybe, but I wasn't in the mood to talk to any of the neighbours, or locals for that matter.

Hmm.

Japan.

My mind drifted back to Tottori, and memories of two very life-defining years. I had stayed in touch with a few people on social media, but only enough to like posts from time to time. Zoe and Jei Pi shared photos from time to time. But what about—

Shinichi?

Naoki?

Shinichi. At least I had ended with him on amicable terms, unlike the last time I had seen Naoki on San-in beach, unwilling to risk his family reputation over my acquaintanceship with Shinichi. After a quick search, his profile appeared. Looked like he had changed his hair back to its natural black colour, though it was still closely cropped. Should I send him a friend request, connect with his 'private' profile?

My finger answered for me, with a quick tap.

After a few minutes — surprising, given the time difference between England and Japan — he accepted. My notification button lit up red a few minutes after that.

Hi was all it said, in a direct message.

Hey I typed back.

Hisashiburi, he wrote in romaji letters.

Yes, long time no see, I answered.

How's life in London?

Southampton, I clarified.

Back and forth, the three dots wriggled, as we took turns to talk. He was single again, after breaking up with his long-term girlfriend. Probably cheating on her, but I didn't text that. I told him I was divorced, and he told me it was Chris' loss. I didn't see it that way. Chris was a good guy. It simply wasn't meant to be.

What was meant to be? Me and Shinichi? Had fate made us single at the same time for a reason?

The Wabi-sabi Doll

Silly thoughts. He was Mr Wrong five years ago, and was still Mr Wrong.

What about other people we had known? I wanted to ask. It was as though he had read my thoughts:

Hey, you know what? Remember your ex, who had the two kids with Shiori?

My breath caught in my throat, my thumbs suspended above my phone before punching a reply.

Yeah, Carl? What about him?

Hopefully divorced too; the bastard didn't deserve a happy family.

He's the CEO of a school in Tottori called Natterbox. It's a rival school of that one you worked for, Voyce.

I stared at Shinichi's text, almost in disbelief at the words. What? How could Carl have worked his way up into such a position. To teach English in Japan required a degree; never mind to work as a CEO. Carl only had high school qualifications. How could my toxic ex-boyfriend, former janitor at Luton airport, and security man in the retail store where I had met him on Oxford Street, now be a successful CEO of an English language school? It beggared belief.

But he embezzled funds and now he's on the run in Thailand.

Hmm. That seemed more the calibre of a man like Carl. But still, it seemed unbelievable.

What about Shiori and the girls?

She's standing by him. Took the twins and they're all on the run together.

Imagine that. Carl, a scoundrel to the very end. After a minute, Shinichi sent a follow-up.

Just joking! He's doing bar work over at Club 365 but I heard he drinks too much on the job. Still married to Shiori.

That seemed more like the Carl I knew. I burst out laughing as I read the message.

What about Naoki? I wanted to ask, but wasn't sure Shinichi would know him by name. He seemed to have read my mind, for the three wiggling dots appeared, and then his message.

Your other ex is the opposite. He's quite a straight-laced family man.

Family man. My gaze crashed to a halt on the penultimate word.

Naoki's married? I let my thumbs hover, while I thought of what to write. *And has kids?*

Yeah, his wife is from Kobe. They have two kids, boy and girl.

I didn't know what to reply, and let one of my hands fall to Millie's head, as my sweet pug had stopped by for a cuddle. It shook as I stroked her.

He runs Yasuda Ramen. You wouldn't recognise him. Not quite – debu – but got a beer gut as you English would say.

Naoki? Fat? He had been so attractive.

Maybe too much time cooking and eating in his restaurant and not enough time exercising, I texted, following on with a laughing-crying emoji.

No more wiggling dots, for now. I'd had enough of hearing how my exes were happy family men – albeit one a criminal family and the other perfectly boring – while I was divorced, childless, and my psychotherapy business was on the verge of struggling. Everyone was doing better at life than me, it seemed.

Not Shinichi, though. Like me, he was newly single. I let my memories slide back to an image of him, that he had sent to me by mistake, instead of to my neighbour Eri, who he had been cheating on me with. His bare-chest under a black bomber jacket and Calvin Klein boxers caused a tingle that I hadn't felt for some time.

What are you looking like these days? Not fat like Naoki, I teased.

A few minutes later, he pinged a selfie back.

Looking good, I ventured, *though even better if you unbuttoned that shirt...*

Another text, obliging. Oh my days, he was still smoking hot.

Now your turn, came the reply.

I was on the thin side, after the stress from my divorce, but I whipped off my top and squashed my boobs together in my bra, to rummage a nice cleavage. I held my arm out and snapped a selfie, then pinged it back.

Still hot as ever, Kim Thatcher.

This was going better than expected. What if I took it up a notch? Why not? We were both single; and far from being happily adjusted, I was happy to be a *hentai*.

I stretched back on my bed, ready for a show, then typed, *There's this thing I want you to do.*

Also by Leilanie Stewart

Novels
The Buddha's Bone
Gods of Avalon Road

Belfast Ghosts trilogy
The Blue Man
The Fairy Lights
Matthew's Twin

Short story collections
Love you to Death
Pseudologia Fantastica
Diabolical Dreamscapes

Poetry collections
Toebirds & Woodlice
A Model Archaeologist
The Redundancy of Tautology

www.leilaniestewart.com

About the Author:

Leilanie Stewart is an award-winning author and poet from Belfast, Northern Ireland. She writes ghost and psychological horror, as well as experimental verse. Her writing confronts the nature of self; her novels feature main characters on a dark psychological journey who have a crisis and create a new sense of identity. She began writing for publication while working as an English teacher in Japan, a career pathway that has influenced themes in her writing. Her former career as an Archaeologist has also inspired her writing and she has incorporated elements of archaeology and mythology into both her fiction and poetry.

In addition to promoting her own work, Leilanie runs Bindweed Magazine, a creative writing literary journal with her writer husband, Joseph Robert.

Aside from publishing pursuits, Leilanie enjoys spending time with her husband and their lively literary lad, a voracious reader of sea monster books.

www.leilaniestewart.com

Acknowledgements

Where would I be without my super hubby and editor, Joseph Robert? Thank you for all the fabulous editing and polish and also your feedback on the graphic design of the cover. Love you!

Thanks to my lovely ARC readers and book bloggers who support my work: Laura at the Bookish Hermit and Hannah at Hannah May Book reviews.

And, many thanks to you for buying my book. Having readers keeps me motivated to write more stories, so just to let you know that I appreciate you taking the time to read and review my books. It means more than you know.

Printed in Dunstable, United Kingdom